10369204 5

C000135774

Adult Fi

5/12/18

HA

Printed in the United Kingdom

First Printing, 2013 Alfie Dog Limited

The author can be found at: authors@alfiedog.com

Cover design: Katie Stewart www.magicowldesign.weebly.com

ISBN 978-1-909894-05-1

Published by
Alfie Dog Limited
Schilde Lodge, Tholthorpe,
North Yorkshire, YO61 1SN
Tel: 0207 193 33 90

DEDICATION

To
Mum and Dad,
my guiding lights and closest friends.

ACKNOWLEDGMENTS

I am deeply indebted to the wonderful Katie Stewart for bringing some of the characters to life in the cover of this book.

My sincere thanks to my husband, Chris Platt, without whom this book would never have happened.

CHAPTER 1

Who wouldn't want to investigate a death threat if they were given the opportunity? It was more interesting than the usual marital infidelity that came his way. Connor Bancroft put his camera bag down on the stone doorstep of the Victorian semi, grimaced as he saw the reflection of his two-day old stubble in the door knocker and rang the bell. The warm autumn sun was on his back as he waited.

Through the small panes at the top of the door, he could see a lean man approaching; his movements appearing jerky through the distorted glass. The man opened the door onto a cautionary chain.

"Steve Daniels? I'm Connor Bancroft, reporter and private investigator. I covered the Lifetracer story in *The Press*." Connor held up a laminated press card for Steve to see.

A look of relief spread across Steve's gaunt face. "Come in." He removed the chain and opened the door.

From his own height of 6', Connor judged Steve was around 5'10" tall. He looked physically fit without being athletic. If he did play sport, Connor imagined it was squash or tennis, although he could see him as a solitary runner. His hair was dark and his swarthy looks and puppy-dog brown eyes would melt any woman's heart. The small white scar below his right eye stood out against his tanned skin. Steve was dressed in chinos and an open necked shirt. However, despite the casual dress, he looked anything but relaxed. He led Connor through the dimly lit, narrow hallway which had a picture of York's Millennium Bridge on the wall and into the lounge. In contrast with the shabby furnishings, the room looked newly decorated with navy walls and white coving and overlooked the main road at the front of the house. Connor could see the nose of his pickup on the opposite side of the street. The road was full of parked cars, he'd been lucky to get a space. He sat at the far end of the settee, removed his notepad and pen from the pocket of his denim shirt and looked up at the awkward figure standing in the doorway.

"Why don't you sit down and tell me what happened?"

"I don't know where to start." Steve, removed a stick of chewing gum from his pocket, unwrapped the gum and started to chew. He moved across to a matching, battered, leather armchair. "I don't think I can describe the man. It wasn't anyone I knew. The package was addressed to me. I was expecting it. I didn't look at the delivery bloke. You don't do you? I signed the paper and he went." Steve looked dejected as the circular object continued ticking away on the table in front of them. It sat alone like some object of worship, on top of a plinth box that had once been its original packaging.

"I remember thinking it was strange that he hadn't parked outside my house, but as you can see, the road's often busy and he probably had other deliveries further along. I didn't pay that much attention." His brow furrowed as he appeared to think.

"Mr Daniels, Steve, you must understand it's

important to tell me any details which might give me a lead. Just run through the events once again from the beginning." Connor flipped to the start of his notebook.

"If the police had taken me seriously when I reported this to them, it would have been fresher in my mind. It was seeing your article about the Lifetracer, in *The Press*, which made me wonder if you could help." He took a deep breath and began from the beginning. "I saw the Lifetracer in a magazine. It looked brilliant. As you know, it's a gadget that counts down and reminds you of all the special occasions that you otherwise forget, so I ordered one from an internet site. I've bought things from that site before and they're always very good. It took three days to come. The doorbell rang at about 10.30. I remember thinking I'd got ten minutes before going out, to collect my next lesson. I'm a driving instructor. The delivery driver was wearing a jacket. I remember that because I thought he must be sweltering, given that it was a warm day. Anyway, when I opened the package, everything was still in its sealed bags as you'd expect and the instruction book was on the top."

Connor turned the page of his reporter's notebook and asked, "Was there any way the package could have been opened before you got it?"

Steve shook his head. His brow remained lined even now he'd stopped frowning. He looked as though he took life quite seriously. "No, I'm certain it was one of those cardboard packages where you tear along the perforated bit to open the box. You can't re-close those without being able to tell. I took the Lifetracer out of its bag and it was already turned on. There it was, 'TIME TO DEATH 36 DAYS'. I was shocked and got the manual out to see if it was an error message. There was nothing there, so I rang the helpline and asked whether it was some sort of joke. I had problems getting the woman on the helpdesk to understand, so she passed me on to her manager who told me 'the device had been checked before leaving the factory and if I thought the device might have been tampered with in the post, I should call the police'. When I rang off from them, I dialled the police. That was no use. Maybe it was the way I explained it. My call wasn't taken seriously. I think the words were 'It sounds like a practical joke. Whose birthday have you forgotten recently?'"

Connor picked at a hole in the knee of his jeans and avoided commenting on the police response, instead he asked, "Did you keep the external packaging?"

Steve shook his head and fiddled with a pen that he'd picked up. "I didn't think it was important, at least not at first. It was later it occurred to me that the cardboard might be used to trace anyone who had tampered with the package. I just presumed that it had come straight from the supplier. By the time I thought about it, the rubbish had already been collected."

Connor took a deep breath. "Are you aware of anyone who might bear a grudge towards you?"

Steve shook his head. "I can't think of anything. I suppose there might be a learner that failed their test and thinks I'm to blame, but otherwise . . ." He shrugged.

"Do many of your learners fail?"

"No. Not really. There are always going to be some, but I've got a pretty good pass rate." He looked pleased with himself.

Connor looked round the room for inspiration, as Steve sat chewing gum and staring at him. The police were right, it did sound like a practical joke, but what if it were for real? Nowhere in all his manuals on police procedure and crime could be remember a section on handling death threats.

"I need you to tell me a little bit more about yourself, your family, your work, what you do in your spare time."

Steve snapped. "There isn't any dirt. I've lived on my own since my housemate moved out in April. I work for myself and live a quiet life. There's nothing to tell. We're getting nowhere. And what's worse - it now says 25 days."

Connor could see the story slipping away from him before he'd even started. Maybe there was no story. Steve could just be a crank, but Connor was intrigued. He would have taken the case on as a private investigator but Steve said he couldn't afford to pay.

"You say you had a lodger. What can you tell me about him? Why did he leave?"

Steve's shoulders hunched. "He bought his own place. Moved in with his girlfriend."

"How long did he live here?"

"Two years. Something like that. He stayed in York after university and wanted somewhere to live while he trained as an accountant. His name is Andrew Bentley. Look, I may as well tell you. I'm sure you'll find out anyway. We had a bit of a disagreement before he left."

"Oh?" Connor looked up from his notepad. "What was it about?"

"He thought I was drinking too much. He was worried it would still be in my bloodstream when I went out on lessons. As if I don't know my own limits." Steve snorted. "That was all there was to it. He's nothing to do with this."

Steve had said all he was going to about Andrew Bentley. Connor wondered whether there was any more to it than that, but given how emphatic Steve had been, he chose not to follow it up until later. He made a note to talk to the lodger as soon as possible.

"And do you have a girlfriend, Steve?"

Steve shrugged, "I suppose so. If you can call her that now. Emma, I've not seen her since all this started. She's scared about her kid. She doesn't want to be around me in case something happens. There's support for you. Ungrateful cow."

Connor noticed that there were no photographs around of Steve as part of a couple. In fact the only photograph was of a lady in her late fifties with straw coloured hair, cut neatly but without much style.

"Ever been married?"

Steve shook his head.

"Any family?" Connor got up and went over the photo on the mantelpiece. He was surprised by the lack of dust. "Is this your mother?"

Steve's eyes flicked up and back before he answered. "Yes, that's Mum. My dad lives locally. He's on his own since Mum died and then there's my sister Claire."

Connor could see no pictures of either Steve's dad or Claire. "Would you mind if I talked to them?"

Steve looked shocked. "They won't know anything."

"But it might help me to get a better grasp of the situation."

Steve shifted, looking uncomfortable. "Could I be there?"

It was Connor's turn to shrug. He couldn't help thinking that having Steve present might inhibit what they said, but it was a means of introduction.

It was starting to look as though working on this would run into the weekend, but no doubt his son, Mikey would find that fun and they had some free time. "I'll need the details of where you bought the Lifetracer, a phone number for your girlfriend, details of your former lodger, meetings with your family and a list of your learners who've failed their tests."

"I don't think I should be giving that information out."

Connor got up. "I'm sorry, Steve. If you don't want me to follow this up, I'm wasting my time. I'll see myself out."

"Wait! I'm sorry. I'm not thinking straight. Of course you can have those things. I shouldn't give them to you under that data law thing, but I think they'd understand. Please don't go?"

Connor sat down again. He was starting to reappraise his initial impression that Steve might be quite attractive to women and was starting to see him as a pitiful character. He picked up the Lifetracer off the table. It was no more than about 3" high and consisted of an upturned face like a clock with the message written across the centre. "How do you programme this thing?"

"The instruction book's in the box. Can I get you a cup of coffee?"

"That would be great. I take it black."

Whilst Steve was out of the room, Connor started making a list of questions. *Does Steve have money? Who are his enemies? What's the story about the family? Was there bad blood between Steve and the lodger?* Then he turned his attention to the instruction book for the Lifetracer. He was still reading it when Steve returned carrying a tray with two coffees.

Connor established that the device was straightforward to set the times, but it would take more detailed knowledge to change the messages. It meant that at the very least, whoever had done it was computer literate, but in this day and age that barely ruled out anyone over the age of four. It was far too late to be thinking about fingerprints, not that he had the means to check them against any database. He'd got friends in the police, but none that he could push quite that far. If he was going to take on work like this, he was going to have to develop his contacts.

He made a note to talk to the internet company that had sold the device.

"If I'm going to make any progress at all, you're going to have to be prepared to tell me more about your life." Connor looked at Steve's hands shaking as he held his coffee cup.

Steve looked round the room as though in search of inspiration. "I suppose I've just assumed it's a random attack. I did wonder if it might be a small bomb, set to go off when the timer runs out."

Connor chose not to point out that it would be unusual for a random attack to be quite so premeditated or to ask why on earth he'd got it sitting on the coffee table if he thought it was a bomb.

"It doesn't look as though it has been tampered with, but perhaps we should get it checked. If nothing else it looks like we've got another few days before it goes off." Connor laughed but Steve Daniels didn't seem to appreciate his joke. "Why don't you start with your life story?"

"I was born in Pocklington, here in York, in 1974. Claire, my sister, is three years younger than I am. I've had a pretty ordinary sort of life. I got a limited number of qualifications before I left school. I've always done something driving related, right from when I rode a moped and delivered pizzas. I became a driving instructor ten years ago when I got bored with delivery driving. Mum was so proud of me. I don't see much of Dad and I never found the right person to marry. You know how it is."

Still smarting from his divorce, a couple of years previously, Connor was sure he didn't know how it was, but chose not to interrupt.

"Emma and I had been seeing each other for about eighteen months until this arrived. We've been together since just before Mum died."

"Were you close to your mother?"

Steve gave Connor a warning look that suggested this was an area he wasn't prepared to talk about, but said "Yes." His eyes were fixed on Connor's, challenging him to take it any further.

"Do you have any debts?"

Steve shook his head. "Mum left me some money when she died. I make a reasonable living driving and I don't spend a great deal."

Connor looked around the room at the out of date television and worn furnishings and guessed Steve was telling the truth. Perhaps he should push harder for this to be a paid investigation. He'd wait to see what it threw up before having that conversation again. He got the impression that there was rather more Steve wasn't telling him. Whatever it was, Connor was determined that paid or unpaid, he was going to find out.

CHAPTER 2

Connor's four year old Border collie, Tammy, started barking with excitement as he approached the pickup. Connor and his dog went almost everywhere together. He patted her head as he got back into the car then drove off in the direction of Clifton, Bohemian Rhapsody blaring from the stereo.

Was this guy a crank or was he for real? Why would anyone give you warning that they were going to kill you? He'd never understood why someone would issue a death threat, rather than get on and kill the intended victim. It had to be worth finding out if there were any other cases involving a Lifetracer. Maybe the Lifetracer was being used as a signature by a killer who wanted to be noticed. How different could this type of investigation be to researching a story? It was time for him to branch out.

He was pulling up at the lights when his phone rang through the hands-free kit. Tammy barked a greeting towards the phone. "Hey, Maggie, just the person I need." Connor smiled, picturing of his own beautiful Maggie.

"I bet you say that to all the girls, Con. How is my blue-eyed wonder? I was just checking you're still on for tonight."

"I'll be there. While you're on the phone, Maggie, could you do me a favour? Do you remember the article I wrote last week on the Lifetracer?"

"How could I forget it?"

"Ok, less of the sarcasm, it was a fine piece of journalism. Can you do a search for news stories in which a Lifetracer is mentioned? National as well as local, over the last couple of years."

"Are you looking for anything specific?"

"Oh, I love it when you talk dirty. No, at this stage I'm looking for anything. Can you email them over to me? See you about 19.00."

There were advantages of having a relationship with the newspaper's librarian, quite apart from those long slender legs and her beaming smile. It had taken him a long time to move on from his marriage, but after a year with Maggie, he felt as though he was making progress.

The music came back on as the phone cut out and he resumed his singing. There was just time for a late breakfast at McDonald's before finishing the piece on the expected increased interest in cycling since the Tour of Britain passed through the city. He turned onto the ring road and then right again past Tesco's.

***

As Connor sat in McDonalds, tucking into his egg McMuffin, he flipped open his netbook and started to look on the internet for the Lifetracer. There were thousands of references and as he paged through the results, all he could conclude was it was an easy gadget to get your hands on, with a wide choice of suppliers everywhere in the world. He picked the site that Steve had bought his from and went to the homepage of giftitatry.com. He despaired of the corny names that filled the corners of the internet. He could order a Lifetracer for £14.99 plus postage and they would have it with him within three days, just as Steve had said. There was little else of interest, except that the company was based in Derby. He was just noting down the details when his mobile rang again.

"Con, it's me, Maggie. What are you getting into?"

"Why? What have you found?" His heart beat faster as he waited for her to answer.

"Other than write ups of the product, I can find one actual news story. There was a murder in Birmingham. A Lifetracer was found with the body. I'm sending the story through to you now. Take care, Con."

"Cheers, Maggie. I'll take a look." He broke into a broad smile. Perhaps Steve Daniels wasn't such a weirdo after all.

He opened his Outlook account and waited for the morning's email to download. He grinned as he looked round at the yellow and red decoration of his surroundings and moved his empties to make way for a pad of paper. He liked the independence of the freelance life, being able to pitch office anywhere he chose, but sometimes he'd swap it all for a plush office with a comfy chair all at someone else's expense.

The story from the Birmingham Mail started to filter through. The victim had been found, strangled, on the Lickey hills by an early morning dog walker. The police had little to go on and although a Lifetracer had been found on the body, there was little or no clue as to how it tied into the inquiry. The body was that of a man around seventy years old. At the time of the article, no name had been released to the public. So what was the link between Steve Daniels and a seventy year old man in Birmingham, or wasn't there one?

Connor made a note to get Maggie to look for follow up stories. Then he finished his coffee, cleared his tray of empties into the bin and headed back to the pickup, where Tammy was waiting to find what remains of breakfast he'd saved for her. He scratched her behind the ear. "I don't know what we're getting into, old girl but it all looks mighty strange."

He was about to drive when he remembered that morning's unopened post in his pocket. There was just the one letter, from the solicitor representing Jayne, his ex-wife. He hated those letters. They almost always asked for more money, but most of that was settled now. He sat back in the seat and tore the envelope open. He read the letter then thumped the steering wheel, accidentally hitting the horn.

Money he could cope with, he didn't have any, but this! How dare Jayne mess with their arrangements for when he could see Mikey? He would now see Mikey every other weekend and not every weekend as they had agreed. Connor felt as though someone had slapped him. He wanted to drive straight round to see Jayne to tell her what he thought, but that would have to wait until she came home from school later. It would be better to see her without Mikey being around, but those opportunities were limited. He could feel the anger thumping through his veins. "How can she do this to us, Tammy? We agreed."

Connor drove out of the car park more hastily than was wise, tyres squealing as he cornered. He slowed down when he nearly hit a lorry turning into the delivery entrance of B&Q. As he pulled up, Tammy fell forwards off the seat into the footwell, making Connor sincerely glad that she was wearing her seatbelt. Access to Mikey was bad enough, he didn't want to lose Tammy as well.

***

Later that afternoon, he drove round to the estate where Jayne lived with Mikey. He sat watching outside the modern detached house for Jayne to return having collected Mikey from school. This wasn't a bad area, but he wished that Mikey could grow up with him in the village atmosphere of Haxby. It would have been good too for Mikey to be closer to open fields and the wildlife it brought. He supposed housing estates had their advantages, but nothing would make him swap.

He hoped this wasn't the day of an after school shopping trip, but he couldn't wait any longer than necessary to talk about access to his son. He breathed a sigh of relief as he saw Jayne pulling up in her green Citroen. Tammy's tail thumped as she saw Mikey getting out of the car. "Hey," Connor called across to them, smiling at the sight of his slender eight year old son. Mikey's fair hair was messed up in a carefree fashion as though he'd been running round. The grass stains on his school trousers confirmed the picture.

"What do you want?" Jayne, ever blunt and to the point, replied. Her shoulder length brown hair was tied back in a businesslike fashion.

"I got your letter."

"This isn't the time."

"So when is the time? It's all right for you to change your mind on when I can see my son, but there's nothing I can do about it."

"Mikey, go inside." She gave him the keys to the house.

He came over and hugged his dad, "Hi, Dad. Can I take Tammy out?" His innocent blue eyes warmed Connor's heart.

"Mikey, go inside." Jayne snapped. The look she gave

Connor through her black framed spectacles was enough to freeze a polar bear.

"Do as your Mum says, Son. I'll see you on Friday, as long as your mum agrees." He pulled a fierce expression back at Jayne, although it was a long way from rivalling hers.

Mikey dragged his feet along the path and opened the front door.

"I thought we had an agreement. Every weekend, we agreed with the judge."

"No, we agreed with the judge it would be times that were mutually convenient and that's no longer mutually convenient."

"It's still mutually convenient to me. Why are you being so selfish?"

"Need you ask? You take him on those sordid cases with you."

"Mikey loves playing spy. We have a great time."

"Playing. That's the thing he should be doing. Not getting involved in the worst aspects of other people's divorces."

Connor bit his lip rather than ask what she thought their own divorce might have done to him.

"Jayne, he loves it. I don't tell him all the background."

"And what will it be this weekend?"

Connor felt himself blushing as he thought about the murder he wanted to follow up. Maybe Jayne had a point and he should leave Mikey out of this, but they were partners. Ok so Mikey was eight, but what else would they do together? He didn't want to become one of those fathers that just took his son to McDonald's every week, because they had nowhere else to go. To be fair they did seem to end up in McDonald's each week, but he told himself it was by choice rather than necessity. They liked McDonald's.

"Please, Jayne."

"We'll see how it goes."

"Can I have him this weekend?" He tried to force the smile that might stand some chance of melting her, but he didn't feel much like smiling right now, not in Jayne's direction. He hoped his boyish but rugged good looks could still have some effect on her. After all, even when they'd split up she'd never said she'd stopped fancying him.

"Ok, I'll see you Friday."

Connor breathed another sigh of relief as he went back to the pickup. He lived for his times with Mikey. They were the best days of all.

CHAPTER 3

Charles Gumby took his hat from the hall table. He smiled, thinking how Lillian would have admonished him for leaving it there, even though stretching up to the shelf above the coat rail would have pulled on his aching limbs. His smile creased his face like a well-worn letter. Years of enjoying his work had etched many happy lines around his eyes and mouth. He placed the hat on his shock of grey hair.

He lifted the photo of his precious Lillian from the table and ran his finger along the line of her cheek. "Thank you for the forty-seven wonderful years we did have." A wistful look entered his eyes as he heard the impatient toot of the car horn outside and checked his watch. *Why couldn't his son have had his mother's placid temperament instead of his own impatient one?*

A stickler for appearance, he glanced in the mirror before going to the door. If it weren't for the rheumatism, he might be said to do well for his age, although even he had to admit that he'd aged since losing Lillian two years ago. It was depressing when you could see the aging in yourself.

He didn't ask for much out of life these days. A car was just too expensive for the few occasions he needed it and there was a limit to the number of times he wanted to call out the breakdown people for a flat battery. He could catch a bus when he wanted to go to the shops, but other than that his home was his castle. His mind was as sharp as ever and despite the loneliness, he enjoyed the fact that after all these years he had chance to catch up on the reading he'd been meaning to do.

"Morning, Raymond."

"It'll just be the three of us for lunch today, Father." Raymond drummed the steering wheel with his fingers as he waited for the old man to make himself comfortable.

"No girls this Sunday?"

"Stephanie's started to develop a life of her own. You know what they're like at fourteen."

"And her sister?"

"Out at some friend or other. I'm sure her mother knows." Raymond shrugged as he started to drive. "Sorry we couldn't take you to church this morning."

Charles wondered why his son bothered to say sorry if there wasn't any reason for it, unless it was to salve his own conscience. He liked the weeks they went to St Laurence's Church before going back for lunch, but that meant lunch wasn't on the table until 14.00 and he knew how Raymond hated his mealtime being delayed. He'd been a regular worshipper years ago, but that was before he moved to Northfield.

"Hello, Dad." Dora greeted him with a peck on the cheek. "I'll just finish doing the veg while Raymond gets you a beer."

Charles sipped the beer while Raymond ranted about an awkward client he'd dealt with the previous week.

Charles was quiet as he chewed his beef. He didn't feel hungry. He did his best to finish the plate so as not to disappoint Dora. She was so good to him. Having her around provided a calming influence on Raymond.

It was when they moved on to dessert that Charles said, "I wanted an opportunity to talk to just the two of you."

Raymond looked up from his lemon meringue pie. "Oh?"

"I've got an appointment to see the solicitor next week. I need to make some changes to my will. I've not done anything about it since your mother died and I've been thinking I ought to." He felt himself relax having got the words out.

"Doesn't everything stay the same as it would have done?"

Charles hesitated. "You and your sister are adults now. You've built your own lives. I think with people living longer, leaving money to children is less meaningful. Don't you?"

"Oh," Raymond sounded disappointed.

"I'm thinking of leaving some for my grandchildren and giving the rest to charities."

"Dad!" It was Dora who came out with the exclamation. "Well, of course, it is up to you, but have you thought about it?"

"I'd have liked a chance to talk to Elizabeth about it before going ahead, but when I rang her the other day she was too busy to talk to me. At least my granddaughters visit me. I like it when they call in after school. They're always willing to humour an old fool, listening to stories from my teaching days." He laughed. "I know things have changed since my day, but they always listen politely. They even tell me about their friends if I'm lucky."

"Well that's kind of you to say." Dora was twisting her hands, "and of course it is up to you, Dad, but..."

"And I want to leave some to the hospice that looked

19

after your mother at the end."

"Well, I'm sure that would be very nice." Raymond appeared strained.

Charles looked at his son. "You're not in debt are you? Your mother and I brought you up to live within your means."

"We did remortgage the house," said Raymond fidgeting with his napkin. "It's nothing."

"Good," said his father. "You'll have no objection to my plans then."

The meal was quiet after that. Charles thought his son appeared to be brooding, but chose not to make further issue out of it. At the end of the day, it was his money and he would choose how he spent it.

As he was leaving Dora said, "I could take you shopping tomorrow if you'd like me to."

"That's very kind, but I only need a couple of bags of things. I'll be fine on the bus. I don't want to trouble you."

"Always the independent one," Raymond snapped as they got into car. "I'm surprised you didn't say you'd walk home."

"I like to stay active, but I know my limits. I've had an independent life. You'll be old yourself one day and then you'll understand the frustration of not being able to do everything for yourself."

Raymond was quiet for a while. As they approached the house he seemed to be searching for something to say. "Garden's looking nice."

"I do my best. I don't dig it as much as I used to, but it still yields a good crop of flowers and I'm proud of my vegetables. At least they don't have to travel far to get to the table."

"Bye then, Dad. See you next week."

Charles waved as Raymond drove away, but received no wave in reply. *Perhaps it was his independence that meant they didn't call by during the week, confusing it with wanting his own company. He and Lillian hadn't been like this with their parents when they were old.*

He and Lillian were supposed to be travelling the world now he was retired, but it wouldn't be the same on his own. He had thought of spending his children's inheritance, but a life of frugality was hard to shake off.

***

It was Wednesday evening of that week in early December and he was sitting in his favourite armchair reading about the Crimean war. It was a period of history that interested him. He sometimes thought he should have specialised in history during his teaching days, but he'd studied science and it had served him well. He still subscribed to *New Scientist* to keep up with what was going on, but his main love was history.

He jumped as the phone rang.

"Mr Gumby, Sir, I don't know whether you remember me, it's Eddie Stanton, you were my headmaster many years ago."

Eddie Stanton? It was impossible to remember all his former students, He'd taught hundreds if not thousands of children over his forty year career. He'd taught more than one generation of some families. He was sure there had been an Eddie Stanton, or at least a Stanton family, but for the life of him he had no absolute memory. He'd know him if he saw him. At least he would if he saw a picture of him as a child. There was so much change between children and adults.

"Eddie, how are you? There's no need to call me 'Sir' anymore."

"Right, Mr Gumby. I was wondering if I could take you for a drink, to thank you for all you did for us back then. It's amazing how you come to appreciate your teachers later in life."

He never tired of meeting old students and hearing what they'd done with their lives. The life of a retired headmaster seemed so quiet compared with his working life.

"Well, Eddie, that would be very nice. I don't go out a great deal these days so if you're in the area it would be nice to see you." He did go and stay at his daughter's house every once in a while, but mostly he stayed around Northfield. He couldn't even remember the last time he'd been into the centre of Birmingham or back to King's Heath, where he and Lillian had lived for so long.

"How about tomorrow? I don't think the Black Horse is far from you. I could see you in the lounge at around 20.00."

Charles Gumby hesitated, how did Eddie know where he lived? He wasn't in the same house he'd lived in when he was teaching and he wasn't near the school. He reasoned that if Eddie Stanton had managed to get his phone number then the address had gone with it. "Yes that's fine. I'll see you there." He hesitated, "I probably won't recognise you after all these years. I do find students have a habit of changing."

"I'm sure I'll recognise you, sir. I'll see you there. I look forward to it."

**

As Charles Gumby went through the heavy door of the Black Horse lounge, a figure by the window seat stood up and beckoned him over. He was right, he didn't recognise Eddie Stanton, but then with his thick-rimmed glasses, woolly hat pulled down almost to his eyes and his dense beard, it was impossible to see the pre-pubescent boy of thirty years ago.

Eddie Stanton had walked to meet him near the bar. He offered his hand to Mr Gumby. "Hello, sir. I'm Eddie Stanton. I don't suppose you recognise me with the beard. I wasn't even shaving in those days. What can I get you?"

"A pint of bitter would go down a treat, thank you." He wasn't too good standing for very long, so he headed to the table that Eddie had left, while Eddie got his drink. He wasn't looking when Eddie slipped the Rohypnol into his beer and he didn't see the grin spread across Eddie's face as he came back to the table. He sat and waited taking in the faded surroundings and feeling an affinity with this aging watering hole.

"So remind me Eddie, when did I teach you?" The conversation continued awkwardly with Eddie recounting stories of playground japes and lessons which had proved useful in later life, but had gone unappreciated at the time. The more Charles Gumby sat there, the less certain he was that he'd met Eddie before and the less it seemed to matter as he found himself filling in with stories from the staffroom that should have stayed well out of the hearing of the students and he would usually have been too professional to mention.

By the end of his second pint, Charles Gumby couldn't remember having such an enjoyable evening in a very long time. The conversation flowed, moving on from schooldays to their families and the achievements of Eddie's own children. When Eddie offered him a lift home, it was natural to accept. They went outside to Eddie's red Nissan Micra and were soon heading out of the car park and onto the Bristol Road.

"Oh, I think you'd have been better to go left there," he said as they headed in the wrong direction for his house.

"Don't you worry, Mr Gumby, I'll get you home." Eddie remained focussed on the road ahead.

He felt tired and relaxed in the passenger seat. His house was a couple of streets away. It would only take a minute. He felt the car picking up speed and opened his eyes.

"Where are we going?" He tried to sit up a little straighter, but without success.

An unhealthy grin spread across Eddie's face as he continued down the Bristol Road and away from Northfield.

"This isn't the right way. You need to turn round."

Even then it didn't dawn on him that Eddie had no intention of taking him home. The world was a little hazy round the edges and he had an overwhelming urge to close his eyes. At Rednal they took the Lickey Road and headed out of the built up area past Cofton Park.

Once Eddie parked, he assisted Charles Gumby out of the car and began to propel him up the hill.

"Are you feeling a little confused?" A leer played across Eddie's lips. "Still, there's no loss of face. There's no one around to see you. Just a few more steps Mr Gumby. That's it shuffling's fine."

The going was slow up the side of the Lickey Hills; the dampness of the air gave him problems with his rheumatism, as he clambered and stumbled over the muddy ground. Eddie Stanton was grabbing his arm and dragging him forward every time he hesitated.

Charles tried to twist his arm out of Eddie's grasp, but the younger man was much stronger.

"Now, now, Sir. There's no need to struggle and no

one can hear you. But just in case ..." Eddie removed Charles Gumby's tie and forced one end into his mouth and then used the remaining length to act as a gag tied behind his head.

There was no one to hear the muffled pleas as the gloved hands of Eddie Stanton wrapped around Charles Gumby's throat and throttled the life out of the weakened old man. And there was no one to see Eddie Stanton place the Lifetracer on the dead man's chest.

Back in the Nissan Micra, Eddie started to drive, removing his hat, beard and glasses as he went and placing them on the back seat with the gloves. He smiled to himself as he headed away, it had almost seemed too easy.

CHAPTER 4

If it hadn't been for the meeting he'd arranged for later with Steve Daniel's family, Connor would have opened a bottle of wine, or maybe several bottles. It always got him like that when he and Jayne fought over Mikey. He headed to the bathroom in search of a razor to tidy up his appearance before he went out.

Ok, so he was impossible to live with. Maybe he did work too many hours and bring his work home with him, who didn't? What he couldn't deal with was how that could be used to take his son away from him. He'd kidded himself that it was Jayne and Mikey that he'd worked so hard for before, but now they were gone he worked even longer hours. The truth was he liked what he did.

He looked in the mirror and smiled at the sight of the chiselled features he had unearthed from below the stubble.

He realised he hadn't rung Maggie to tell her he'd be late. There was another relationship he was messing up. He grabbed a towel to dry the water off his face and went into the bedroom where he'd slung his mobile into the middle of the bed. He'd said he'd be there by 19.00 but if he wasn't meeting Steve's family until 19.30, it was going to be gone 21.00 before he got to Maggie's. This was going to be painful. He deserved everything he got and more besides, but being in the wrong didn't make it any easier.

He breathed a sigh of relief when Maggie's phone diverted to the answer machine. "Maggie, it's me, Connor. Something's come up. It's about the murder case. I'll get to you as soon as I can, but it'll be after 21.00." He hung up relieved to have at least deferred the dressing down that he expected to receive. Maybe he could ease the pain by moving things to the next level and letting her meet Mikey. He hadn't wanted to introduce Mikey to their relationship until he was sure it was going somewhere, but now seemed as good a time as any and if Maggie could see that he was trying, then maybe she'd be more forgiving of the times work got in the way.

He took a clean pair of jeans off the back of the chair and went in search of a shirt. He would have been happy to go to Steve's house for the family meeting, but Steve had been insistent that they met at a bar in town. Connor grabbed his jacket and Tammy's lead and bundled her into the car. "Here we go again, old girl. Me and my intrepid partner. You know the ropes. If I don't come out in a reasonable time then raise the alarm. You can either howl or press this button here that sounds the horn." She didn't understand a word he was saying, but somehow it calmed Connor knowing that she was there and might summon help if needed. Border collies were bright. It was just a question of how bright.

He was lucky to find a free spot in the pay and display spaces right outside the pub. He searched through the loose change he kept in the car for enough to cover the two hour maximum. He shouldn't need more than an hour, but he didn't want to interrupt the flow of conversation to feed the meter. He left Tammy in charge of the pick-up and headed over to the small brick building opposite. He tried to arrive early, to size up the people he was meeting as they came in, but he was late as he walked into the bar. It was a busy place and Connor was surprised by the choice. Steve was already sitting at a table in the far corner. He was with a man in his fifties or sixties who was staring into his pint, shoulders rounded and sunken as though wanting to blend into his surroundings. Although given that the surroundings were quite distinctive, he was always going to stand out. Then there was a couple who looked around Steve's age. The man sat straight backed, his imposing shoulders overlapping the personal space of the slim, mousy haired woman sitting next to him. He presumed this was Steve's father, sister and her husband. He waved a hand to Steve then went straight to the bar to get a glass of scrumpy, before joining them at the table.

He held his hand out to the older man. "Connor Bancroft."

The man looked startled to have been addressed.

"This is my dad, Harry Daniels and these are my sister Claire and my brother-in-law David Suffolk."

It was David who spoke first. His voice was deep and booming. "What's this all about then? I hope we aren't being dragged here under false pretences. I was supposed to be at a poker game this evening."

Steve looked round as though concerned that other drinkers might have stopped to listen, while Harry Daniels shifted in his chair, but the pub was noisy with lots of conversations crammed into a small space and as a result afforded a strange privacy.

Connor was surprised to find himself on the defensive when he had been under the impression he was there to help the family. "How much has Steve told you?" His eyes narrowed as he looked at David. David's thickset jaw and dark eyes were off-putting. He imagined him to have been a rugby player in his youth, come to that he might still play. Either way, he wasn't someone to fight with.

Steve wrung his hands, "I thought it better to leave it to you to set the scene."

Connor shook his head. He decided he wouldn't tell them about the piece from the Birmingham Post and would just see where the discussion went.

"I presume Steve has at least told you that he has reason to believe that his life is in danger?" He looked round the table at the small group for a reaction, only Claire made eye contact with him.

It was David who spoke. "Well, he's mentioned something about receiving the message on that thing, but where do you fit in?" He seemed to be the self-appointed lead for the family and was setting about it in a brusque fashion.

Connor wondered if it would be easier to recognise this and address his questions through David or whether to address Harry as the senior member. He got the impression that if he did, David could become quite belligerent. He tried to take them all in with his look as he said "Steve received a Lifetracer through the post and called me in to investigate. He wants me to see if I can find out who's behind it. I'm presuming he's already told you about the message it delivered. "

David leaned forward and stabbed his finger towards Connor as he said, "And where do you think we fit in?"

Connor held his hands up in submission. Events weren't going quite the way he'd imagined. "I'm sorry, if there's a problem here then I think you should sort it out between yourselves. I'm just here to get some background so I can follow up the investigation on Steve's behalf. I'm not thinking you fit in anywhere, I was rather hoping that between you there might be more of an idea of anyone that could be responsible." Connor made a mental note to do a thorough follow-up on the background of David Suffolk.

Claire put her hand on David's arm. "It's ok, Mr Bancroft. We're all worried about what's happened. That's all. What do you want to ask us?"

Connor smiled at her and opened his pad. "Well, I'd like a bit of background on the family and whether you know anyone with a grudge against Steve."

Claire started talking before anyone else had the opportunity. She had a narrow chin and delicate mouth that looked to Connor like a tulip coming into bloom. "We're quite a small family. In terms of those of us that are close anyway." David shot Claire a warning look, which made Connor wonder what they weren't telling him. "Dad has one brother, but he's lived in America for years so he's in the clear. There are some cousins, but we aren't in touch with them. I don't suppose they even know where we live. Dad can speak for himself, but he's on his own since Mum died."

Harry stared into his beer. His sandy hair was thinning. He wore a sports jacket and tie, which although smart, suggested that little money had gone into achieving the appearance. Connor reflected on his faded jeans. He couldn't help but think of 'pots' and 'kettles'.

"It's been hard." Harry shook his head as he spoke.

Connor hoped that he was not about to hear the father's sob story.

"Then there's us," said Claire moving on. "What you see is what you get."

Connor doubted that very much.

"He shouldn't be such a useless instructor." David was brooding over his drink.

"That's not fair," said Claire, trying to soothe her husband.

"It's his own damned fault. Look at him sitting there. Butter wouldn't melt in his mouth. Why don't you ask him about our wonderful family? Ask him how come he's the one who can afford a housekeeper."

"I don't think this is getting us very far," said Harry clearing his throat. He looked up at Connor for the first time. "Perhaps it would be better if you asked us some more specific questions."

"Other than the learner angle, which of course I'll follow up," he looked around the walls at the old fashioned adverts and memorabilia of a bygone age and then up at the board listing the real ales and fruit wines available, searching for inspiration. "Do you know of anyone that might bear a grudge against Steve?" Connor wasn't sure how much more specific than that he could be.

"What apart from all of us?"

"David!" Claire appeared shocked by his outburst.

"Why would you bear a grudge, Mr Suffolk?" Connor kept his voice level as he spoke.

"Ask him where his money came from." David glared at Steve.

Claire stood up, "David, I think we'd better leave."

Connor wondered just how many pints David Suffolk had had before the one in front of him. He'd like to hear more, but he doubted he'd be getting much further by talking to them, not as a group anyway. To Connor's surprise, David had risen from the table and despite taking a moment to give a fearsome look to Steve, Claire was already leading him away when Connor turned to Harry Daniels. "How would you describe your relationship with your son?"

Harry flashed Steve a nervous look. His moustache twitched as he spoke. "Fine. He's my son. We get along fine."

"Can I ask you about the money that David mentioned?" Connor was looking at Harry, but it was Steve who answered.

"It was from my mother. She left it to me when she died." Steve said.

Harry was once more staring into his drink, looking as though he wanted no part in the conversation.

"Did your mother leave money to Claire as well?"

"No," Steve looked away from Connor as he said it.

Connor made some notes. He turned to Harry. "Mr Daniels do you know anyone, outside the family, who might have anything against your son. Anything at all."

He shook his head.

This whole meeting was going nowhere. Connor couldn't believe he'd given up part of his evening with Maggie for this. Still if nothing else it had confirmed that there was something funny about the whole business. He just didn't know what it was. All families had their skeletons if you dug deep enough, with others you didn't need to dig that far.

***

"You know, Maggie," Connor said when he was sitting eating his delayed Chinese takeaway. "I'm starting to wish I'd never got involved with Steve Daniels. I'd walk away if I weren't so convinced there'd be a story in there somewhere."

Maggie's flat was spacious, with the advantage of

being near the centre of York. It was always useful to stay there when they went out. He wasn't sure that she was supposed to have pets, but Tammy stayed when he did and no one seemed to mind. Maggie was sitting with her feet up on the couch, chestnut hair framing her face and shining in the light of the spotlight that was angled just behind her.

"I got you the follow up stories on the Birmingham murder." She grinned at him, "Although why I'm helping you to spend even more hours working is beyond me."

He ran his fingers through the long strands of hair at the side of her face. "You know I'll make it worth your while." Sitting on the edge of the sofa, he leant across and kissed her. Hoping that was all the reprimand he was going to get.

"What's this, sex for favours? Have you no scruples Connor Bancroft?"

"None that I can think of." He started unbuttoning her blouse and kissing her neck. He was just getting to the nape and left shoulder on his way down when his mobile rang.

"Leave it," said Maggie, sounding hopeful.

He carried on kissing her for a moment, until the insistent ringing had spoilt the moment. He answered the call.

"It's Steve Daniels, I wanted to say sorry for earlier."

"Ok,"

"And," he hesitated, "I just wanted to know if you were still working the case?"

Connor sat up straight. "Tell me one thing, Steve. Why did you tell me you couldn't afford to pay for me to carry out the investigation?"

"I," there was a long pause, which Connor chose not to

fill. "I didn't know how much it would cost. I thought it might be a lot and I don't have a huge amount."

"You could have asked. Why don't we start again? This time we'll start by discussing my fee. I'm still working for you if you want me, but it won't be for free."

"Ok,"

Connor punched the air. "You also need to be prepared to answer my questions honestly."

"Do you want to start now?"

Connor looked at Maggie, still sitting with her unbuttoned shirt. "No, I'm busy right now. I'll call you tomorrow." And with that he finished the call and turned his phone off. "I'm all yours," he said to Maggie, smiling. "Now where were we?"

CHAPTER 5

It was late for Tammy's breakfast by the time they both got out of the car back at Connor's house. "Ok, I should have taken your food with us. You know I never think that far ahead." They went through to the kitchen and Connor put a scoop of food into her bowl and turned his attention to the coffee machine.

Whilst the coffee brewed, he spread the stories from the Birmingham Mail out on the lounge table and glanced over what Maggie had managed to find. There were three stories. The first when the body was identified, the second when they did a reconstruction of the crime and the final one, a follow up story, a little while later. Connor got his fresh Colombian coffee and started to read the first story.

'Police have confirmed that the body found on the Lickey Hills is that of retired headmaster Charles Gumby.

Mr Gumby who lived alone in the Northfield area of Birmingham was last seen alive on Monday last week, although his body was found on Friday morning. Police are appealing for anyone who may have seen Mr Gumby between Monday and Thursday to come forward.'

The article went on to talk about his life and the family he had left behind.

By the time of the second story, the police had managed to discover what Charles Gumby's movements were on the evening of his death. The police were still trying to trace the person he had met for a drink in the Black Horse public house in Northfield. This seemed important as he was seen to leave with the man in a small red car. The description of the man accompanying him had been vague. No one had taken the registration number as there was nothing unusual at that stage. Even if they had, Connor supposed it would have been unlikely to match the original record of the car. That was the last time that Charles Gumby had been seen alive. The reconstruction had assumed that it was this car that took him out to the Lickey Hills, but no one could be certain. There was no reference to the Lifetracer in this story.

The final story gave a bit of detail about Charles Gumby's life and appealed for anyone with information to come forward. He had lived his whole life in the Birmingham area and taught at a number of schools, latterly as headmaster of a school in King's Heath. He and his late wife moved to Northfield when they retired, to be near their son and his family. He hadn't told his son that he would be meeting anyone on the night he died. It appeared that the police had no real leads, but what was clear was that if the murderer was the man in the pub, then it was someone who Charles Gumby knew.

Connor scratched his head. How did a headmaster in Birmingham link to a driving instructor in York, or was the Lifetracer an unfortunate coincidence? He wasn't sure he believed in coincidences. In his experience if there appeared to be a link, then however tenuous it was, it was probably real. After the debacle in the pub, he was in no hurry to start asking Steve Daniels any questions about Birmingham. He needed an alternative approach. Perhaps he could follow up on the girlfriend and the failed learners. He also needed to track down the lodger and obtain some background information on David Suffolk.

He dialled Steve's number. Today he intended to start on the front foot. "I'm guessing it now says 24 days, so we need to keep the investigation moving. If you're ready to talk money then I'll come round. You can have the details of your failed learners, your girlfriend and your former lodger ready for me. I'd also like to ask you a few questions."

Steve had agreed and arranged to see Connor in an hour. "Come on Tammy, this is no time for napping, we've got work to do." The faithful dog got up and followed her master out to the car.

As Connor drove out of Haxby through Wiggington, his mind turned to the role that David Suffolk played within the family. He'd complained about missing a poker game for their meeting and Connor wondered just how often he played and whether he tended to win or lose.

A woman of about sixty, in jeans and sweatshirt was coming out of Steve's house as Connor arrived.

"You'll be that Conan," she said as he smiled at her. "I'm Betty, Betty Lloyd. I expect he's told you all about me. I was a friend of his mother's you know. Dreadful business, still I expect you'll sort it. I don't suppose you'll need to speak to me..." She looked hopefully into Connor's eyes.

Connor knew not to disappoint her and couldn't help but think that her chatty style might be a useful source of information. "I would like to talk to you, very much. I can't imagine I'll be more than half an hour here. Could I call you after that?"

"You can do better than that. I live six doors down. See the one with the green door, that's me. Why don't you call round?"

"Thanks, I'll do that." Connor smiled again and she scurried away.

The Lifetracer was still sitting on its plinth on the table in the lounge. This time Steve was more compliant than the night before and Connor managed to get him to ring and effect introductions to both his girlfriend, Emma Price and his former lodger, Andrew Bentley. He also had the assurance of payment for his services, including an advance of £500 and a list of around fifteen learners who had failed their tests with Steve in the recent past. Some of them, Connor noted, had failed a number of times. He wondered why at that point they hadn't changed instructor or given up, but then some people were just thick skinned.

Having obtained the other things he needed, Connor took the risk of turning the conversation to David Suffolk. "You're brother in law is an interesting character."

"Devil incarnate more likely."

"I take it you don't get along."

"Nothing I can't handle."

"What does he do for a living?" It was going to take more direct questions to elicit any useful information.

"Pushes people around, I imagine. He's some type of manager, though God help anyone working for him."

"Your sister seems to have him under control."

"Yes," Steve looked into the distance. "Odd that," but said no more.

"Do you know if he has any gambling debts?"

"You'll need to ask him that one. Good luck."

This was going nowhere. Connor got up to leave. "I'm off to see your housekeeper now. I met her as I was coming in."

Steve snorted. "Are you sure you've left yourself

enough time? You'll be there until tonight. She's harmless enough, but boy can she talk."

Connor smiled. That was what he was hoping for.

Betty Turner's house was similar in design and layout to Steve's, however there the similarity ended. Betty's house was crammed full of photos and knick-knacks which looked as though they had been bought from every seaside resort from Bognor to Blackpool and many more besides. As he looked at the table, Connor wondered what one person could do with so many letter openers and not a single item of post in sight.

"I was saying to Steve the other day, he ought to find someone to follow this up. It isn't right, the police not being involved. What his dear mother would have said, God rest her soul. We were friends you know. Had been for years. I met her when she lived in Gloucester, not that she was there long. We always stayed in touch. I was happy to look after Steve after she died, what with my own son being so far away."

Connor wondered whether it was polite to interrupt when someone didn't even stop for breath or whether he should just wait until she ran out of steam, whenever that might be.

"Dreadful state of affairs when you can't even live peacefully in your own home without someone threatening to kill you. And him living down the road. Doesn't leave you feeling safe does it? I mean they could get the wrong house. I don't blame that girl of his staying out of the way. I've thought about it myself. But then where would my promise to Paula be if I left him to it at a time like this? Of course she wasn't still alive when I made the promise. I wasn't expecting her to go so young. You know how it is."

At last Connor saw his opportunity. "Do you know anyone who might have a reason to threaten Mr Daniels?"

"Why would anyone want to do that? He's such a lamb and so like his mother you know. You only have to look at him to see he's got his mother's genes. She doted on him. 'Her little soldier' she used to call him. What she must think of someone threatening him like this. God rest her soul.

I remember the photo of him she sent me when he was about five. It would have been his first school photo. Such a handsome little chap."

Connor realised that Steve's description of Betty had been all too accurate and the rate she was going, he would have lost the will to live long before he obtained any useful information.

"I'm afraid that's all I've got time for at the moment Mrs Lloyd, perhaps if you give me your phone number I could arrange to come back another time."

"Please, call me Betty. Haven't you got time to stay for a nice cuppa? I can have the kettle on in a jiffy. It wouldn't be any trouble."

"No, I'm sorry but I'd already arranged to meet someone for lunch. You'll have to excuse me." And before Betty had had chance to write her phone number down, he was making his way towards the front door.

She stopped by the hall table on the way out and jotted it on a piece of paper. "Can't have you forgetting this now, can we?" She said thrusting it into his hand.

"No, thank you." Connor made his escape without causing offence and was relieved to be back in the fresh September air and freedom.

***

Connor headed off to meet Emma Price in her lunch

break. The sun was shining and the air was warm. They had agreed to meet at the café outside the art gallery. Despite the passing traffic he always found it a good spot. The view was inspiring with the city walls standing solid and magnificent beyond the fountain. The people watching opportunities were unrivalled as queues of tourists formed for the guided walks and the open topped bus tours of the city.

Connor was already seated when a blonde haired, blue eyed, woman of around thirty came tottering over, looking out of place amongst the more practically dressed tourists, in their flat shoes and carrying their rucksacks. "Emma?" said Connor, getting up to meet her.

She smiled a baby doll smile that lit up her face and made it easy to see why Steve was so attracted to her.

Once she was settled with a sandwich and coffee, Connor began. "I don't know how much Steve's told you?"

She shot him a look as though measuring up whether she could trust him. "He's told me everything. Why do you think I'm not seeing him anymore?"

"Yes, he did say. I'm sorry. You've got a little girl?"

Emma's face clouded. "I'm not here to talk about my daughter. Let's start with you first. What are you doing for Steve?"

Connor smiled, she was no dumb blonde and could hold her own. "I wrote a story in *The Press* about the Lifetracer. I'm a journalist and private investigator and Steve thought I might be just what he needed. To be fair, most of my investigations are into wayward husbands and the occasional errant wife, but the principles are much the same."

She nodded. "So, what do you want from me?"

"I'd like you to give me an independent view of Steve. Maybe an idea of anyone who bears a grudge towards him."

It was Emma's turn to laugh. "That would be a long list. We've been together since early last year. It was just before his Mum's suicide. If it hadn't been for her dying I can't see we would have lasted so long if the others are anything to go by."

"Wow, slow down there. Let's start with his mum's suicide. Do you know very much about it? Does anyone know why?"

"Oh, I'm sure the family have got some idea, but they never told me. They keep their family secrets guarded." She gave a snort of derision.

Connor made a note to dig out any stories on the mother. "What did you mean when you said it wouldn't have lasted?"

"Steve was a real mother's boy. From the stories I've heard, not from Steve you understand, whenever there was a new girl in his life, the mother would drive her away. She'd insist that everything was done her way. She just had to click her fingers and Steve would go running. I'm sure I wouldn't have been able to stand it if it had still been like that. When she died, he was lost and I suppose in some ways I replaced her. He'd do anything for me. Sometimes it felt a bit oppressive. He has quite an obsessive personality."

"Do you know anything about his mum leaving him some money?"

"Oh, sure. You can't believe the fuss. Harry thought she was leaving everything to him but that didn't happen. She left some to Steve and some to another bloke, but I never found out who he was."

"Did you get a name?"

She scowled. "It was like another big family secret."

"What about Claire?"

"No, nothing. David was spitting tacks. You just wouldn't believe the problems it caused in that family. They weren't speaking at the funeral."

Connor could imagine from the reception he'd had the other night that things may have been a little frosty. What he couldn't see was how this all fitted to a headmaster in Birmingham, unless he was the other man to whom money had been left. Perhaps he was a childhood sweetheart of Paula Daniels.

"How well did you know his brother-in-law?"

"David? He's a pussycat. All bluster. Throws his weight around like he's someone important, but as soon as his wife opens her mouth, he's like a spoilt puppy. It makes you think she's got something on him, if you know what I mean."

"Any ideas what?"

"No, I've thought about that, but the only thing I can think is that he's nicking money from somewhere to pay for his gambling."

Connor nodded. There seemed no shortage of people that might have a grudge against Steve, but he thought he'd better ask if Emma could think of anyone else. "I presume you knew his lodger, Andrew Bentley?"

"Andy's a sweetie pie. He wouldn't' hurt a fly. Not that Steve saw it that way when he accused him of drinking. Andy couldn't bear the thought of any harm coming to us learners. I must say he had a point. I'd never have arranged my lessons for any time after lunch." She shook her hair back as she laughed.

Connor chose his words carefully. "Do you think Steve

has a problem with drink?"

She shook her head. "Oh he likes a glass or two, but I wouldn't say he has a problem. Not a real problem anyway."

"Do you know of any of his learners that might have a particular reason to scare Steve, or whether there was anyone else outside of the family?"

Emma smiled. "If every learner who failed their test were to threaten him, he'd need permanent protection. He's got a good first time pass rate, but there are always some that just aren't up to it. He's got one woman, who's still having lessons with him and she's failed eight times. I don't think she blames Steve. If she did she'd have gone somewhere else. You ought to hear him when he's got to go out for a lesson with her. He hates it. She terrifies him. Even after all this time, she's lethal at roundabouts. Well, any junction. I'm guessing she's got a bit of a crush on him."

"How did you meet Steve?"

She gave a coy look. "He taught me to drive. Well I suppose that's not the whole story. He'd been out with another girl I knew through work. It was quite a while ago. She couldn't cope with his mother. Anyway, she knew I liked Steve and suggested I should book my lessons with him and flutter my eyelashes a little. I did and the rest is history."

"Do you know how much money Steve's mum left to him?"

Emma shook her head. "He's pretty guarded about that. I know it ran to thousands but I don't know how many. Everyone wondered where she'd got it from, but I don't think they found out."

"And how does Steve get on with his family now?"

"They don't talk to each other if they don't have to. They refuse to set foot in his house. Oh, they were civil to me, most of the time anyway, but you wouldn't describe them as close! I need to be getting back. It's been nice meeting you Mr Bancroft. Do feel free to give me a call." She fluttered her eyelashes at him.

"It's Connor," he said with a weak smile. If he didn't know better, he'd have sworn she was coming on to him. He tapped the pen on his notebook, wondering if there were more to her break up with Steve or whether that was another story that no one was talking about.

He sat watching the passers-by scurrying to their destinations, wondering how many took the time to look up at the remarkable architecture and history that was surrounding them. He looked over at Bootham Bar and watched people going to and fro beneath it, oblivious to the amazing structure.

He relaxed enjoying the sunshine and thinking. How had he become involved in a murder investigation? He was a photo-journalist who dabbled in investigations into peoples marital problems. Perhaps it wasn't too late to pull out and go back to what he was used to, but he was being drawn in. He was fascinated by what he was going to find. Could he find out what had happened? Besides, a cheque for £500 was always welcome.

CHAPTER 6

After he left Exhibition Square, Connor went to fetch Tammy from the car for a walk. He was in search of inspiration. Everyone and no one had a reason to threaten Steve Daniels, but did any of them have reason enough to kill him? He sat on a bench in Museum Gardens, listening to the clicking of the squirrels chattering to each other across the trees. It wasn't something you heard very often and it was amazing how similar it sounded to the way people clicked their tongues to wildlife, at least to his untrained ear. He walked past the observatory and down to the river. The tourists were queuing for the river trips near Lendal Bridge, as they always seemed to on a fine day, but he contented himself to walk along the bank back towards Clifton.

"We need to ask some questions of the company that sold the Lifetracer, see if there is a link to the one left with Charles Gumby and whether there was a delivery address. I suppose we've no way of knowing if the first one was bought from the same place and given that it's a different police force, I don't fancy my chances of finding out what they already know." As usual, Tammy wagged her tail in reply.

He flipped his phone open as he walked. "Trevor, it's Connor Bancroft. How are you?" He'd been friends with Trevor Whitworth since school days. The fact he was now

Detective Inspector Trevor Whitworth served to ensure Connor stayed in regular contact.

"I was wondering if you could do me a favour."

"Do I ever stop doing you favours? What have you got in return?"

"Nothing yet, but I'll let you know when I have."

"Before you ask, I can't access mobile phone records or credit card histories without the appropriate authority. We've been through that."

"I know. I've found someone else that can do that for me. Not that I should be revealing that to a copper. I want to know if you can tell me something about a case in Birmingham."

"Birmingham! You know, it's far easier when you ask about the cases I'm working on. It depends what you want to know. I'll try."

Connor explained about the Lifetracer and asked Trevor if there was anything on file about the one that was found with the body of Charles Gumby."

"Do you know what you're getting yourself into, Con? This isn't your usual kind of thing. Shouldn't you be leaving this to our lot?"

"I'm just branching out a little."

"I'll take a look, but you've got to give me something. Why do you want to know?"

"Fair enough. There's a bloke here in York that thinks his new Lifetracer may have come with a death threat. He did try telling you guys, but whether he wasn't very clear in what he said, I don't know. What I do know is that he wasn't taken seriously, so he came to me. I want to know if his Lifetracer and the one left with the body of Charles Gumby might have been bought from the same place and whether there's a link between them. I don't think we're looking at a copycat, unless the murderer saw the story in Birmingham, as it hasn't been covered anywhere else. At least, not as far as I know. You couldn't do a search to see if these things have turned up anywhere else could you?"

"Yeah, sure. It's not as though I'm busy fighting crime or anything. Meet me for a drink in The Fulford Arms. If I've got anything I'll bring it with me. About 18.30?"

With that out of the way, Connor headed for home. He wanted to speak to David Suffolk and he wasn't keen to ask Steve for the number.

There was only one D Suffolk listed in the phone directory, so he decided to take a risk.

"Mr Suffolk, it's Connor Bancroft, we met last night."

"You!"

Connor had anticipated that this would be a difficult call and he wasn't disappointed. At least he knew he'd got the right person. "I wondered whether I might ask you another couple of questions seeing as you had to leave early last night." He could imagine the volcanic reaction beginning to bubble at the other end. "Do you see much of your brother-in-law, Mr Suffolk?"

As Connor listened to the dial tone he concluded he wasn't going to have the opportunity to ask the more personal questions he'd lined up. He rang Andrew Bentley the former lodger and arranged a meeting with him for the following morning.

He'd been off the phone for about five minutes when it rang. A hushed voice the other end almost whispered, "It's Claire Suffolk here, I think you rang my husband."

"Yes, I wanted to ask you both a few more questions."

"I know what it looks like, but it wasn't him. He wouldn't do something like that. We've got our problems and he doesn't get on with Steve, but he wouldn't go as far as that."

"Mrs Suffolk, how often does your husband play poker?"

"A couple of times a week, why?"

"Does he win?"

"Sometimes."

"What time does he come home when he plays?"

"I don't stay up. He's learnt to be very quiet when he gets back."

"So a couple of times a week, your husband comes home in the middle of the night."

"It's not what you think. I know he isn't having an affair. I'm his wife. I'd know if he were."

Connor raised an eyebrow. That wasn't what he thought, but it was an interesting response. "Do you share a car, Mrs Suffolk?"

"No, he's got his own car. Why?"

Connor wondered what distances he drove when he went to his 'poker games' but thought better then to ask. "I was just interested. Mrs Suffolk, who might want to kill your brother?"

There was a long period of quiet before she replied. "I don't know. He's infuriating, but none of us would want to go that far."

"May I ring you again if I have any more questions?"

"Ring my mobile rather than the house phone. It isn't wise to talk to David. He's got anger issues."

Connor thought that was a bit like saying that Tammy was a dog, but bit his lip.

***

Connor had been surprised that Andrew Bentley wanted to meet at his place of work. He wondered how he would pass off the meeting to his employer. Perhaps

Connor would be passed off as a client or a prospective client. He felt compelled to dress up in keeping with the subterfuge and even went as far as having a shave.

He arrived on the dot of 10.30, feeling awkward in his navy suit that had last seen the light of day for a family wedding some months ago and a silk tie that had been a present from Jayne some years before, when she was still trying to convince him to smarten up his appearance. She had of course failed and as their relationship was a thing of the past, he felt safe to dress like this for one short meeting, without the fear that someone was going to try to make him stay that way. God forbid!

Connor smiled when he met Andrew Bentley in the accountant's reception and thought that his suit was even more ill-fitting on him than his own felt. He wondered if anyone fitted a suit. At a little over 6' in height, he thought that maybe Andrew would still broaden out to fill his. All Connor could look forward to was the benefits of middle aged spread.

Andrew looked as though he was still recovering from teenage acne and looked barely old enough to be out of school. For a moment Connor felt old. He thought of his mother saying that the police had started to look young and smiled.

"Thank you for coming in. I'd have met you out of work, but I'm afraid I've got other engagements for the next day or two and I presumed you wanted to see me urgently."

Connor was ushered into a small meeting room with a window overlooking the city. The view was the room's redeeming feature. He waited while Andrew poured them both a drink of coffee before getting down to business.

"How long did you live with Steve Daniels?"

"About two years. It was after I'd finished university. I moved into a shared flat first, but I wanted a bit more space, so when I could afford it I found the house share with Steve."

"What was he like to live with?"

Andrew put his head on one side considering. "He was out quite a lot. When he was there, everything had to be done in a certain way. He was one of those people that would lock the front door twice to make sure it was locked and then check it again later."

"Why did you move out?"

Andrew looked straight into Connor's eyes. "I suppose he's told you we fell out. He probably thinks it's me threatening him, but it wasn't like that at all. I'm sure his girlfriend, Emma, would vouch for me. She's one of his learners. It was nothing personal. I was just worried that he was putting his learners' lives at risks by drinking too much before he took their lessons. In the end I said something and we had an almighty row. I'd already been thinking of moving out before that. I was earning a bit more and looking at getting my own place. It made my mind up."

"Have you seen Steve since you moved out?"

Andrew shook his head. "We were never mates, even while I was living there. In fact Steve always seemed like a bit of a loner. When his mother was alive he was often round at her house, but other than that and his various girlfriends, he didn't seem to have any real friends. The girlfriends never seemed to last long either. I think his mum saw to that."

"Did you know his brother-in-law, David Suffolk?"

"Apart from his mum, who used to come round and tidy up for him, I didn't meet any of his family. He was a real mother's boy." Andrew was fiddling with a paperclip that had been sitting on the table.

Connor smiled hearing that from someone who looked so wet behind the ears themselves. "One final question, do you know anyone who would have cause to threaten Steve's life?"

Andrew shook his head. "Sorry, I'm not being much use to you am I. I have been thinking about it since you rang me, but he just wasn't the sort of person that anyone had strong feelings about. A nobody."

Connor thanked him for his time, thinking that his observations appeared ironic.

With an afternoon to kill before seeing Trevor, Connor decided to leave the case and focus on some photographs he needed to accompany an article on York. He wished more than ever that he was in his usual jeans as going round in a suit with his camera made him feel too much like a Japanese tourist. He was grateful it was a compact city and it was a few of the more hidden features that he needed to photograph before he went home to complete the writing. He'd already taken pictures of most of what he wanted, but he needed a good one of the statue of Minerva, the Roman goddess of wisdom who sat on the corner above the doorway of what had once been a bookshop. As Connor headed towards Stoneygate he couldn't help but think how much he needed her powers right now.

CHAPTER 7

"You off to Bob's do?" Paul called to Dav as he locked the back door and wandered past the forklift trucks to the car park.

"Free pint. What do you think?" Dav stubbed his cigarette out with his boot and pushed his hands deep within his pockets.

"Want a lift?" Paul gestured towards the passenger seat.

Dav shrugged and got in.

"Nothing like a pint at the end of a boring day."

"Pallets don't look much different to this morning. I sometimes think you lads just give the illusion of working." Paul grinned.

"'Ere, just cause you're the boss! We've moved 'em in, we've moved 'em out. I'm not saying we might not move the same ones sometimes, but I wish it was me retiring. Least I can do is have one or two drinks with the lads." Dav laughed.

"Sixty five and still a lad. He's got something right. But then when you're all together in the warehouse that's how you seem. I may not come to work in overalls, but my days are just as exciting. It pays the bills. Bob must have moved a lot of pallets in the last fifteen years. I'll just stop for the one. Barbara'll be expecting me. I said I'd be about an hour."

The noise level in the Bull's Head was way too loud for Paul to hear himself think, but then to his knowledge, the warehouse lads didn't tend to do much thinking. He looked at the peeling paintwork. It wouldn't have borne anything more than the subdued lighting that failed to brighten the dreary interior. The dark wood and worn red velvet chair covers looked as though they'd been there as long as the pub. With the lighting, there was little hope of hitting treble top on the frayed dart board, unless you'd practiced blindfolded. As long as the beer was cold, available, sold by a pretty barmaid and there was somewhere sheltered outside to smoke, there wouldn't be a lot of complaints. He got himself a pint and went in search of Bob Minton.

"What are you going to do with yourself now, Bob?" Paul asked with a hint of envy.

"Well there's me garden and when Marge's not around I imagine I might put in the occasional appearance at the bookie." He winked at Paul.

"Not planning lots of trips to the sun then?"

"Nah, me roots are here in Derby. I suppose I'll still be down Pride Park on match days, for what it's worth. Over the last few years, the team has been awful. But the results don't matter. There's still the crack with the lads. That's what it's all about."

Paul let out a sigh and nodded. "Now if it were me. I'd be off to Spain as quick as you could say, well as quick as you could say retirement. I know Barbara would appreciate that. I don't know that we'd go there to live, just an extended holiday. There's the grandchildren to think about." He looked wistful. He'd got a few years left until his own retirement and they couldn't go quickly enough as far as he was concerned. Working was a mug's game, but someone had to pay the bills and he wasn't the sort to want charity or to live on benefits.

"I'm sure we might manage the odd trip abroad, I can't see Marge letting me off without that. She loves the sun."

Paul was getting through his pint easily when a youngish man came up to him. "Are you Paul Tranter?"

"Yes, who's asking?"

"Oh you don't know me. My dad used to work with you years ago. Said you were the best boss he ever had."

Paul could feel himself standing straighter. He'd have asked what the father's name was, but he was hopeless with names and although it might have been the polite thing to do, he'd never have remembered.

"Can I buy you a drink?"

Paul looked at his glass and smiled, "Go on then, but just a half." He turned back to listen in to the conversation that Bob was having with one of the new trainees, teasing him about just how long he'd got until he could have a good time again. He didn't watch the man in the hoodie go to the bar and buy his drink. He didn't see the drug being slipped into the glass.

"Cheers," he said, tipping the half into his pint glass when it was handed to him. "So, are you looking for work?"

"No. I don't live local anymore. I moved away."

Paul thought that might explain the different accent. It wasn't a Derby one, but he couldn't place it. "So what brings you to Derby?"

"Oh, just visiting my folks. Dad said there was a do on here tonight, so I thought I'd come down. He remembers Bob."

They began to chat about nothing in particular and Paul noticed his glass was empty once again.

"Here, I'll get you another," said the stranger.

Paul thought for a moment. He was having a far better time than he thought he would, perhaps he'd stay for just one more and get a taxi home. He didn't usually do this sort of thing, Barbara wouldn't mind this once. He could give her a quick ring and tell her he'd be later than he'd said.

Paul nodded, "Ok, if you insist. I'll have a pint. The car will be safe here until the morning. Barbara can drop me back here on her way to work."

The stranger smiled. Paul tried to remember what the man's name was, but drew a complete blank. He ought to pay more attention to the start of a conversation, but maybe the man hadn't said. It was too late to ask now, he'd feel stupid. He did wonder why anyone would want their hood up indoors, but then maybe that was the fashion, although he'd have put this chap as being too old for the fashion conscious stage.

"This is Daniel he'll be going to senior school this year." Paul passed the photo out of his wallet to the stranger. "This is Sophie, she's my granddaughter. She just loves her ballet." Paul took out the last photo and laughed. "And these are Cane and Ryan. You've never known such tearaways, but in this they look angelic." Paul looked at his watch. "Good heavens! Is that the time. I must be off." He put his wallet into his pocket missing it altogether and then had to retrieve it from the floor. The room swam as he stood up again.

"Steady." Said the stranger supporting his arm.

"I'd better order a cab."

"Don't worry about that. Let me give you a lift. I switched to soft drinks after the first." The stranger held up the glass of coke as if to prove a point.

"I can't put you to that trouble."

"It's no trouble. Please it would be my pleasure. I presume you don't live far away."

"Long Eaton."

"Almost on my way."

Paul wobbled again as they headed out to the car park and the stranger guided him towards a small dark car.

"I'm going to feel rough tomorrow." Paul tried to focus on the door handle of the car to open it, but the stranger did it for him. "It's a long time since I've had a hanver, hangver. Oh, you know what I mean."

The last thing he remembered was sinking into the passenger seat and the stranger starting the engine. After that there was nothing.

***

The stranger parked in a dead-end on the industrial estate, away from prying eyes. The light would fade eventually. He sat drumming on the steering wheel, shooting a look across to Paul ever few minutes to make sure the drugs were still working. "Come on, come on." He got out and walked round the car, watching for any signs of unwelcome observers.

He looked at his watch again. He should have plenty of time. He took a deep breath. *No need to worry.* The dose of Rohypnol should last several hours. Paul wouldn't be coming to his senses just yet. "Not just yet." He sneered. "And here you are missing out on seeing the perfect location. Such a shame. It took me so much trouble to find it. And all for you. You should be honoured. I spent a day 'sightseeing'. You should have been here. I had a nice little train journey and all on your behalf. You would have liked the waste land the other side of the river from Pride Park. But I couldn't find a way in, so you'll have to make do with here. Such a shame, but I think you'll like where I've chosen." He started the engine. "Shall we go?"

By the time they parked in Darley Park Drive, Paul Tranter was too wobbly on his feet to move unaided. The stranger helped him out of the car, supporting most of Paul's weight as he did so.

"Gently does it. Just a couple of drunks swaying our way home after a good night out." The stranger shot darting glances around them, but there was no one around.

With Paul leaning against him as they walked, he steered a course across the park away from the main paths and he hoped away from any courting couples. It was well past midnight. His heart raced as he made slow, steady progress to his chosen spot.

The park was dark, although the horizon was suffused with the faint orange glow of the city's street lamps.

"No pretty lights for us, just lovely darkness." He checked his pocket for his Mini-Maglite, it felt comforting to him. The air was still and silent, except for the occasional hoot of an owl. He stopped, his ears pricked. It sounded eerie as he focussed on the task in hand. Even a killer could find a setting creepy. He smiled thinking how scared Paul Tranter ought to be, if he knew what was happening, but the stranger had saved him that fear, which made him the good guy. He nodded in self-satisfaction.

It was hard trying to carry Paul as well as the tripod camping seat. He had hoped that Paul Tranter would be able to manage his own bodyweight for long enough to complete the task, but at least this way there was no struggle.

Even in the darkness he could see the silhouette of the

tree, with its bough extending forwards at just over two metres in height, perfectly positioned. He didn't so much put Paul down on the grass as allow him to fall in a heap. Then the stranger tied Paul's hands in front of him.

"Not too tight now. I don't suppose you're going to do a lot of struggling." He knotted the rope and let it fall. Then he took the other rope from under his hoodie and threw one end over the branch of the tree pulling it to the desired length.

"And this is why you needed the stool." He continued to address Paul as though he were a willing part of proceedings. He climbed up and secured the rope to the branch.

"Now we come to your part. This could be a little tricky. I did want you to stand on the stool." He kicked the slumped form lying on the ground below the tree and got little reaction. "I can see you aren't going to be doing this for yourself. Such a shame. Shall I help you? Just like threading a needle." On the third attempt Paul's sagging head went through the loop of the rope. "Now all I need to do is pull the thread tight, just like my mother would have done." The stranger pulled Paul's body forward so that the noose started to tighten and then lowered his body allowing the rope to pull tight.

"Now all we need is the finishing touches and voila!" He climbed back onto the stool and placed the Lifetracer on the branch, then stepped back down to admire his handiwork.

"Job done." He picked up the stool, and walked on through the park to exit through a different gateway. Then he walked round the edge of the park seeing no one, got back into the car, removed his gloves and drove away.

CHAPTER 8

David Suffolk coughed and waved away some of the smog of cigarette smoke that was lingering above the table. The cough echoed around this disused part of the warehouse, bouncing off the concrete walls as though the rest of the group had joined in. None of them but Richie would have smoked in their own homes, but here at the back of Frank's business they were different people. He swirled the amber whiskey round the base of his glass then brought it up to his nose to inhale. It almost brought tears to his eyes. Just how he liked it, neat.

This was freedom. Admittedly, it was freedom that came at a high price, but you couldn't measure the value of everything. Of course, when he went home to Claire he'd blame the smell of smoke on the others, but she wouldn't be fooled. He'd blame a lot of things on the others, but she'd still see his weakness. He didn't talk about who he played against when he was at home, or for that matter how the night turned out. What Claire didn't know, she couldn't moan about.

Seeing tonight as an opportunity to repay some of his debts, he'd introduced the newcomer to the group, assuring the others that he had money to lose and the personality to lose it. At least that had been David's assumption. What else could you expect from someone who wouldn't tie a shoelace without checking with his mother first? But things weren't turning out that way and once again, David was down on the night.

Richie took up the deck of cards, his cigarette hanging from the corner of his mouth. He split the pack and with a nimble arch and flick of the hand, merged the two halves together, like a pro. He'd had enough practice. Even David could just about perform the trick, give or take the odd stray card. Richie smiled the toothless grin of an aged alligator and flicked away the ash that had fallen on his over filled Leeds United t-shirt, burping with what David imagined was contentment.

Joe and Frank put in the small and big blind and then Richie dealt the cards round to the expectant players. David looked at his cards, considering the odds of them turning out to be a decent hand. The room was silent as each in turn placed his bet.

Richie discarded a card and dealt the flop. A round of betting followed, with all six players keen to see what cards would come next. It was the final hand of the night and no one wanted to be the first to fold, least of all David. Richie burnt another card and then dealt the turn. Eddie Stanton was sweating. This gave David no clue to his hand as he always sweated. He was the sloth of the gang with body hair to match. Every move he made was laborious.

Richie put aside the card from the top and dealt the river. Now it was a question of nerve but the stage of luck was behind them. A round of betting followed. He could feel the thrill of optimism thudding hard against his chest. Luck was rarely with him, but he had nerve.

David saw Joe as the gazelle of the table. He drove up from the outskirts of Derby for the game. Some nights the drive was worth it, while other nights like tonight were a different matter, but he was quick at reckoning the odds and was more often up than down. He seemed at home in the warehouse. This one might be empty, but David presumed that it was little different from the one Joe spent every day of his working life in.

"Fold." Joe put his cards down and got up from the table. David watched him wander over to the window to look out at the passing traffic. He always stayed to the bitter end. At this time of night there'd be little traffic to hinder his journey home. It would take him about an hour and a half, less if he pushed it. He'd been part of this group of players since before he moved south, although he joined them less often than he used to.

Frank folded and went to join Joe by the window. David saw him as the tortoise of the group, retreating into his shell as soon as he wasn't satisfied with a hand. There was no bluster to Fred. If he stuck at it, you knew he had a winning hand. In many ways he was no poker player at all, but he seemed to enjoy the crack.

Richie as dealer had raised a further twenty and another round of betting had started.

"I'll raise you fifty." David lifted his eyes from his cards and stared into the eyes of the newcomer. David had him down as a snake; not a venomous one and lacking the power to crush someone. He was just one of those slippery characters that seemed to slither everywhere without any useful purpose. The man didn't flinch but moved a pile of money forwards. Eddie followed suit and they were round once again to Richie.

Richie shook his head "I'm out of it," he looked down at the empty space where his money had sat. "Fold." The alligator moved his chair away from the pond and watched from the bank.

David lifted an eyebrow. This was his game. He could feel it. He was holding the king of spades and the ten of hearts. The community cards were the king of diamonds, the jack of diamonds, the ten of spades, the ten of diamonds and the six of spades. That gave him a pair of kings and three tens, a full house, tens full of kings. He fancied his chances of winning back some of what was rightfully his. "Raise you a hundred." He pushed a £50 to match the previous bet and five £20 notes forward. David ran a finger round his collar. He was down to his final £200. He already owed another £500. He needed this pot if he was to buy any breathing space on the thousands he now owed.

The brown eyes facing him barely registered what he said. The man pushed his own money into the middle. Matching the bet and raising a further £100. "All in." The pressure was still on.

Eddie waited what seemed an interminable amount of time before he shook his head and sat back. "Fold. It's between you two."

If they'd had the money, they'd have been there all night. Neither was willing to give in. It was time for a showdown.

"I'll call," said David matching the previous bet.

As the cards were turned. David was horrified to see that his opponent was holding the queen and nine of diamonds, a straight flush.

Steve Daniels gave a sly smile. "I guess I win again gentlemen." He drew the money towards his side of the table.

"You son of a bitch." David threw the table towards his brother-in-law. Reaching over and grabbing his lapels before Eddie pulled him away.

Frank called over from the window. "Not here. You settle your scores somewhere else."

David was fuming. He'd introduced Steve to the group because he'd assumed, as it turned out wrongly, that he'd be hopeless at holding a poker face. It was supposed to have been an easy way to win back Claire's inheritance and with it his self-respect. Instead of which, he was now indebted to the little snake and in no hurry for Claire to find out.

***

Connor looked at the bills piling up on the hall table and grimaced. He went through to the den, which was formerly the dining room and pushed aside some papers to make a space for his mug of coffee. There was a drinks mat around there somewhere, but like everything else it had long since been buried by writing debris. He sat at the computer and finished the article on York, then returned to a piece on organic farming that he had been researching the previous week. He'd often thought if he hadn't been a journalist that he might have tried his hand at farming organically. Farming was in his blood and he still leant his father and brother a hand once in a while, but true organic farming was difficult to achieve. He found it hard enough with his small garden.

He'd been working for a couple of hours and had also found time to arrange a visit to Derby, to the offices of Giftitatry, for the following morning. He was sitting back in his black leather swivel chair wondering what further research he could do on the case when Maggie phoned.

He loved the sound of her sultry voice, with just a hint of the north-east still in her accent. He drifted into thoughts of the feel of her touch.

"I think I might have another one for you,"

"Another what?" Connor asked.

"Another murder. I thought that's what you were working on."

Connor sat up straighter. "Sorry, yes of course it is. I was miles away. What happened?"

"It was in Derby. Another man. Middle aged, found hanging from a tree. There was a Lifetracer on the branch of the tree next to him."

"I can't believe the police haven't linked them." He began jotting some notes on the back of a sheet of paper on the pile. He turned it over to see if it was important. Finding it to be a reminder to submit his tax return, he pushed it aside and took another sheet.

"Maybe they have. I suppose it depends on what key details were input to HOLMES. It still doesn't mean that the York force would take seriously someone who received a death threat on a Lifetracer sent through the post. I suppose it would depend if they were aware of the other cases at the time and how Steve Daniels described it to them. They must have crank calls all the time."

"Can you email the stories over to me? What paper were they in?"

"Derby Telegraph. It was June of this year."

"Ok, I'll take a look. I'm going to Derby tomorrow. I might be able to talk to some people while I'm there. I love you Maggie."

"There's no need to go quite that far," she said laughing.

He was editing the organic farming article down to the required length when the stories from Maggie came through. There were just the two of them. Both were taken from the same paper, a week apart. In the first piece, it said that a body had been found hanged from a tree in

Darley Park. It was surprising that no one had seen the incident, but it had happened late at night and initially the police thought it might be suicide. Although why a suicide would leave a Lifetracer was beyond Connor's understanding. In addition to which, suicide in such a public place would be most unusual and as the victim had his hands tied, it would have taken some effort to stage the display.

The second article provided more detail. The victim had been fifty-two year old Paul Tranter a resident of Long Eaton who managed a warehouse in Derby. He had lived all his life in the Derby area and as far as Connor could tell from the story, he had no apparent links to either Birmingham or York. What he did have was a Lifetracer. Connor wondered if there was a remote possibility that he had any connection to either Steve Daniels or David Suffolk, but that would be harder to find out.

He called a cab, got his stuff together and headed back towards York to meet Trevor.

It was an odd time of day passing round the town centre. The daytime shoppers and tourists had given way to the evening crowd, with young people now in the majority. Connor felt old as he passed short skirted teenage girls spilling out onto the pavements, trying to light the cigarettes that were denied them inside. He loved the atmosphere of the historic city. While he sat in rush hour traffic, he tried to imagine what sort of crowd would have frequented York a hundred years previously and suspected that if nothing else their skirts would have been rather longer. Fashions might change, but the shadow of the Minster had remained much the same for centuries. It was visible from so much of the city, towering over the neighbouring buildings. The cathedral's architecture never ceased to make Connor take time to stand in awe of the engineering feat it represented.

Trevor was already nursing a pint when Connor arrived and from the beaming grin, Connor suspected it wasn't his first. Connor got a glass of Chardonnay and went over to join him.

"I've got another one for you?" Connor watched for his friend's reaction.

"Another what?" Trevor looked confused, holding his hands out as though expecting another pint of beer.

"Not drink, murder!"

"Con, I spoke to you a few hours ago. Slow down will you. We're not short of work as it is. Same thing?" Trevor had made a success of growing into his well-built body. He could have moonlighted as a bouncer, but looked every inch the policeman. Connor wondered if he ever went on undercover work and how on earth he managed to disguise his occupation.

He nodded. "Looks like it. It was put down as suicide to begin with but the hands were tied in a way that meant it was either an assisted suicide or murder. From the location and the Lifetracer, my money's on murder."

"Where was it? Not here in York, I'd know about it."

Connor shook his head. "Derby this time." He passed a copy of the newspaper article across to Trevor. "Our murderer seems to get about. I don't know what that tells us."

They both fell silent. Connor was lost in thought. Now he needed something that connected the locations. There was of course the railway, but that would make it look as though the attacks were random. However, the presence of the Lifetracers told a different story. "Did you find anything?"

"Yes and no. The devices are mass produced. There's no accessible serial number that could have been used for tracking. There is no way of knowing where that particular one came from. It could have been second hand on Ebay for all we know. What we do know is that they could find no evidence from Charles Gumby's effects of it having been sent to him by post. They are presuming that it was placed at the scene by the murderer."

"So there was no advance warning?" Connor made a note.

"Doesn't look like it."

"Looks like our murderer has changed his approach," said Connor tipping his glass and watching the viscosity of the wine as it ran down the side of the glass.

"If it's the same guy."

"Yes there is that. I know where the one that was sent to Steve came from. I'm paying them a visit tomorrow. It's in Derby, same as the second murder. It seems odd that your guys aren't linking them."

"It may have got confused by the second one looking like suicide. Though I don't know of many people who choose to hang themselves in public. I suppose he may not have wanted to spoil the family home, but when it's assisted it's usually something less dramatic than a hanging. Con, do you think it's wise to get involved in this?"

"When have I ever done what's wise? Besides, your colleagues weren't interested when Steve came to them."

"Well, maybe we would be now. Can I get you another?" said Trevor raising his empty glass.

"I thought you'd never ask."

CHAPTER 9

By the River Fosse, the dew lay heavy on the grass, but that would soon dry out as the sun gathered heat through the day. Connor walked in companionable silence with Tammy, who darted to and fro. It was good to stretch their legs before the long day in the car to Derby. He remembered he hadn't asked Maggie whether there were any stories on the mother's suicide. He looked at his watch. It was still too early to ring. He was due in Derby at 09.30. He would ring Maggie on the way.

He drove through the centre of York rather than going round the ring road. At this time of day it was quicker. As he drove out the other side and past the race course he saw the sign for the next meeting. He had a thought on how he could say thank you for all the information Maggie was pulling out for him. They could all go to the races.

He drove on, singing along to "Under pressure", with Tammy wagging her tail every time he looked across to where she was sitting next to him.

It was nearing 09.00 when he arrived at the ring road around Derby. Thank goodness for sat nav. He could remember the last time he was there, driving round the ring road twice and still missing his turning. This time was different. The sat-nav gave him perfect directions and with a mile to his destination, he pulled up at the side of the road on an industrial estate and called Maggie.

"Now what is it?" she asked in a voice of mock resignation.

"The mother. I want to know if there were any stories when she committed suicide. Anything that might tell me why she did it and what her state of mind was."

"How is that relevant? She can't be the one threatening Steve."

"I don't know. It just feels like a loose end at the moment. There was one other thing."

"Go on," she was clearly expecting more work.

"Would you like to go to the races on October 10th?"

He could hear the smile in her voice. "That would be lovely." Then cottoning on that it was a sweetener for the extra work, "you know I'd dig these out for you anyway, don't you?"

"Thanks, Maggie. I just thought it would be nice."

"Yes, it will. Will you have Mikey that weekend?"

"Yes, it will be all three of us. He loves watching horses. He'll be in his element."

"It'll be nice to spend a bit of time with him. That'll be great. Do you think he'll like me?"

"Maggie, he'll love you. Just be yourself."

"Ok. I'll ring you with those stories later. Oh, Connor there was one other thing. Have you followed up with any of the learners yet?"

"No, I've not started with that line of enquiry."

"I can't see how it could be any of them."

"Why not?"

"Well, they can't drive yet. At least not on their own. How has the murderer got his victims to their final locations?"

"Well, presumably by car. Aah, I see what you're

getting at. If they drove to the place they picked the victims up, then they must be able to drive on their own. Someone who has repeatedly failed their test isn't competent to do that. I wonder if there's another angle with the learners?"

"What's that?"

"It's just that his girlfriend, or ex, whatever she is, was picked up by Steve when she had driving lessons. Perhaps he's come on to others of his learners and they may not appreciate it."

"I can't see how that connects to these others though."

"No, that's a fair point. I'd better go. I'll talk to you later."

Connor took Tammy out of the car and walked her round before setting off for his destination. Warehouses all looked much the same as each other and the one occupied by Giftitatry was no exception. The functional, white-stuccoed office unit was at the front with the warehouse attached behind. Parking for visitors was to the side of the building close to the entrance of the warehouse.

As Connor drove round the side, his path was blocked by a fork lift truck that had been left in the middle of the driveway. Connor honked the horn of his pickup to draw attention to the fact he was trying to get through. An ungainly, overweight man in overalls with thinning sandy hair, his pudgy hand holding a cigarette, stared at him from a canopied area at the edge of the warehouse, but made no move towards the vehicle. Connor pushed the horn again and still there was no response. He cut the engine and got out of the pickup. He walked over to the man.

"Excuse me."

The man drew a deep breath through his cigarette, but gave no response.

"Is that your fork lift?"

He lurched a large pace towards Connor, stood towering over him in an intimidating fashion and blew the cigarette smoke out directly at his face. "What's it to you?"

Blinking to clear his eyes, Connor held his ground. "I need to park in the visitor spaces that are just there."

"Then you'll have to wait."

"I'm sorry, would you mind moving your vehicle? It's just that I have an appointment with the managing director and I don't want to be late."

"I've got a cigarette to smoke. I don't want to be late for that."

Connor looked at the name badge sewn on the overalls, Patrick Coltrane. "Look Mr Coltrane," he was starting to feel annoyed. "If you don't move your vehicle, I'm going to have to make a complaint about you."

As Patrick Coltrane leaned across him, the acrid smell of stale tobacco and bad breath forced Connor to take a step back. "As I said, you're going to have to wait. We're not allowed to smoke in our vehicles and no one comes between me and my cigarette."

Connor noticed another man standing a little way off, looking uncomfortable and trying to signal to him to back off. Connor's shoulders slumped. This was all he needed, a run in with the warehouse loon. He thought twice about leaving Tammy in the car. He always left the windows down for her and he wasn't sure if he was more concerned that something would happen to her or to his vehicle. On the hottest of days she sat in the back of the pickup under a makeshift shade canopy. Perhaps he'd be as well to park on the road outside. He was just getting back into his vehicle and about to reverse when Patrick Coltrane moved his fork lift back towards the warehouse and allowed him through. Connor parked the car, told Tammy to stay where she was and headed off to the office block.

Connor was ushered through to the managing director's office.

"Sorry I'm a few minutes late. I've just had a run in with your Mr Patrick Coltrane over parking."

Josh Thompson couldn't have been much older than thirty-five, dressed in jeans and an open-necked Oxford shirt. He didn't fit Connor's image of a managing director. He wondered whether his own career should have been something to do with the internet. Perhaps he could have made his fortune and retired young, instead of doing something he loved and scraping a living.

Josh gave a knowing smile. "I'm sorry. Yes, he can be a bit brusque. He's a good worker though. He lost his last job through some sort of run in with his manager. We try to work through these things with him, but it's hard going. Now, how can I help you? All my diary said is that you're a journalist writing about one of our products."

Connor shifted. He wondered whether he should have been a bit more truthful at the outset. "I did write about the Lifetracer, a couple of weeks ago in The York Press."

"Ah, that's one of our best sellers. Heaven knows why. It doesn't do anything you can't do on your computer. Still we sell a lot of them, so who am I to complain?" He laughed and shrugged his shoulders.

Connor wondered how to explain what he was working on. "The thing is, I've been asked to investigate a case where one has been used as a means of providing a death threat."

Josh stiffened up and folded his arms across his chest. "And how does that affect us?"

"Well, the one that was used had been despatched from here. Your helpdesk explained to the man who received it that there was no way it could have been interfered with before leaving the warehouse, but several more have turned up, linked with actual murders and I wondered if there was any way of tracing whether they had been supplied from here too?"

Josh looked angry, so Connor ploughed on before he had chance to answer.

"Please, don't misunderstand me. We aren't suggesting any wrongdoing by yourselves. We are just trying to trace who ordered the devices and who the recipients were."

Josh stared at him for a moment, looking as though he was trying to measure whether Connor was telling him the whole story. He shook his head. "We ship dozens of them every week. It's been one of our best sellers. We get orders from all over the world. There's no record of serial numbers. We get them in and ship them out. The computer keeps track of how many we've shipped and automatically reorders. Can you tell me anything more about the murders they're connected to? If you've got the names of the victims and the approximate dates we can look up on our systems whether the victim received it from us. One thing's bothering me though, why aren't the police involved? It should be them I'm talking to."

"I'm working for the man who received the threat. The police weren't interested when he reported it, so he called me in. I'm a private investigator as well as a journalist. The police don't seem to be following up the connection with the Lifetracer. I don't know why." Connor handed him a sheet of paper with names and dates. "These are the cases that appear to be connected. There may be others, but I haven't found them yet. One of them was here in Derby; I have an appointment to talk to someone at Higgins and Sons later this morning. That was where he was employed. It seems he'd gone to a work leaving do and the murderer took him from there. The other was in Birmingham."

Josh nodded, "I'll get somebody to take a look. Can I get you a coffee while you're waiting?"

It was half an hour before Josh Thompson came back to the meeting room. "No go, I'm afraid. There were no deliveries to the men who were murdered from us and there were so many despatches around those dates that it would be impossible to work out if any of them matched. There are a number of suppliers of this particular product. I can't see you being successful in tracking down specific Lifetracers. I'm sorry."

Connor got up. "Well, thank you for your time. It was a long shot, but worth a try." He wondered whether the manufacturer would keep a record of which serial numbers went to which reseller, but at best he would narrow it down to a supplier and a date that the purchase must have been after. It was possible with some detailed analysis that a match might be found, but it all relied on the murderer using the same name and address details for each order. The first problem would be to track down the Far Eastern country that had made the units.

He went out to the pickup, where he found a dent in his rear bumper. Tammy was waiting to see him. She must have wondered what was happening when someone drove into the car. Connor was seething. He looked round for Patrick Coltrane, convinced that this was his work, but without a witness, what difference was he going to make? He spotted a cctv camera on the roof at that corner of the building. He marched back to reception to make a complaint, hopeful that the act of violence had been captured on film.

CHAPTER 10

Connor had time for a coffee before his visit to Higgins and Sons, if he could find somewhere suitable. Eventually he found a McDonalds and bought an apple pie to go with the coffee, saving a corner of the pie for Tammy.

"What do you make of all this, old girl?" he asked when he returned to the pickup and she had devoured the apple crust. "I've got this feeling that there's a key piece of information that Steve Daniels isn't telling us. Either that or the whole situation is very strange." He shook his head. He let out a little sigh wondering why he had taken it on in the first place.

Higgins and sons was on a similar industrial estate to Giftitatry. There were varying sizes of units off driveways on either side. Connor was pleased to find car parking at the front of the building, saving him from the fork lift trucks that were manoeuvring at the side. He waited in reception for Cynthia from personnel.

"Sorry to have kept you," Cynthia breezed into reception. Despite the electric blue eye-shadow standing out on an otherwise scrubbed English rose face, it was the long purple finger nails that drew Connor's attention. Here was someone who didn't do the washing up. "Do come through, Mr Bancroft isn't it?"

"Please, call me Connor."

He was escorted into a functional meeting room, a

circular table and four chairs dominating the small space.

"Coffee?"

"No, I've just had one thanks."

She poured herself a cup, "Well I will if you don't mind. It's been one of those mornings. Now how can I help you?"

Connor wasn't sure what to make of her. She had an air of being in a hurry and bustling, but he got the impression it was more a case of trying to make herself appear busy than any reality.

"It's about Paul Tranter. I'm investigating another situation that could be related to the circumstances of his death. I wonder if you could tell me a bit about him and about the company."

"Well, of course, I've told the police everything I can. Isn't it better that you talk to them?"

"My client wasn't taken seriously when he went to the police, so he asked me to investigate for him. Am I right in thinking there was a Lifetracer found with Mr Tranter's body?"

"Well, yes."

"But that isn't a product that you sell."

"No, that isn't our sort of thing at all."

"How long had Mr Tranter worked here?"

Cynthia sipped her coffee before replying. "He'd been here about eight years."

"Do you know where he was before that?"

"No, I'm sorry. I know very little of his personal life. You'd be much better speaking to his wife, Barbara. I'm sure she'd be willing to talk to you if she thought it was going to help. She's desperate for her husband's killer to be caught. As are we all." Her smile was winsome.

"Can you give me her details?" He forced a smile back,

hoping that she might feel some sort of rapport.

Cynthia hesitated. "No, I'm afraid I can't, but if you'll leave me your card I will ask her to give you a call, if she doesn't mind."

"Thank you. That would be great. Can you tell me what happened at the leaving do before Mr Tranter was murdered?"

"I wasn't there. I have evening classes in aromatherapy and I knew Bob wouldn't mind. He's always been very interested in my little hobby. It might be worth talking to him too."

"Who's that?

"Bob Minton, it was his retirement do." Connor knew there was no point asking for his contact details.

"Could you ask him to call me too?"

"Yes, that's not a problem."

"One other thing, do you know if Mr Tranter had any enemies?"

"Paul was a lovely man. I can't imagine anyone wanting to kill him. It all seems very strange. I would have thought that Barbara would be a much better person to ask than me."

"Just one other thing. Do you know of any reason he might have gone to Darley Park?"

"I have no idea. It's not the sort of place I would imagine him choosing to go to at that time of night. You never know what's going to happen." Cynthia stopped herself. "I, well that is, Oh dear, me and my mouth, it's going to get me in trouble one day."

Connor nodded to reassure her that she was doing the right thing, while thinking to himself that she was probably right. "Thank you, if you could ask his wife and Mr Minton to call me that would be very helpful."

Cynthia resumed her air of bustle as she showed him out and Connor started to get the impression it was more for the benefit of the other staff than for him. He could imagine Cynthia doing aromatherapy. He pictured her in a floaty, flowery skirt or kaftan, still with those purple nails. He smiled and walked back to where Tammy was barking and wagging her tail in delight that he was back.

Before he drove away, Connor programmed Darley Park into the sat-nav. He wasn't sure what he hoped to see, but if nothing else Tammy could have a walk. He stopped at a sandwich van that was parked on the roadside of the industrial estate and bought a bacon lettuce and tomato sandwich, as always he would throw the tomato in a bin, he was never quite sure about the lettuce either. He wondered why they never seemed to sell just plain bacon sandwiches.

Darley Park was a mixture of open grassy areas and a number of patches given over to trees, where it would be possible to walk unnoticed, especially at night. Connor walked along by the river to the weir and wondered why such a public place had been chosen to stage a murder. Was this just a convenient location or was the killer trying to make a statement? He sat on a bench and ate his sandwich. Tammy had her head on one side, waiting for a crust. As always, she wasn't disappointed.

Connor could see nothing in particular that he could learn from the park and decided the best thing he could do was head back to York. In his mind he was building a profile of the killer. Someone who could travel round the country and who, if he did have a family, was able to come home late without raising suspicions. Connor thought of David Suffolk's poker games and wondered what time they went on until.

He was still on the A38 approaching the M1 when his phone rang.

"Hello, it's Barbara Tranter here. I had a call from Cynthia Appleby to say you wanted to talk to me about Paul." She sounded tearful.

Connor looked for a lay-by to pull in.

"Yes, I would like to if that's possible."

"How soon can you come? I'm free this afternoon."

Connor looked at the clock. He'd got enough time to turn round and head back to Derby and still be in time to collect Mikey later. "Whereabouts are you?"

As she gave him the address in Long Eaton, he programmed it into the sat-nav. "I should be there in half an hour. I'll see you then."

He drove on until he came to the motorway and then headed south towards Long Eaton instead of north for York.

Barbara Tranter lived in a small, tidily kept house on an estate. The front garden was immaculate with rows of flowers sitting amongst displays of conifers and heathers, Connor wondered whether the order was Barbara's way of dealing with grief. He walked along the weed-free, cobblestone path to the front door and rang the bell. Tammy was standing up at the window watching him go.

Connor's first impression of Barbara was of a china doll of around fifty, who would break if she so much as sat down too heavily. Her make-up was struggling to hide her grief. She forced a smile and spotted Tammy. "Oh, do bring her in. I love dogs. I've been thinking of getting one myself, since, well since Paul, you know."

Connor went back to the car and opened the door for Tammy who jumped down tail wagging and trotted up to the front door. She looked back at Connor for permission before going inside.

The house was as well tended as the garden. Connor wondered how the grandchildren were coping with their Grandma's new found tidying obsession, or maybe she had always been this way.

He sat down on the settee and Tammy lay down at his feet. "It's very good of you to see me, Mrs Tranter." He looked round at the photograph frames all around the room. Some were of the grandchildren, some of the children but many of them included Paul and Barbara Tranter. It was almost as though Mrs Tranter had developed a shrine to her husband's memory. The rest of the room was more conventional, with elegant curtains held back by matching ties, a modern flat screen television and racks of DVDs. The decorating was a little too chintzy for Connor's taste but he dismissed it as he didn't have to live there.

"Please, call me Barbara. Why wouldn't I want to see you? I'm hoping you may be able to help. Cynthia says that you're investigating another murder that may be related to that of my husband."

"Well," said Connor. He didn't want to raise Barbara's hopes, but he didn't want to dash them either. He needed all the information she could give him. "At this stage it is a threat of murder, rather than the actual thing."

Barbara sniffed, "I don't think anyone had threatened Paul before. . ." she was having difficulty referring to the death itself. "I just don't think they had."

"I'm sorry if my questions are difficult for you, but there are one or two things it would be helpful to know. Did your husband own a Lifetracer before his death?"

"A what?" She shook her head.

"A Lifetracer, there was one found with his body. It's a

sort of diary."

"Oh, you mean that thing. No, the police asked me about that. I'd never seen it before. I don't think it was Paul's. It couldn't have been, I'd have known. I suppose he might have had it at the office, but I can't see why. I think they asked about it at Higgins & Sons too. I don't think anyone there recognised it."

Connor made a note on his pad. "Had your husband ever lived in Birmingham?"

"Birmingham! Good heavens no. What's Birmingham got to do with it?"

"I thought the police might have told you, although I'm not sure they're working on the connection. There was a murder in Birmingham, six months before your husband died, where a Lifetracer was left with the body as well."

Barbara gasped. "You mean, this may be a serial killer?"

Connor stroked Tammy's head for inspiration. "Yes, I'm afraid it looks that way. Is there anything to suggest that Paul was selected? Could his killer have known that he would be at that pub on that night?"

"I suppose if they knew Bob was retiring, they might have guessed Paul would be there. At least for some of the evening. He'd been the boss for quite a time. It was appropriate that he went."

"Did he normally go to things like that?"

Barbara shrugged. "He used to tell me he'd much rather come home to me, but there were some he went to, where he'd known the person for a long time. What happened in Birmingham?"

"In that case the victim went along willingly, so we have to assume that he knew the murderer. The victim had been a teacher and headmaster, but always around

83

Birmingham."

She pursed her lips, thinking. "Paul grew up in Derby, then we moved to Long Eaton when we got married. As far as I know his family didn't have any connections with Birmingham. I believe there was a man at Bob's do that was talking to Paul, buying him drinks. That's what Bob said. It wasn't someone he knew. The police want to trace him as he may have been the last person to see Paul alive. Bob said he thought he saw them leave together, but couldn't be sure. You'd be better talking to Bob."

"Cynthia was going to call him for me as well." Connor stroked Tammy's head. He felt uncertain how to ask such difficult questions of someone who was grieving.

"I think he and his wife are away at the moment. I often see her in the post office. I think she said they would be back next week." Barbara was screwing a tissue up in her lap as she was talking to Connor; every so often she tore a tiny piece off it and was building a little pile of tissue bits on her leg.

"Barbara, I know this is very difficult, but can you think of anyone who would want to kill your husband?"

The tears began to drip down Barbara Tranter's cheeks. "Definitely not. Paul was a lovely man. He always had a kind word. He was great with the children when they were young and adored his grandchildren. Why would anyone want to kill him?"

"I don't know, but I'm going to do my best to find out." Connor's outward confidence masked the uncertainty he was feeling. He just didn't seem to have much to go on and wondered what his next steps needed to be.

CHAPTER 11

Connor hoped he wasn't going to get stuck in Friday rush hour traffic as he left Long Eaton that afternoon. Mikey would be expecting him at 19.00 and he didn't want to be late. Although the traffic was heavy outside Sheffield, he was thankful that it was still moving. He got home with just enough time to have a drink and feed Tammy, before going out to collect Mikey.

Jayne's house seemed still and silent when he arrived. There were no cars on the driveway and he rang the bell in trepidation. There was no reply. Damn her. How could she do this to him? He felt sick at the prospect that she was stopping him from seeing Mikey.

He took out his mobile and rang Jayne's mobile number to see where they were. As she answered he could hear children shouting in the background.

"Didn't you get my message?" She was shouting above the noise. "He's got a party with a school friend. I'll drop him off when we finish about 20.30."

Connor felt his shoulders relax. She must have rung the house phone and he hadn't had time to check for messages. He'd been steeling himself for her to say that he wasn't having Mikey that weekend. At least that hadn't happened. He got back into the car and hugged Tammy in relief. Then he drove home to rustle up something for dinner.

He was just sitting down to eat when the doorbell rang. He bounced to the door, presuming that it was Mikey, earlier than Jayne had thought. He was surprised to see Maggie standing there. The low hung jeans and sparkly t-shirt indicated to him that she hadn't come straight from work.

"Maggie, come in. I was just eating." He was flustered. If Maggie stayed then she was going to meet Jayne. Come to that, she was going to meet Mikey. Perhaps it would be a quick visit. He took a deep breath and reminded himself that he was an adult and these things were permissible. Maggie was still standing on the doorstep, looking at him.

"You look as though you've seen a ghost. Are you all right? You've not got someone else here have you?" For a moment Connor wondered if Maggie had been hurt in a previous relationship or whether it was just a joke.

"Of course not. I'm fine. It's great to see you. Go through to the kitchen." He kissed her on the cheek as she passed.

His plate was set on the breakfast bar that ran from the wall out into the middle of the kitchen. Maggie climbed onto the stool the other side. "I found some stuff on the mother's suicide. I thought you'd want to see it. It looks as though the paper covered it quite comprehensively."

Connor moved a pile of books aside to make space for Maggie to put her things down. "I hope you don't mind if I finish this before it gets cold?" He pointed to the plate of pasta.

"No, sure. Where's Mikey?"

Connor breathed a sigh of relief realising that Maggie was ready and prepared for meeting him. "He's at a party. He'll be here in half an hour. There's a bottle of wine open in the fridge if you want a glass."

"What, Dutch courage?" Maggie got up and helped herself to a glass of wine. She looked at the label, "South African. That makes a change for you."

"I got a case of it as a present last Christmas. I've just got round to drinking them. It's not bad. So what have you found out?"

"I think you should look for yourself." Maggie spread half a dozen sheets of paper out on the work surface.

The first one that Connor picked up was a very small article about Paula Daniels' will. "Hang on. This says she left amounts to both her sons. Surely, it doesn't mean David Suffolk, Claire's husband? Steve said there had been no money left to his sister that presumably means the brother-in-law too at least that's what you'd think from David's response. Steve didn't mention having a brother. Is there any more about a brother in any of the other pieces?"

As Maggie sorted through the pile, looking for another of the articles, the doorbell rang.

"That'll be Mikey." Connor rushed to the front door and threw it open. He flung his arms wide ready for the flying hug he would receive from his son. Mikey didn't disappoint him. Jayne was standing behind.

"I had to park on the road. There's another car on your drive." She sounded as though she were accusing him.

"I'm sorry, is it a great inconvenience to you if I have visitors."

"Who is it?"

"I don't think that's any of your business."

"This had better not be work related. I don't want you involving Mikey."

Jayne marched past him towards the kitchen.

"Why don't you come in?" Connor said, following her.

Maggie was gathering up the papers on the breakfast bar as Jayne strode in.

"Look," said Connor. "Mikey's fine," he hated having to justify himself. She'd got herself a new man and he hadn't had any say in the matter. "This is Maggie."

"Cool," said Mikey, holding out his hand to shake Maggie's. "I'm Mikey. This is my Mum. Don't mind her, she worries about me."

"I'll bring him back Sunday around 17.00," said Connor trying to usher Jayne back out of the kitchen.

"Aren't you going to say goodbye to Mummy?" Jayne shouted through after Mikey.

A little voice called back, "Yeah, bye Mum," but Mikey continued to introduce himself to Maggie.

Once Connor had closed the front door, with Jayne safely on the outside, he went back to the kitchen.

"What are you reading?" Mikey had climbed up onto a stool next to Maggie and was trying to see the papers that Maggie had covered with the envelope.

Maggie put the newspaper stories back in the envelope. "Oh, it's nothing, just something your dad asked me to do."

"Is it work? Can I see?"

Maggie looked across to Connor for help.

"Mikey, why don't you go and show Maggie all your dinosaurs? I'll just finish eating this and I'll come through. Do you want some juice, Mikey?"

"The triceratops is my favourite." He had taken Maggie earnestly by the hand and was leading her through to the lounge, where his toy box sat in the corner of the room, overflowing with the paraphernalia of childhood.

Connor followed shortly afterwards carrying the bottle

of wine and a glass of orange juice for Mikey. He raised the bottle to Maggie to ask if she wanted a top up, not wanting to disturb the explanations of all the dinosaurs that Mikey was giving her. She shook her head and mouthed that she had to drive. Connor hesitated. He'd like Maggie to stay, but perhaps none of them was ready for the situation that would occur in the morning when Mikey came to get into bed with him for a cuddle. He hoped Maggie would stay until after Mikey had gone to bed, but he'd have to wait and see.

"Can Maggie stay for the weekend too?" Mikey asked looking up at his father.

"Well," said Connor not knowing what to say.

"I'm sorry, Mikey," said Maggie, coming to the rescue. "I need to go home tonight. Maybe I could join you both sometime tomorrow. Would you like that?" Her eyes darted across to Connor for confirmation. He nodded.

"I'd like that. Will you stay to read me my bedtime story?"

Connor couldn't believe how Mikey had accepted Maggie. He wondered what he'd been worried about. He marvelled at how flexible children are when they're young.

"What shall we do tomorrow, Mikey?"

"Haven't you got some big case that you're working on? I wanted to play detective."

Maggie shot a look across to Connor, who shrugged. "Well it's a bit difficult. What I'm working on at the moment isn't very nice. I don't think Mummy would be very happy if you were involved in it."

"Is there lots of blood?"

Children, always get straight to the point. "No," said Connor. "It's funny that, but there isn't any blood. I wonder if that's relevant?"

"So, if there's no blood, can I help?"

"I don't think so, Mikey. Not this time." Connor was petrified that if Mikey went home to Jayne telling her what his dad was working on, then Jayne wouldn't let him stay at weekends.

"But Dad, you said we were partners."

"Oh, Mikey," he said, scooping the boy up in his arms. "We are partners, but I just don't think I should involve you in this particular case. Why don't you help me write one of my articles instead?"

"But that's not as much fun as playing cops."

"Another time, Mikey. Now go and put your pyjamas on and clean your teeth. I'll get Maggie to choose a story and we'll be up in a minute."

"But I'm not tired."

"Mikey, I don't want an argument. Please just go and put on your pyjamas."

"Ok." He scuffed his shoes along the floor as he left the room. Tammy followed him out and went upstairs with him.

"He's adorable," said Maggie after he'd left the room. "You know he looks like a miniature version of you. I know his hair is fair, but his face is just the same."

"Yes, everyone says that. I think it annoys Jayne. My hair was fair as a young child. We seem to get more alike as he gets older." He went over to the bookshelf and pulled out a couple of Mikey's favourites. "Now which do you prefer, Horrid Henry or Michael Morpurgo's *Billy the kid?*"

Once Connor had finished settling Mikey, he and Maggie returned to the lounge.

"Shall we look at those newspaper cuttings now?" said

Connor, refilling his wine glass and bringing Maggie an orange juice. He felt a wonderful peace from having a family around him. Having Maggie there just made everything perfect.

He began to read. "So, she took an overdose. Not that that tells us anything. The inquest returned a verdict of suicide, so it was clear-cut. What the inquest did find was that she had been reunited with her estranged child from a previous relationship. I wonder if that's the other son. No names are given so we have no choice but to ask Steve Daniels. There seem to be a lot of things he's not telling us, but it's going to have to wait until after the weekend if I'm not going to involve Mikey." Connor began to put the cuttings back in the envelope. "How do you fancy a day on the North York Moors Railway tomorrow? Mikey loves things like that and the forecast is good."

"That's a brilliant idea. I've not been up there for ages. Shall we take a picnic? I could pick some stuff up on the way over here in the morning."

"Ok, what time can you get here? Our mornings start about 7.00 when Mikey's here."

"I never see that time on a Saturday morning. Let's say 8.30." Maggie started to get her things together to go.

"Maggie."

"What?"

"Just, thank you. You were great with Mikey this evening. I appreciate that. I'm glad you're coming tomorrow. It will be great to have the three of us."

"I enjoyed it too," she said kissing him. "I love his innocence and interest in the world. When you look at all these murders, you wonder where it all goes wrong."

CHAPTER 12

Connor was woken by first Mikey and then Tammy scrambling into bed along-side him. He settled down in the hope they might let him go back to sleep for a while. He could tell from the light suffusing the room through the curtains that it was already a sunny morning and he was looking forward to their day out. When Mikey wouldn't stay still, Connor got up and went to get everyone's breakfast. He left Mikey tucking into a bowl of Coco Pops while he went to get a shower. By the time he came down, Mikey was plugged into the Playstation with Tammy dozing at his feet.

"You need to get out of those pyjamas and put some clothes on young fellow. We're going out for the day."

Mikey jumped up, leaving his on screen car to crash into a wall. "Where are we going? Is Maggie coming?"

Connor smiled. "Yes, Maggie is coming and we're going up to the North York Moors Railway to see the trains."

The little boy's face beamed. "Can we go on a steam train?"

"Yes," said Connor lifting him up. "We can go on a steam train. Now go and get dressed before Maggie gets here."

Mikey came downstairs wearing a dinosaur t-shirt and a pair of jeans. He was still barefooted and Connor knew that getting him to put socks on was going to be a battle.

He had just settled himself back in front of the television when the doorbell rang. He got up again and scurried through to answer it. It was still locked and Connor came up behind him with the key. When they opened the door, Maggie was standing there with a Tesco bag in each hand.

"Morning. I've brought provisions."

"What are we having?" Asked Mikey, jumping up and down with excitement.

"Do you like doughnuts?"

Mikey nodded, a beaming grin spreading across his innocent face.

Maggie followed Connor through to the kitchen and began to unload the bags on the kitchen worktop.

"For someone without children, you've done a pretty good job," said Connor admiring the haul.

"I've learnt by looking after my sister's children. They have very clear ideas on what they like and what they don't like. Woe betides me if I get it wrong." She laughed.

By the time the picnic was packed and they had driven to Pickering it was almost 10.30. They bought tickets for the train to Grosmont and then walked along the platform admiring the steam train and carriages before getting on. Mikey was in his element and was trying to explain to Maggie how the steam train worked. "It's like the one in the museum," he said at the end.

"He loves the Railway Museum. We've spent many wet Saturdays in there, wandering round and going on the model train they've got."

The train was chugging its way along the line when Connor's phone rang.

"Good Morning, Steve, no I'm not working on your

case today."

"But the timer is now saying 21 days."

"I'm well aware of that. To be honest, I don't know how much more I can do until you are prepared to be straight with me."

"What do you mean?"

Connor looked round at Maggie and Mikey. "I'm not having this conversation now. I'm having a day out with my son. Perhaps I can see you on Monday, when you might like to tell me about your brother."

There was quiet at the other end of the phone. Connor chose not to fill the gap.

"How did you find out?"

"I read the stories about your mother's death." Connor turned his head away from Mikey before speaking again. When he did he spoke quietly. "When I see you, you might also like to tell me what you know about the reasons your mother committed suicide."

"Oh," was all Steve replied.

"I can see you at 10.00."

"That's no good. I've got a lesson. Can you do 11.15?"

"I'll be there," and without waiting for a reply, Connor hung up and turned his mobile off.

At Grosmont they piled off the train and went to have a look round the engine sheds and shop. Tammy was startled by the loud noise of the engine letting off steam and Mikey went down to her height and wrapped his arms round her neck to comfort her. "It's ok. They always do that. You just need to stand a little further away." Connor smiled at Maggie, enjoying having someone to share the moment with.

They wandered up the stairway to the shop. Mikey was thrilled with his *Train Driver* badge, while Connor got one that said *Station Master*. Maggie settled for a postcard to send to her mother in Durham.

They sat in the autumn sunshine eating their picnic before going back on the 13.30 from Grosmont to Pickering to find the car. Mikey wanted to lean out of the train window to see the steam going backwards away from the engine, but Connor made him settle for the fantastic view of the front of the train as they went round a bend and saw it stretching out before them.

Mikey was exhausted but happy. He had spent the whole day asking questions and Connor was tired from having to think of replies. He wondered whether Maggie had enjoyed it as much as he had, but from the contented look on her face he thought he might know the answer. By the time they were in the pickup on their way back, Mikey and Tammy were sound asleep in the back, leaving Connor to enjoy Maggie's company in the front.

"How did Steve react to your comments?" Maggie asked Connor.

"He was quiet. I don't know what's going on. I don't feel in control. I don't understand why it's all such a family secret, but then I suppose I don't come from a family with skeletons in the cupboard. I suppose my family had its share of crises in the past, but we did a good job of hiding them. You can join us for tea, if you want to. That is if you can stand the thought of sausages, beans and potato smiley faces."

"Yes, I'd like that. Will it mean I get to read another instalment of Horrid Henry?"

"Probably."

When they got home Connor turned his mobile on to see if there were any messages. He went to put in his diary the time he'd agreed to meet Steve and realised he already had a dentist appointment for that time. He tried ringing Steve to delay their meeting, but there was no reply from his home. He looked at the number Steve had rung him from earlier and realised it was a mobile. He tried calling and went straight to answer-phone. He left a message and said he'd try again later in the weekend.

Connor was sorry to see Maggie go on Saturday night. He was enjoying having her around and wondered if she felt the same. Mikey asked if she could see them again on Sunday, but Connor had to explain that they were going to his parents' house

"We've got a big family meal for Mum's birthday. I ought to take you there sometime, but I think I need to at least warn them first."

"Well, what do you know? I get to meet your parents as well as your son. I am honoured."

"I said maybe," he said kissing her. "If you want to."

"I try not to introduce people to my family if I can help it. Mum always tries to marry me off."

Connor laughed. I don't think it's quite as bad with boys, but I must admit my mother thinks I need someone to look after me."

"Don't we all?" Maggie said snuggling into his embrace. "Today's been good. Thank you."

"No, thank you. I'm just glad you and Mikey get on so well. You're a real hit."

She nodded, then picked up her bag and went towards the front door. "Take care with this investigation, Con. I don't want anything happening to you."

He kissed her again and opened the door for her. "I will. I promise."

***

"Morning, Tiger." Connor said to Mikey as he drew

the curtains back to let the light in to the boy's bedroom. He'd had to put heavier curtains in here to stop the early morning light from waking Mikey with the lark, in the summer. "You must have been worn out from yesterday," he said sitting down on the edge of his son's bed and leaning down to give him a hug. "It's already 09.00, we're going to have to start getting ready if we're going to pick up Aunty Charlie on the way." Aunty Charlie was his sister Charlotte, her husband Peter was out watching their youngest, Timothy, playing football and would meet them all at Connor's parents' house. Conner had agreed to pick up Charlie and their elder child, Zoe.

"Is Uncle Graham coming too?" Graham was Connor's brother. He was a brooding farmer and for all his distance, Mikey worshipped him.

"Yes, he'll be there and Aunt Michelle." It would be quite a family gathering, but then it was their mother's sixty-fifth birthday and their father insisted that this meant they were now retired and able to start enjoying their old age. Connor's mother wasn't so sure she wanted to be labelled old, but if it meant Jim would spend less time working on the farm then she was all in favour.

"Bath time for you first, though." Connor got off the bed and headed for the bathroom to run the bath and float the boat and ducks amongst the bubbles. Mikey was growing out of this sort of thing, but Connor still loved the little touches of childhood. "Come on, Mikey, the bath's ready."

A sleepy Mikey stumbled into the bathroom behind him.

"Right, you wash yourself all over and I'll come back and dry you." Connor left him to it for a few minutes and went to take the *Sunday Times* off the mat.

"Dad," a little voice shouted down to Connor.

Connor retraced his steps up to the bathroom. "Yes, Mikey."

"Will you wash my hair for me?"

The upturned sleepy angelic face couldn't fail to melt Connor and he cupped his hands in the water and wet Mikey's hair, then reached for the shampoo and started massaging it into Mikey's scalp. "Does your mum do this for you?"

"No, she makes me do it myself. She says I'm a big boy now and shouldn't need things like that, but it's nice when someone else does it for you."

Connor smiled. He was more than happy to take care of his son for as long as the little boy would stand it.

CHAPTER 13

"Happy birthday, Grandma." Mikey held out the present that Connor had given him to hand over.

Grandma gave Mikey a big hug and began to remove the paper. "Oh, Mikey," she laughed. "*1001 places to see before you die* are you trying to send Grandpa and me off travelling?"

Connor grinned. "It wouldn't do any harm, now you're both retired."

"Everyone's in the kitchen. Go through, Darling."

"Thanks, Mum." Connor led Mikey along the flagstoned passageway to the farmhouse kitchen, which had been little changed over the years. A traditional Sunday lunch was cooking in the range, even though it was late summer and everyone was sitting around looking warm.

Mikey ran outside to play with his cousins and Tammy followed.

"How's things?" His brother, Graham, asked Connor.

"Not bad. I'm working on a very strange case at the moment. I don't know what to make of it."

"If it doesn't involve the price of wheat I'm not much use to you." Graham thumped him on the back and wandered over to where their father was reading the paper.

"How's Mikey doing?" Connor's Mum asked as she

bustled over the cooking.

"Great," said Connor beaming. "Jayne's being a bit difficult, but when we're together Mikey and I have a wonderful time. I introduced him to Maggie, yesterday." He bit his lip, waiting for his mother's reaction.

"And when are you thinking of introducing us?" She stood up straight, planting her hands on her hips, a wooden spoon sticking out from her left hand.

"I wanted to talk to you about that. I'd like to bring her over one Sunday if that would be all right?"

His mother's face softened. "Of course it's all right. It's better than all right. I'm pleased to see you happy again. How did it go with Mikey?"

Connor turned a chair round and straddled it, grinning up at his mother "He loved her. She's got this way with children. She's a complete natural."

"What's this then bro'?" Asked Charlie coming back into the kitchen from seeing what was going on outside. "You've not found a real girlfriend at last, have you?"

Connor could feel himself blushing. His sister always had a way of getting to him. He was struggling to find an answer when his mobile rang.

"Hello, it's Bob Minton here, you left a message for me through Cynthia Appleby."

Connor got up. "Bob, yes, thanks for calling back. Did you have a good holiday?"

"Yes, we got back an hour ago. As soon as I got Cynthia's message I thought I'd get in touch. Wretched business. If there is any way that I can help I'd be only too pleased. I must have been one of the last people to see him alive and to think that the other bloke he was talking to might be the murderer."

"Can I come down to see you on Tuesday?" Connor

wedged the phone under his chin and patted his pockets in search of a pen and paper. Charlie, seeing what he was doing, passed him both items from the side table.

"Yes, that's fine." Bob gave him the address and phone number and agreed to meet him on Tuesday morning.

Connor wondered if he could make a day of it and go over to Birmingham as well. There wasn't a lot of point in visiting the murder site, but it might be worth going into the pub the victim was last seen in. There was a son somewhere local too. Perhaps Connor could find him.

"So what's this case?" Charlie asked him when he came off the phone.

"Well," said Connor not spotting that Mikey had come back in from outside and was sitting on the floor stroking Tammy. "I seem to have a serial murderer on my hands."

"The police should be investigating if it's a murder."

"They are, but there's a bloke who's been threatened and he's called me in."

"Cool, Dad," said Mikey wrapping his arms around his dad's waist. "When do we start?"

"Oh, Mikey, he said swinging the boy round and sitting him on his knee. "I don't think you should be involved in this one. Besides, I promised your mum."

"Go on, tell me about it, Dad. Is it very horrible?"

"Well, all murder is horrible, Mikey."

"That's enough now," said his mother. "I'm just putting lunch out and this is no conversation for my birthday."

Connor smiled, relieved to have been given a way out of a difficult situation. He got up to clear the table ready for the meal and give his mother a hand. It seemed unfair that it was her birthday and yet she was still doing all the work. It was hard to stop her. She loved taking care of her family and there were precious few occasions on which everyone got together these days.

Connor took pleasure in choosing a bottle of wine from the rack and pouring it out for the adults.

"Can I have a bit?" Mikey asked

"Just a sip," said Connor watching him. "That's enough now. You'll be in no state for the afternoon."

Mikey laughed.

"A toast," said Connor. "To the best Mum in the world." They all raised their glasses and repeated the toast.

Connor's mum was beaming with pleasure and embarrassment. "Now tuck in, before it gets cold. There's plenty more if anyone wants seconds."

The afternoon passed quickly and all too soon it was time to take Mikey back to his own mother's.

"But I don't want to go. I want to live with you Daddy."

"I want you to as well, Mikey, but at the moment you live with Mummy and I don't think that's going to change for a while." Connor put his hand behind the driver's seat and gripped Mikey's hand.

"But Mummy hasn't got a dog and I love being around Tammy."

"Tammy loves having you around too. At least you can see her on weekends."

"Will you tell me some more about the murder?"

"No, Mikey. If you go saying anything about that to your mother, we'll both be in trouble."

Mikey was in tears when Connor pulled up outside his mother's house. Connor leant across and gave him a hug. "Be brave, little man. I'll talk to Mummy about whether I can see you next weekend."

He got out of the pickup and took Mikey's bags off the back seat. "Stay, Tammy. I'll be a minute."

He went round and opened Mikey's door and lifted him down. "Come on, ranger," he held out his hand to his son.

When Jayne opened the front door, Mikey clung to Connor. "I don't want to go?"

"What have you been saying to him?" Jayne snapped.

"Nothing. We just had a good time. Can I have him next weekend, please?" He hated having to beg, but he was desperate for the time with his son.

"We'll see. It doesn't seem to be doing him any good if this is the state it gets him into."

"This state, as you put it, isn't because of spending time with me. It's because he's got to come back to you. He is my son too, you know." Connor could feel the anger rising and was trying to control it before Jayne refused to let him see Mikey at all. "I'll pick him up at 7.00 on Friday." Then before she had chance to answer, he ran his hand through Mikey's hair and then reached down and kissed him. "I'll ring you." He reassured his son and then walked back down the path almost in tears himself.

Sunday evening seemed very quiet when Connor and Tammy got home. He thought about ringing Maggie to see if she could come over, but instead he decided to read through all the cuttings from Paula Daniels suicide. Who was the other son? Why hadn't any of the family mentioned him? Connor was starting to think that his less than ethical hacker friend was likely to be coming in very useful soon. What he wasn't sure about yet was who he wanted to know more about. There was David Suffolk and then Steve's former lodger, perhaps there was more going on there than Connor knew about.

He settled on the sofa with a glass of Chianti and Queen's *Night at the Opera* playing in the background and then he began to draw out a tree of who was related to whom so far. He'd need to talk to Steve in the morning before filling in any more of the gaps. He leant back on the settee, letting the music wash over him. He hoped that leaving his mind to process the available information on its own might throw out a new angle. Instead, he dozed off, exhausted from his happy weekend.

***

Connor was not in the best of moods as he left the dentist on Monday with one side of his face numb from anaesthetic. He hated having fillings as much because it reminded him he wasn't as young as he used to be, as for the reality of the discomfort.

"It's all right for you," he said to Tammy as he got back into the pickup, "you have teeth designed to last as long as you do. I suppose to be fair it's because you don't live so long, but it's good to have all your parts work for as long as you need them."

He turned out of the car park and headed back to the ring road. "Let's go and find out what Steve Daniels has got to say to us this time." Some of the numbness was wearing off and he could start to feel the bruising of having his jaw pulled around.

Steve was looking out of the window waiting for him when he arrived. This time Connor took Tammy in with him and she followed at his heel. Steve said nothing about Tammy as they entered.

"It's down to 19 days," said Steve looking down and wringing his hands as they went into the lounge.

"In which case you'd think you'd have told me everything you know. Come on, Steve. Let's have the rest of the story. Who is this brother? I presume you do know about him."

Steve nodded. "It's not what you think."

Connor didn't know what he thought, so it was hard to agree with Steve.

"He's my half-brother. We didn't know about him. My mother had him before she met my father and he was given away. My brother, not my father." He laughed. "We've known about him for a couple of years. We don't see him at all."

"And your mother left him some money too."

Steve nodded.

"What can you tell me about him? Is there any reason that he should bear a grudge against you?"

"I can't see why," Steve glanced at Connor as he spoke, but then looked down again.

"I think I'd like to talk to him. Can you tell me his name and where he lives?"

Steve shook his head.

"Look, Steve, this isn't a game. Either I'm working for you and you are going to cooperate or I'm off the case." He got up.

"No, don't go. I just meant, I don't know where he lives. Not beyond the fact that it's around Derby somewhere. His name is Patrick Coltrane."

Connor sat down. "I don't suppose he drives a fork lift truck does he?"

"I don't know."

"Well if it's the same Patrick Coltrane that I'm thinking of, I've got a score to settle with him. He dented my car."

"You've met him?" Steve seemed surprised.

Connor wasn't sure how much to say. If it was the same Patrick Coltrane, then he worked for the company that delivered the Lifetracer to Steve. That couldn't be a coincidence? After all, he always said there were no such things.

"How much can you tell me about him and the background to his birth?"

Steve shrugged. "I think it was about a year last November that he came looking for Mum. She'd never mentioned him to any of us, not even to my father. He had no idea."

"Did you meet him?"

Steve nodded.

"What did he look like?"

"He's quite tall. A big man. Sandy, thinning hair. Struck me as a bit slow, sort of cumbersome."

Connor remembered the bloke with the fork lift. It sounded like the same man. There couldn't be two men answering to that description in Derby who both happened to have the same name.

"Did he smoke?"

"I don't remember." Steve appeared to be thinking. "Yes, I think he did. He was overweight too. I remember thinking how little he was like the rest of the family, but then I suppose Claire and I are like our father, for better or worse."

"What happened when he turned up?"

"I don't know. I wasn't there. We met him later. I think Mum thought we could all be one big happy family."

"But you couldn't?"

"That wasn't what he wanted. To be honest I don't' know what he wanted, other than to show her she'd ruined his life."

"What happened?"

"There was an argument. Things got a bit heated. I told

106

him he'd better leave. It's bad enough with David's temper without Patrick throwing his fists about."

"So he left?"

"Not before saying we hadn't heard the last from him."

"Steve, why didn't you tell me all this before?"

"It didn't seem relevant. I thought he was all bluster and then Mum died. I couldn't see that it fitted in anymore. He'd got his money. He never wanted us in the first place."

"Is there anything else you aren't telling me? This does all seem rather important in the circumstances."

"No, there's nothing else. I promise."

"How did your father react to this and your sister? Come to that how did that husband of hers react?" Connor felt a prick of excitement. Like a hound scenting a rabbit.

"David, he was the worst. Particularly after Mum left Patrick some money. Dad was all very quiet about it. It was like he didn't know what to say. David thought Claire had been badly treated and that meant he'd been badly treated."

Connor could see how he might not appreciate that. He wondered whether any threat had been issued to David as well.

"Steve, what made you order the Lifetracer from that company? Did you know that Patrick worked there?"

"Does he?" Steve looked wide-eyed. "I'd used them before. I found them on the internet. I'd no idea he worked there."

"Why did your mother commit suicide, Steve? Was that something to do with all this?"

Steve looked away. "I don't know. She didn't leave a

note. It's not the sort of thing you can ask afterwards. I mean, it's too late by then."

Connor wasn't ready to leave the subject. "But why do you think she did it?"

Steve snapped back, "I don't know. I said that didn't I? I think you'd better leave. If you don't want to investigate this then don't. I'll find somebody else." He got up ready to show Connor to the door.

"I'm sorry. That was insensitive of me. I'll see what I can find out." He got up feeling a little deflated. "Is there anything else you need to tell me?"

"No, I don't think so. This isn't easy."

"No, it can't be. I'll ring you with anything I find out." Tammy followed Connor out.

"Well old girl, what do you make of that?" He asked her when they got outside. "I think we need to know some more about Patrick Coltrane, not that I feel like meeting him again. Perhaps we'll do some background research and see what it turns up." He opened the car for Tammy to jump in. "You wait here. I want another little word with our Mrs Lloyd. She knew Steve Daniels' mother didn't she?"

Connor walked along the pavement and up the path to Betty Lloyd's door. He'd stretched out his hand towards the bell, but the door opened before he had chance to press the button.

"I just happened to see you out of the window."

Watching more likely! "I wondered if I could talk to you about Steve's mother. You did say you knew her didn't you?"

"Oh yes. I was friends with Paula." She continued talking as she ushered him into the house. "We went back years."

"So did you know her when she had her first baby, Patrick?"

For a moment Betty looked uncomfortable. "Well of course it wasn't something she talked about."

"But you knew."

She nodded. Then speaking quietly she said, "It was how we met. It was when I was expecting my son. You know, routine check-ups and the like. She was on her own, well staying with an aunt I think. She needed a friend."

"She gave the baby up for adoption I take it?"

"I think he went into a children's home. I don't know why he wasn't adopted as a baby. He was an odd looking thing. She said it made him easier to give away. She didn't feel a connection with him."

"Betty," Connor took a deep breath. "Do you have any idea why Paula killed herself?"

"Oh will you look at me," said Betty wiping her eyes with a tissue. "You'd think I could talk about it by now. It was a shock to all of us. She hadn't given me any idea she was going to do something like that." She blew her nose like an elephant trumpeting and then dabbed her eyes on her sleeve.

"Did she talk about having seen Patrick again before she died?"

Betty nodded and Connor sat there waiting for her to be ready to speak.

"I remember she said that she'd failed him. She thought if she'd been there for him he could have turned out differently. She said he'd never had a chance and it was all her fault."

When Betty finished Connor smiled at her. "Thank you. That is very helpful."

As Betty reached for another tissue he said, "I'll see myself out."

CHAPTER 14

"Kenmore, did you do ok at school?" Cheryl twisted a strand of her long blonde hair as she stood by the sweet stall.

He let out a deep chortling laugh, "No way. I messed up big time. That's why I'm working with you lot."

"What d'you mean? We're not that bad."

"No, I became a youth worker to help others avoid the mistakes I made."

"Yeah right. I bet you've never done anything wrong."

Kenmore's deep belly laugh was often heard ringing around the youth club walls and tonight was no exception. He stopped laughing and wiped a tear from his eye, then looked serious. "Ok, you want to listen. I'll tell you a story."

Several of the teenagers gathered round, perched on the arms of chairs and on the settee. Kenmore drew up a wooden chair and straddled his long legs around it, with the back of the chair towards the kids.

"I knew plenty of other youngsters, white and black who were finding a career with one foot the wrong side of the law. Some of it minor stuff, like shop lifting, but others were already running drugs and starting to deal. To begin with I looked at them and thought I wanted me some. Then one day my uncle Clyde came round. He'd just come out of prison. He started telling me what it was really like. He'd spent so much of his time inside he couldn't fart without someone telling him what to do. I was about twelve then."

The kids sniggered.

"So what was it like?"

"Well for someone who likes their independence and likes to make their own decisions it didn't seem like a bright idea to be locked up twenty-three hours a day and told what to do for twenty-four. I wanted me a girlfriend and a family of my own and I wasn't going to get me the best of those by being in prison. I didn't start working at school or nothing. I just kept away from real trouble."

"So what did you do then?"

"I left school with no qualifications and no prospects, same as many of the kids round here did. Same as some of you will if you don't stop truanting!"

One or two of the children looked at each other and tried not to react.

"Seven years ago, when I was sixteen I went along to a church service as a bet. It was more a dare than a bet. I found it hard to turn down a challenge, particularly when I didn't need to break the law to do it." He laughed heartily and the kids found it infectious and joined in.

Then he grinned. "I got more than I bargained for from that Sunday. I came away wanting to know more about the Christian message. Oh I'd won the bet and I didn't tell my friends what happened, at least not at first, but by the time I accepted Jesus into my life I was ready to tell anyone who'd listen. Even my most cynical mates."

"So how d'you end up here?" Gav kicked the worn toe of his trainer against the settee as he spoke.

"No one wanted to employ a black teenager with no qualifications. I realised I needed a proper education to do anything with my life. So I went to evening classes and did voluntary work during the day. I decided I wanted to work to help other youngsters avoid the mistakes I made and do something with their lives. So I work with you lot. I know some of you come to church, but where would the rest of you be if you weren't here on a Friday night."

"Same place as every other night. Out with our mates in the streets."

"Exactly! Getting up to no good or at the very least thinking about it. Studying later on was much harder. That's why I try to discourage you lot from skipping school. I know it feels like you're asserting your independence now, but it's you that will pay the price later. You can fight against authority all you like, but in the end they aren't the ones who'll suffer."

There were groans from one or two of the boys. Cheryl said, "We know that. It's just that I hate school."

"You'll hate what not going does to your life even more." Kenmore was about to carry on when Patrick came in.

"What you looking at?" Patrick pushed one of the younger kids out of his way.

"I'm sorry, Patrick you know we don't allow that type of behaviour, man." Kenmore got up off the chair pulling himself up to his full height.

Patrick took no notice of Kenmore and proceeded to push another child off a chair that he wanted to sit in.

Kenmore went over to him. He felt sorry for Patrick. He didn't fit.

"What's the problem, bro?"

"What's it to you?"

"It's quite a lot to me when you start pushing the others around. You know we have rules about respect."

Patrick spat to the side of Kenmore. "No one respects me. Why should I care?"

Kenmore could see his point. Patrick had spent his life in and out of fostering, until moving to Birmingham with a family who had adopted him. The adoption seemed to be as much out of pity as any real fit with their lives. On top of all that, the boy had an inherent difficulty in dealing with the world around him.

"You get respect here." Kenmore said the words, but wasn't sure how true they were.

Patrick was different. Kenmore had no idea why the boy attended. He sat in the corner on his own, staring at the others enjoying themselves, as though watching through a window. He never seemed to want to join in. He never said much. He was large for his age and tended to lope rather than walk. He was ignored by most of the other children. They were too scared of him to say anything he would overhear. It wasn't the same as respect, but it had the same result.

"If you want to stay, you keep to the rules." And with that Kenmore went back to where the group was sitting, but the moment had passed and he wasn't in the mood to retake up his story telling.

Patrick scowled after him.

One of the younger boys needed to walk past Patrick. He smiled at Patrick nervously as he went. With one swing of Patrick's fist, the boy found himself sprawled across the snooker table.

"Hey!" Kenmore rarely raised his voice, but when he did it was loud. He approached Patrick. "Hey, easy man. No one here means you any harm."

Patrick swung his right fist and landed a thumping blow to Kenmore's chest. Kenmore staggered backwards, gasping for breath as the wind was knocked out of him. He doubled over, gulping for air.

Kenmore's voice was controlled when he was able to speak again. "I'm sorry, Patrick," he coughed still struggling, "but you're going to have to leave the youth club. We've been as supportive as we can be, but there's behaviour that we cannot condone. From now on you are barred." He held his chest with his right hand, while pointing towards to the door with his left.

Patrick grabbed a snooker cue, smashing it against the wall. Some of the girls screamed, whilst the boys shrank back into the nearest corners. There was silence as Patrick made for the door, stopping to overturn the table tennis table as he went, a smile of satisfaction curling the edges of his lips.

There was silence.

"Can some of you boys get this straight?" Kenmore clutched his chest to reduce the searing pain. "I think I'm going to get this checked at the hospital. I'll let Ted know I've gone." He staggered towards the door, trying not to show the extent of the pain to the children.

Kenmore said a quiet prayer for Patrick as he headed out. It was times like this that rather than doubt his faith, Kenmore was more convinced than ever of the work that the Lord had called him to do.

***

Kenmore was putting away some shopping, in the kitchen, when the doorbell rang in his terraced property. He walked with his rolling gait towards the door and peered through the spy hole before opening it. It wasn't that he was afraid of who might be there; it was a curiosity to know who it would be before he opened the door. He didn't recognise the man standing on his

115

doorstep clutching what appeared to be a Bible. Kenmore opened the door and smiled.

"How can I help you?"

"Mr Daley, you may not remember me. I used to come to the youth club years ago. It's just that I've found God and I wanted you to know."

"Come in." Kenmore waved the man along the hall. "First door on your right." He then followed behind after closing the front door. "Well this sounds like a cause for celebration. I'm afraid I don't recognise you. What did you say your name was?"

"Eddie, Eddie Stanton."

Kenmore narrowed his eyes trying to remember. "There've been a lot of kids pass through our doors over the years. When would it have been?"

"It must have been about 1982."

Kenmore took a good look at the man in front of him. He must be older than he looked. He was quite a good judge of age, still these days everyone was looking younger.

"Let me get you a drink. Tea, coffee?"

"Coffee, please."

As Kenmore went through to the kitchen the visitor followed him. "Nice place you've got here."

"Thanks," said Kenmore smiling. "My wife's the decorator. She's taken our son off to university today. There wasn't room in the car for all of us, with all the stuff he was taking. My daughter was desperate to go, so I said I'd stay behind. I was waiting for them to call to tell me how it had gone. I expect she'll get something to eat with him before heading back. He's gone to Keele, so not all that far."

Kenmore made two cups of coffee and then found a

plate for some biscuits. One thing he'd learnt working with young people was that they always appreciated a biscuit. The same seemed to be true of older people too. He turned his back to reach up to the cupboard and as he did so Eddie picked up the coffees.

"I'll take these through shall I?"

"Oh, yes that's great."

Kenmore followed later. He was late enough not to see Eddie slipping the tablet into his cup. As time went on, Kenmore became more relaxed.

"So are you still living locally? You said you found God, what happened?"

Eddie smiled, his face close to a grimace. "Oh, I don't live round here anymore. I live a long way away. As for God, he was everywhere and I just wasn't looking."

Kenmore was feeling strangely relaxed. He didn't feel he had full control of his mouth when he tried to speak. There was something not quite right about the man in his living room. If only he could put his finger on what it was.

The room began to swim for no apparent reason and Kenmore found himself lying back in his chair and closing his eyes.

"God is everywhere." Eddie said again, standing up and peering at the inert Kenmore. He took a vial of insulin from his pocket, attached the needle and injected it into Kenmore's arm, feeling grateful for the wonders of the internet and what you could buy from unscrupulous suppliers in other countries. You no longer had to know the right people. You just had to be able to press the right buttons and the world came to you. No one wanted proof you were a diabetic to sell you insulin.

"Just a little present I'd like to give you, nothing special." He lifted the Lifetracer from his pocket, placed it next to the unconscious body and smiled.

Of course there was a possibility that Kenmore would survive, but as long as no one found him too soon, the dose of insulin should be enough to kill him. He'd watched the rest of the family loading up and setting off a little while before he'd come to the house. He'd given them long enough not to turn back for some forgotten item before going to the door, but from what Kenmore had said, he had plenty of time before they would be back.

He put his gloves on and took the cups through to the kitchen to wash. He'd been careful not to touch anything else and as long as he removed the trail, everything was going to be all right. He wondered whether his boots would have left any footprints, but they were two sizes larger than his own feet, so it would be misleading if the police did find them. He opened the front door and went along the street to his car. The Micra was parked round the corner in a side street. He drove off before removing the glasses and the wig of fair hair. As he put the gloves on the back seat, he was glad to put Eddie Stanton away for another day.

He drove away from Birmingham towards the motorway. Everything was starting to fall into place.

CHAPTER 15

Connor moved the open cereal packets aside and spread his papers out on the breakfast bar in the kitchen. He often found that expanding his working environment around the house gave him more space for thinking. However much information he had gathered so far, he needed the services of Terry (Fingers) Thomas to fill in some gaps.

Within the computer world some hackers went into other people's computers for the fun of it, because they could; others did it for illegal gain. There also existed some on the other side of the law, 'ethical hackers'; people who used their hacking skills to assist with law enforcement or to help companies close up any holes in their systems. Somewhere in between sat Fingers. Fingers would best be described as a 'less than ethical hacker'. He worked with law enforcement operations, most usually private eyes and undertook operations that in their nature were not always strictly legal. What he couldn't find out about a person using a computer wasn't worth knowing.

Connor had met Fingers through a friend and had been delighted by the association. As long as the records procured never had to be used in court, Fingers would stay out of prison and earn a tidy sum in the meantime. In matrimonial matters, this wasn't an issue. A murder case might be more difficult.

Connor dialled Fingers' mobile. "You sound like I woke you." Fingers worked irregular hours at the best of times.

"Hey, don't worry. I needed to get up by 16.00 anyway. What's new?"

"I need some information. It's not an errant husband this time."

"Ok, I'm listening." Fingers was about Connor's age and lived alone with his computers.

"I'm investigating a death threat."

"Hey, Man. Do you really need me?" Connor could hear the alarm in his voice.

"Fingers, please, hear me out."

"I'm listening." His voice still sounded half full of sleep.

"I just want a basic history. I've got one or two people who I need to know more about. Where they've lived. Where they've worked. That sort of thing."

"Ok, I can do that. Most of that's public anyway and the bits that aren't, well they'll never know the difference. What names?"

"To start with there's David Suffolk." Connor went on to provide as much detail as he could on David, Steve Daniels, Harry Daniels and Andy Bentley. He paused and then threw in Betty Lloyd.

"There's one other too. A bit of a rogue. The bastard dented my car. Patrick Coltrane. I know he was the son of Paula Daniels, but I don't know much else. He works for Giftitatry in Derby. I'm not certain if that's the same Patrick Coltrane, almost sure, but not certain. I want his whole life story, as much as you can get." Connor tapped his pencil on the pad in front of him, trying to think whether he'd got everyone.

"When do you need it by?"

"Soon as."

"Ok, leave it with me. I'll see what I can find. Should I be charging danger money on this one?"

"Fingers, you always think of a premium to charge. Just bill it as usual." Connor smiled.

"A man's gotta live." And with that he hung up.

***

Connor found Bob Minton's house on his way in towards Derby. It was a mile or two from the warehouse that Bob had worked in and had the benefit of convenience, even if the setting was not idyllic. He wondered whether Bob would think of moving now that he'd retired.

Bob's garden was tidy, with no sign of rotting bicycles and undriveable cars. The same could not be said for his neighbours, either the attached property or the one the other side.

Connor went up the path and rang the bell. It was Mrs Minton who answered the door. She looked about the same age as Bob and was neatly dressed, with an apron covering her skirt.

"You must be Connor. Come through. Bob's just outside at the moment. I'll call him. Can I get you a cup of tea? It's a dreadful business. Bob was quite put out when he heard about it and to think it must have happened not long after Bob saw him." She had a gentle manner and diminutive stature. Connor imagined her to be unprepared for such a traumatic occurrence.

Connor waited for a polite break in the introduction before saying he'd prefer a black coffee if possible and seeing it as her cue Mrs Minton scurried back towards the kitchen to call Bob.

Bob was still holding a pair of secateurs when he came into the lounge. He held out a muddy hand to Connor.

"Pleased to meet you. I've been enjoying the unseasonably good weather in the garden. I couldn't believe it was still so good when we came back from Spain. It was a lot warmer out there, but I can't complain. It beats working anyway." He grinned at Connor and waved him to sit down on the worn flowery sofa. There was evidence of cats having used the legs as a scratching post, but no suggestion that this was recent.

"It's good of you to see me."

"Not at all. I was shocked by what happened to Paul. He wasn't a bad boss. He didn't deserve anything like that. I still can't get over the fact that I was talking to him and that other chap not long before it happened." He shook his head.

"Can you describe him?"

"Who, Paul? Oh, sorry, I see. I don't know. He wasn't one of us. That is, he didn't work at Higgins. I think he said something about his father having worked there, but I can't remember him saying who his father was. I don't think he was very old. Late twenties of thirties. He'd got one of those tops on. The ones with the hoods, that so many people find threatening. I suppose under that he could have been any age. He was clean shaven, that I did notice, but I don't think there were any 'distinguishing features'." He seemed pleased with himself for using the term.

"Did he have an accent when he talked?"

Bob hesitated. "Not that I remember. He didn't sound as though he was from round here, but then, you can't always tell."

"Did he talk to anyone apart from Paul Tranter?"

122

Bob stopped to think. "No, I don't think he did. It struck me as a bit odd in the first place. Why would the son of someone come to my leaving do and not even make himself known to me. I must have known his dad, otherwise how would he have known I was having a do? Come to that, how would he have known Paul? I'd been there longer than he had, unless it was from some previous job. I was trying to think back through all the lads I've worked with over the years and whether any of them had a son of that sort of age, but there've been so many, it's hard to say." He shrugged.

Bob's wife, Marge Minton, came in with the coffee and put it down on the table. She looked as though she was about to speak but Bob gave her a sharp look and she smiled and went back out of the room.

"Was there anything strange about Paul Tranter that night?" Connor was jotting some notes on his pad.

"What sort of thing do you mean?" Bob was playing with the secateurs as he spoke; doing up and undoing the catch.

"Well, was it usual for him to come out to occasions such as yours? Would someone have known he'd be there?"

Bob fiddled with the catch on the secateurs as he answered. "He usually turned out, at least briefly. I don't think I'd ever seen him stay so long or let his hair down so much. He was laughing and seemed to be enjoying himself and I don't think I've ever seen him have more than one drink before. That was all unusual."

"What was he like as a boss?"

"Paul," Bob sounded surprised. "He was all right. He expected the lads to work hard and wouldn't stand for any nonsense, but he was fair. What more can you ask for?"

"Did he ever get on the wrong side of anyone?"

Bob pursed his lips. "I suppose he must have had his enemies. Who hasn't? It's not the job of the boss to be liked." He laughed as though he had cracked a joke. Connor waited for him to get back to the point. "There's always talk. You know how it is."

"What sort of talk?" Connor sat up a little straighter, wondering if he was getting somewhere.

"Well, you know. Sometimes one of the lads would get told off for something and it was always Paul who had to do the telling."

"Can you remember anything in particular?"

"Lad's come and go. You don't always know what happened to them. Every so often there'd be a rumour that someone had got the boot, but most of the lads had been there for a while. They were a good bunch."

"Can you remember any who didn't stay?" Connor felt as though he was panning for gold and just searching for that one elusive nugget.

Bob scratched his thinning grey hair. "You'd be better talking to Cynthia about that one. She'd know all the people who had worked there." Connor made a note to talk to her again.

"Can you think of anything else from that evening?"

Bob sat and thought. "No, not that I remember. If anything does come back to me, I'll give you a ring. Better get back to my roses," he said, raising the secateurs.

Connor got up and headed towards the door. He thought better of shaking Bob's muddy hand again on his way out.

"Birmingham then." He said to Tammy as he got back into the pickup. He decided to go down the A38 rather than back round the motorway. He wondered how he should play the visit to Charles Gumby's family. He hadn't spoken to them and they weren't expecting him. It was foolish. There was a good chance they wouldn't even be in. He hadn't thought about this part of his day. He'd just thought that having already headed south, it made sense to carry on. Ringing ahead might have been more sensible.

He pulled off the A38 at the next service area and pulled out the details of Charles Gumby's family from his satchel. It hadn't been difficult to find an address and phone number on the internet, just from the information that had been given in the newspaper. What on earth was he going to say?

He listened to the ringing tone on the phone and rehearsed in his head how he would introduce himself.

"Oh hello, is that Dora Gumby?"

"Yes, who is this?"

"You don't know me. My name is Connor Bancroft. I'm investigating a death threat in which a Lifetracer has been sent to the victim. I believe there was one left at the scene of your father-in-law's murder." He could sense that she was weighing up if this was a crank call. "I want to find out if it's the same person behind it."

"We've already spoken to the police. You should go to them."

He could tell from her tone of voice that this wasn't going the way he wanted. "Please, don't go. I don't think the police are working on the Lifetracer connection. I don't know that they've realised there's a link. There was another murder in Derby too." He could tell that he'd now got her attention.

"It's awkward. I'll need to talk to my husband. What

do you want?"

"I'd just like to ask you a few questions. I'm trying to work out what the connection is."

"If you'll give me a number I'll get back to you."

"But I'm nearly in Birmingham now. I could come round in half an hour."

"Mr Bancroft, if after what happened to my father-in-law, you think I'm going to invite a strange man round to my house, you are very much mistaken. My husband will telephone you."

Connor felt the sting of the reprimand. It was a fair point. He hadn't thought to put himself into her shoes. He was so used to dealing with marital infidelity that he hadn't thought of the implications of murder.

"I suppose we can at least call in at the pub and then see where he died." Connor said to Tammy as he closed his phone. "Come on girl."

CHAPTER 16

There had been little to gain from the visit to the Black Horse. The bar staff had changed since the night of Charles Gumby's murder and although there were a number of people sitting around the bar, they were lunchtime drinkers who didn't frequent the pub in an evening. Connor had asked around, but got nowhere. Feeling frustrated, he made his way out to the Lickey Hills.

It was hard to imagine on a sunny September afternoon that this had been the scene of a tragic murder. As he and Tammy trekked up the hillside, he wondered where it had all happened, but realised he wouldn't be any the wiser about the course of events even if he knew the location. The view from the top of the hillside was an interesting mix of industrial and rural. Even the fields in the distance were bisected by the motorway, with its moving snake of continuous traffic. Connor took the ball out of his pocket and threw it for Tammy who scampered across the grass in pursuit.

Connor shrugged. "Nothing here to see, girl. We may as well be getting back." They made their way back down to the pick-up, Tammy running ahead and then back with the ball as they went. Once back in the car they set off to join the motorway snake to go home. Connor pulled in for fuel at the service station and bought a copy of the local newspaper to get a feel for what the place was like and to look for freelance writing opportunities. He didn't look at the headline until he was putting it down on the seat. 'Vital Clue in Youth Worker Murder'.

He moved the pickup away from the pump and parked again so that he could read the story.

'Police are saying that the murder of youth worker, Kenmore Daley, may be linked to the murder in December last year of former headmaster, Charles Gumby. As reported in the Mail yesterday, Mr Daley (49) was found dead in his home in Kings Heath on Saturday. Although Mr Daley died of an apparent overdose of insulin the police are treating the death as suspicious and have issued a statement saying that there are similarities to the death of Mr Gumby (70), who was found strangled on the Lickey Hills in December of last year.

Police are appealing for anyone who spoke to Mr Daley in the days leading up to the incident to come forward.'

Connor sat back in his seat and let out the breath he had been holding. While he'd been enjoying himself on the North York Moors Railway, the killer had struck again. At least these two were in Birmingham, so some sort of link was possible, particularly with them both working with children, but how did Paul Tranter fit in?

Connor decided to ring Maggie, but needed to get away from the petrol station first. He started the engine and pulled back onto the slip road. The wonders of technology. He spoke into the phone telling it to call Maggie. The phone started ringing out.

"Hello, gorgeous."

"Con, you old flatterer. Where are you?"

"I'm on my way back from Birmingham. I wondered if

you wanted to come over later."

"Have you got any food in?"

"Not exactly. We could go out."

"Why don't you come to mine? I'll pick something up on the way home."

"Tammy and I will be there. I've got another murder for you."

"With a Lifetracer?"

"I don't know yet. I need to ring Trevor and see if he can get anything. I'll see you later."

Neither Trevor nor Fingers were on speed dial. Calling them would have to wait until he got home, which given the traffic on the M42 could be some length of time. Connor resigned himself to a long journey and turned on Radio 5 for company.

It was 19.00 before Connor got home and once again Tammy was waiting to be fed. As Connor came through the lounge he noticed the answer phone light flashing. He decided for the sake of peace and quiet to feed Tammy first and then deal with the phone. He'd told Maggie he'd be there by 20.00, which should give him time for a quick shower as well as ringing Trevor.

After putting a scoop of food in Tammy's bowl and leaving her to bolt it down, he pressed the answer phone button.

"Yo, ring me. I've got something for you."

Fingers. Connor dialled his number.

"What have you got?"

"Can I email this to you? I've not finished yet, but there's quite a lot to be going on with."

Connor gave him his gmail address. He could take his net-book to Maggie's and access it from there.

"I should have the rest by the end of tomorrow. You're

dealing with some interesting people."

Connor was tempted to look at the detail, but if he was going to stick to his resolution of not letting Maggie down, then it would have to wait. He knew what he was like. If he became engrossed in the detail, he'd be there all evening.

He dialled Trevor's mobile.

"I suppose it's too much to hope that you've rung me because you think I'm good company and you can't bear not to see me?" The policeman was chuckling on the other end of the line.

"Funny," said Connor smiling as he did so. "But no. I'm after some more information on the same case. Well it's not exactly the same case, it's a related one. There was a murder last weekend in Birmingham. Gentleman by the name of Kenmore Daley. I want to know if the police found a Lifetracer at the scene. It's been linked to the death of Charles Gumby, but the paper didn't say how."

"It sounds like our guys are on top of it. Why don't you back off?"

"Come on, Trevor. Firstly, I've got a client and secondly, I want the money. I suppose I'm intrigued with this one now as well and my journalistic instincts are saying there's a story and I'm getting closer."

Trevor grunted. "I'll see if I can find out, but I shouldn't be doing this."

"Not even if I buy you another drink?"

"Hmm."

Connor smiled. He knew his friend wouldn't let him down and besides if it all came together he'd hand it all over to Trevor anyway. It might work out well for both of them.

He went upstairs to have a shower as the phone rang

again. He grabbed the handset in the bedroom.

"I miss you, Daddy." Mikey started to cry on the other end of the phone.

"Oh, Mikey. I'm sorry I'm not there with you. I'll see you on Friday. That's only another three sleeps away."

"Why can't I live with you?"

"It just isn't as easy as that." Damn Jayne. *Why couldn't it be as easy as that?* He wanted it. Mikey wanted it. "I know it's hard."

"Have you caught the bad man yet?"

"No, not yet Mikey, but I'm trying. Can I talk to Mummy?"

"Jayne, it's Connor. Did you know he'd rung me?"

"I can't say I'm all that happy about things. All he's done since last weekend is talk about you and Maggie."

"He misses me, Jayne. It's natural. I can see him this weekend can't I?"

"I was thinking of doing something with him."

"Such as?"

"Oh I don't know. I don't have to tell you everything."

"At least Saturday then. He wants his dad."

"Ok, Saturday. But get him back here by seven."

"Thanks, Jayne."

Why did everything have to be so hard?

***

"Maggie! You've got to read this." Connor turned the net book round for her to see.

Maggie came over with wet hands from preparing the vegetables. "You'll have to read it to me," she said waving her hands towards him.

"I don't know which is more interesting, David Suffolk, who seems to have debts in excess of £150,000 and a penchant for young men or his half-brother-in-law.

Patrick John Coltrane was the other son of Paula Ross, now Daniels, and a father who, if known to her, had been her secret to the grave. I wonder whether she knew who it was. Anyway, he was in and out of children's homes during his childhood, before moving to Birmingham where he was adopted by the Coltrane family of King's Heath."

"So, you're saying . . ."

"I'm not saying anything except he has links to the area. I don't know from this whether he went to the school that Charles Gumby was head of, but if I had to put money on it, I'd guess that he did. But then a headmaster and a youth worker could have known about David Suffolk's weakness too."

Connor kept on reading. His mind was racing. Was this the point at which he should hand what he'd got over to the police? He was too much of a coward to want to be a hero and prove all the links. For a start he was not enthused by the thought of meeting either David Suffolk or Patrick Coltrane again in person.

"Wow, Maggie. You're not going to believe this. It says here Patrick worked for Higgins and Sons. That gives us a link to Paul Tranter." He sat back in his chair and breathed out. He could feel his hand shaking with the excitement and tried to take control. "We need to know whether Patrick was seen in the areas of the murders or whether he has any alibis for those dates. He didn't strike me as the gregarious sort. I'm guessing it could well be a case of him being at home on his own and no one to verify his story. I should be more suspicious if he were with someone. It's looking less like David Suffolk, although by the sounds of it, he's guilty of other things!"

"Con, you can't just approach Patrick. He was the one

who drove into your car. If that's what he does for starters, what else is he going to do to you?"

"You're right, but I could do some background research. Find if he has connections to all of the people and whether he had any motive for finishing them off. What we've got so far is that Patrick Coltrane works for the company that supplied the Lifetracer to Steve, he worked at the same company as Paul Tranter and he grew up in King's Heath, the same place that both Charles Gumby and Kenmore Daley worked with children. You've got to admit, it doesn't look good for him. Perhaps I should follow him, watch his movements. I'm good at that sort of thing and I do enjoy covert operations."

"What do you think you're going to find?" Maggie sounded exasperated. "You don't think he's planning any more murders do you?"

Connor shrugged. He felt sulky having his idea ridiculed by Maggie. "Isn't there supposed to be a pattern to the frequency of murders by serial killers, or is that just in the movies?"

"Well, what have you got so far? The most recent was this month."

"Before that I've got one in December last year and one in June of this year. That either means they're getting more frequent or there are other murders we don't know about yet."

"Do you want to check there wasn't a full moon while you're at it?"

Connor got up and gathered his things together. "If you're not going to take this seriously then I'm going home."

Maggie came over and rubbed his cheek with her hand. "I'm sorry. I didn't mean to poke fun. I'm not used to this stuff. Please don't go." She put her hand on his neck and stroked it.

He could feel himself melting under her touch. He was torn. He wanted her to take what he was doing seriously, but that touch. He lent forwards and kissed her. The investigation could wait; perhaps it was worth accepting her apology.

CHAPTER 17

Connor wanted to find out how much Steve Daniels knew about his half-brother. He wondered if the family had come together before their mother had died. It looked as though Patrick Coltrane had some connection to the murders, but if Steve didn't so much as know the guy, why would Patrick threaten him? Ok, so they'd met, but was it any more than that? Was it jealousy for a lost upbringing with his mother? Jealousy was a powerful motivator. Connor headed straight round to Steve's house when he left Maggie's.

The road was busy with rush hour traffic as Connor drove out of the city towards Clifton. He was glad he was going in the opposite direction to the commuters. As he approached the house looking for a place to park, he spotted Steve getting into his own car and preparing to drive off.

Connor's car was pointing the opposite way. Steve didn't see him as he drove past. He appeared to be engrossed in opening the car. In that moment Connor's curiosity took over and he decided to follow Steve. He turned left down the next side street, hoping that it would give him the opportunity to go round the block and come out in time to see which way Steve went. He'd chosen a dead end. He turned round as quickly as he could in the pickup before pulling back onto the road in search of

Steve. Steve's Nissan with its learner driver sign prominently standing on the roof was nowhere in sight. Connor was disappointed. He reasoned that Steve was probably off to collect his first learner of the day and that following him was unlikely to have yielded anything useful, but he was hooked.

His plan was thwarted, but the adrenalin was still pumping, he parked the Mitsubishi and headed back towards Steve's house. He had no idea what he was looking for without Steve there, but he just wanted to have a poke around.

He walked up the path to the front door. There was no point ringing the bell. He knew that Steve was out. He peered through the lounge window. The Lifetracer was still sitting on the coffee table. If his calculations were correct, it must now say 17 days. There was nothing else of interest to see. Connor was just wondering whether he could get round the back of the house when the front door opened. He pulled away from the window.

"I, I was just …" He was relieved to see Emma Prince standing there. The colour drained from her face, she looked as startled as he was.

"Sorry, did you ring the bell? I was upstairs. You can't always hear."

Connor relaxed. "Yes, I thought there was nobody home, I was just having a quick look to be on the safe side. I was looking for Steve." He realised it must be obvious that he was looking for Steve, but he'd said it without thinking. Then a thought struck him, "I don't suppose he's said much to you about his half-brother, Patrick Coltrane has he?"

Emma seemed to have recovered from her surprise. She shook her head. "No, sorry. He hasn't talked about him at all."

"Do you know when he'll be back?"

"He said he'd got lessons all day today and wouldn't be back until tonight."

Connor wanted to ask if her being there meant they were seeing each other again, but wasn't sure how to pose the question. "If you see him, can you tell him I called? Thanks." Then he made his way back to the road and the safety of his pickup.

"Well, Tammy, we nearly blew that one." He started the engine and rested his forehead on the steering wheel for a moment. "I need to be a little more careful if I'm ever to be a proper private eye. It's far easier as a journalist. You don't need to be as furtive at least not with the stories I write. Where to now?"

Tammy wagged her tail.

"Ok, home it is. Let's go and make some phone calls. Do you fancy breakfast first?" And with that, Connor headed off to McDonalds.

He was just turning into the road to McDonalds when his phone rang. It was Raymond Gumby, Charles Gumby's son.

"My wife said you'd called. Who are you?"

Connor noted the abruptness. "Mr Gumby, I'm sorry to intrude, but I'm investigating a death threat to my client which I believe may be linked to the murders of your father and Kenmore Daley."

"Why don't you talk to the police? They're dealing with it. I don't see how I can help you."

"I'd just like to ask you a few questions about your father, to see if there is anything that might help. Did you know Kenmore Daley?"

There was quiet for a moment. "I went to the youth

group he helped run when I was kid. We lived quite near there."

"Did your father know him?"

"I suppose so. As a parent you try to take an interest in where your children are."

"Did they ever work together?"

"Not that I know of. I suppose there might have been events that the youth club did in conjunction with the school, but I don't remember any."

"Would there have been many people who knew both your father and Mr Daley."

Raymond laughed. "Over the years probably hundreds."

"Did you get on well with your father?"

"Now look here, if you're trying to imply that I had anything to do with this I will speak to my solicitor about it. Just because my father was changing his will, everyone seems to think I might have had a reason to wish him dead. Well it's not true."

"Mr Gumby, I'm sorry, I didn't mean to ..." But Connor realised he was talking to the dial tone, so hung up. That hadn't gone as well as he'd intended. There were still questions he wanted to ask Raymond Gumby, but it was unlikely that he'd be prepared to answer if Connor rang back. He wondered whether there were any way he could get hold of a copy of any transcript of the police interview with Raymond Gumby. He'd need to ask Trevor. He could at the very least get Fingers to do some background checks into the son's financial situation.

Connor chided himself. If he managed to get hold of Kenmore Daley's widow, he needed to tread rather more carefully. That was two errors of judgement in one morning and there was still the rest of the day ahead.

Sitting in his parked car outside McDonald's he no longer felt hungry. He started to wonder if there were a possibility that Raymond Gumby might have any links with Paul Tranter and Steve Daniels, but it was too late to ask any more direct questions. Patrick Coltrane may not be the only one to connect to all three of the victims.

He dialled Cynthia Appleby and arranged to go back to Higgins and sons to talk to her later that day. Then armed with a takeaway they could eat along the way, he set off.

It was 11.30 by the time he got to Derby and once again he was shown into a meeting room with Cynthia Appleby flouncing behind him. He wasn't used to people trying to be so showy and it was wasted on him. He wanted to know about Patrick Coltrane and get out of there again as soon as possible. He realised he would have to go through the polite formalities if he was to come away with any useful information. Besides, after the journey the cup of coffee was very welcome.

"Have you found anything else out?" At last Cynthia signalled that she was ready to talk about the matter he was there for.

"I'm following up a lead on a former employee of yours. Do you remember a Patrick Coltrane?"

"Patrick Coltrane," she repeated appearing to search through her mind. "Oh, yes," she said. "If it's the one I think it is, I do remember him."

"Is it possible that you could dig out his file? I need to know why he left."

"It's going back a little while now. His file may have gone to the archives. I shouldn't disclose any information out of it anyway. Tell you what, I'll look it up on the computer and if it's the one I think it is, I'll tell you as much as would be publicly available."

Connor groaned. Now wasn't the time for her to go all procedural on him. He just wanted to know what happened. He hoped that the information he was given would be sufficient.

She left him in the meeting room and went out. He poured another coffee and sat back and waited. If he could get finished here in time, perhaps he could go and see what Patrick Coltrane did at lunchtime. He might eat his sandwiches at work with the lads, but if he didn't then maybe Connor could learn something. On balance, he was reluctant to reintroduce himself to the thug. A dented bumper was one thing, but if this guy was a murderer there was no end to how far he might go if he got annoyed. It struck Connor that the style of the murders didn't suit someone with an aggressive reputation. In fact there had been no brutality at all, if you discounted the inherent violence of strangulation and hanging. Perhaps it wasn't violence that was missing, so much as blood. He couldn't see Patrick taking such a bloodless approach. He was still thinking about it when Cynthia came back.

"Just as I thought." She put a file down on the table. "I can't let you see his file, but I don't see any harm in showing you this."

She took out a pile of company newsletters from the folder and started to sort her way through until she came to the one she was looking for. She smiled. "It was run as a caption competition. It's a good job that Paul Tranter had a sense of humour."

She turned the newsletter round and Connor saw the picture of Mr Tranter sporting a black eye, with a purple tinge to the edge.

"But it's not Paul Tranter's background I'm after. I

want to know about Patrick Coltrane."

"Exactly." She beamed at him.

Connor realised what she meant. "Am I right in thinking that Patrick Coltrane did this?"

Cynthia nodded. "It was all a bit of a misunderstanding over cigarette breaks. Paul tried suggesting that Patrick should go back to work before he'd finished his cigarette. He was a bit of a chain-smoker as I remember. Mr Coltrane just lashed out. Of course he was fired for gross misconduct. Paul had to go for an x-ray. They thought he'd fractured his cheekbone to begin with."

Connor resolved not to have another run-in with Patrick Coltrane.

"Was there any come-back on the incident afterwards?"

Cynthia shook her head. "It made it difficult to do a reference for the guy. In circumstances like those we would just issue our standard reference that Joe Bloggs worked for us from date A to date B and not answer any specific questions. You have to be so careful these days."

"So there's no need for me to ask whether Patrick Coltrane had anything against Mr Tranter. It looks as though he wasn't that keen on him at all. Thanks." Connor got up to go. "I don't suppose you know if Mr Tranter ever heard from him again after that, do you?"

Cynthia shook her head. "I have no idea, sorry."

Once he was outside Connor felt confused. Everything seemed to be pointing him towards Patrick Coltrane, but none of the murders seemed to fit with his tendency to immediate violence. Was it possible there were two sides to him? There was the violent first response and then a more calculated revenge at a later date.

He got Tammy out and walked her around the car park. "We're going undercover, young lady, at least as much undercover as you can do in this thing." He pointed to the Mitsubishi, not that Tammy was taking any notice, she was more interested in the smell she was trying to follow across the tarmac. "I suppose you'd rather we were tracking a suspect, but I think we might be too obvious doing that. Come on." They got back into the vehicle and set off towards Giftitatry.

"Tammy!" Connor was alert. They were driving down a side street looking for parking "Am I imagining things or does that look like Steve Daniels' car to you?"

The L-plated car was empty, but the logo and phone number on the back marked it out as Steve's. "It looks like we didn't need to follow him. So what's he doing in Derby? Stupid question. I'm guessing he's seeing his half-brother, but why?"

Connor needed a different side road to park in, to make sure that Steve didn't see the car, particularly with Tammy sitting in the passenger seat. Then he headed off on foot, assuming that he'd be less conspicuous as long as he was careful. As he walked back towards where Steve was parked, he turned up the collar of his trench coat. Now he felt like a real detective.

CHAPTER 18

It struck Connor that he didn't actually know where Steve had gone and there was only a remote chance of finding out. He walked back to the road that led to Giftitatry and looked around. There was nothing except other industrial buildings, a few bits of waste ground and a sandwich van. The road curved and he walked as far as the corner. From there he could see the front of Giftitatry where there was a man sitting on the wall in front of the building. The man looked about the right build for Steve. *Bingo*.

Connor was in two minds about what to do. If it was Steve, he could surprise him and ask what he was doing there or he could wait and watch. He suspected he would learn more by watching, but there was no opportunity to get close. He stayed near the corner, feeling conspicuous in the largely people-free surroundings. He sat perched on the wall, the sharp edge digging into his leg even through his jeans. He could just see Steve on the limit of his vision. He'd had just about enough time to take in every detail of the surrounding buildings when he saw a man loping towards Steve. He could tell from the gait that it must be Patrick. He seemed to be signalling along the road, fortunately in the opposite direction to Connor.

Connor followed the men from a discrete distance. They made their way along the pavement. Apparently talking, Steve and Patrick had an easy manner together. This certainly didn't appear to be a first meeting. They came to a line of parked cars, Patrick going round onto the road side. Then Connor heard the rasping of an engine turning over and sparking reluctantly into life. There was nothing he could do on foot and being too far from his own car to take up the chase, all he could do was watch them go.

He began to walk in the opposite direction, back to where he'd left Tammy and the car. He hunched his shoulders to reduce the risk of being recognised when they passed and then stooped to tie a shoe lace so that he would be out of normal view. As the car passed, he looked up and noticed that it was heading back to the entrance of the estate. They could be heading anywhere.

There would be little benefit to be gained from waiting for them to come back and instead Connor decided to have a look at where Patrick lived, although after bumping into Emma at Steve's house that morning, he wasn't so sure his snooping skills were good enough. He programmed the sat-nav for Reeves Road and set off.

The road was to the south of the city. It was an area of small terraced houses with little distinguishing one from another, except the paint colour of the door. He decided to leave the pick-up round the corner in Rutland Street and walk round to Patrick's house. From the estate agents' boards around, it was a mixture of rented and owned property. From the apparent size, Connor guessed that most of them would have been two-bedroomed. There was little if any greenery to the front of the properties, just pavement and roads of parked cars.

Patrick's door was peeling blue paint, in need of redecoration and there looked to be a small amount of rot on the window sills, but grubby net curtains prevented Connor from seeing inside. He thought about ringing the bell. If Steve and Patrick were there, apart from catching Steve out as to knowing his half-brother, Connor had no idea what he might say.

He was just thinking about heading back to the car when the door of the neighbouring property opened and a middle aged woman looked out.

"Are you looking for someone?"

"I was trying to find Mr Patrick Coltrane's house." Connor said feebly.

"I don't know the bloke's name that lives there. It could be him for all I know."

"Thanks," said Connor, hoping that she wouldn't take the conversation further.

"I'd tell him you called, but I've not spoken to him yet and I can't imagine I'm going to start now." She closed the door and left Connor alone.

Connor was by now feeling hungry and conscious that Tammy would need to stretch her legs, he headed back to the car and went in search of a pub for lunch.

Once he was settled with a drink and had ordered homemade steak and ale pie and chips, Connor decided to ring Steve to see what reaction he got.

"Hi, it's Connor here. I was wondering if I could come round to see you. There are some things we need to discuss."

"I can't really talk now. I'm out on a lesson. I should be back about 17.00 if you want to call round then."

"Right. I'll do that." Out on a lesson indeed!

Connor had only just hung up when his phone rang.

"Connor, it's Trevor Whitworth, are you still working on that case?"

145

"I was going to ring you. Yes. I've found a possible connection between all three if you're interested."

"Go on."

"A gentleman by the name of Patrick Coltrane, he's my client's half-brother. He grew up in King's Heath and worked for the company in Derby where the bloke was hanged."

"I'll certainly pass it on. I was really ringing to see if you wanted to go for a drink later in the week."

Connor hesitated. "Could you get me a copy of the interview that was done with Raymond Gumby, the first victim's son?"

"Is the drink dependent on it?"

"No, but it would help. How about one lunch-time?"

They made their arrangements and Connor started to tuck into his pie, which was rather too mass produced to have been made at 'home'. All he could think of as he chewed was that he really needed to talk to Patrick Coltrane or at least someone who knew him well.

The drive back to York was uneventful and he arrived at Steve's house shortly after the agreed time. He was surprised to see Harry Daniels ringing the bell as he approached. It seemed to be a day for strange meetings. He took a deep breath and then called out a greeting.

Steve's father looked startled, as though he had been caught in the act of doing something he shouldn't. "I was just calling on Steve."

Connor couldn't help but think that was fairly obvious. Before he had time to answer, Steve opened the door to them both. "Dad! I wasn't expecting you. This may not be a good time."

"Oh don't mind me," said Connor. "I wouldn't mind talking to both of you." He saw an opportunity to ask

Steve some questions and watch the father's reaction to them.

"Come in," Steve sounded rather more hesitant. They went straight through into the lounge and all stood rather uncomfortably in the middle.

"Sit down," Steve moved a pile of papers off the seat of the chair and put them on the floor. "I was going to make some coffee," he gestured awkwardly towards the door as though he didn't want to leave the room.

"That would be really nice," said Connor grinning. "I'll have mine black, please."

Steve continued to move from one foot to the other. His father looked up from his intense gaze at his hands. "I wouldn't mind having one too, if you're making some."

Appearing reluctant to go, Steve left the room.

"Look," said Harry as soon as Steve left. "I know how this must look."

Connor felt confused as he was struggling to work out how it looked.

"I was concerned for my son. I've been ringing him for the last few days and got no reply. I just wanted to check he was ok."

Connor nodded in understanding. He supposed that if your son was issued with an apparent death threat, it would be a very odd father who wasn't worried.

"I'm here to ask him one or two more questions about Patrick Coltrane."

Harry Daniels looked up sharply. "What's he got to do with all this?" He spoke with a considerable amount of venom.

"I wanted to know how well Steve had got to know him. After all, they are brothers."

"He's got no place in this family," Harry almost spat

the words out.

"How did you feel when you found out about him? After all, it was before you and Paula got together."

Harry opened his mouth to answer, but Steve came back in at the same moment carrying a tray. His father got up. "Here, let me help you with those."

Now he was in full swing, Connor didn't want to lose momentum. "I was just talking to your dad about Patrick Coltrane. I was asking him how he felt when you all found out."

Harry Daniels looked at his watch. "Is that the time? It was only supposed to be a flying visit. I'll see myself out." He got up and left the room without any further comment.

"Dad is very sensitive about Patrick. He couldn't bear that Mum had never told him and it didn't go down well when Mum didn't leave all her money to Dad. He thought they'd got everything in joint names and it would automatically be his, but Mum had been moving money into accounts of her own for several years."

"Were your parents happy?"

"Oh yes, very." Steve answered too quickly for Connor's liking.

"Do you know why your mother left her money to you and Patrick?"

Steve sounded indignant. "We were very close. She was entitled to leave it to whoever she wanted to."

"Do you know why she left it to Patrick and not Clare?"

"Perhaps she didn't want David getting his filthy hands on it." Steve snapped back.

Connor looked at Steve's face as he asked, "How well do you know Patrick?"

He thought Steve coloured slightly as he replied. "I barely know him at all. Why would I?"

"When did you last see him?"

Steve shrugged. He hesitated as though he were thinking. "Probably at Mum's funeral. I don't think I've seen him since then."

Connor sat and weighed up whether to challenge him directly. He took a deep breath before saying. "I was in Derby today, I thought I saw you. I must have been mistaken."

Steve fumbled for the diary from his pocket. "I had lessons all day, here in York. Look!" He showed Connor the page where in small writing a number of names of learner drivers had been pencilled.

"Right. It must have been someone who looked like you." Connor couldn't think what to say next. He decided to see what Steve's reaction was to some of the things he'd found.

"I've come across three murders so far where a Lifetracer has been left. I don't know if any of them had the device sent to them in advance."

"Right," said Steve.

Connor thought he could have been telling him about when his shopping was going to be delivered for all the reaction it got.

After quite a pause Steve added, "It looks like I've got another seventeen days unless you find out who's behind it."

"Oh, I plan to find out in that time," said Connor getting up. "If you'll excuse me, I'll go and carry on with the search." He went through the hall and let himself out of the front door.

Connor rang Maggie from the car. "I need to pick your

brain."

"Oh good and I thought you were ringing to arrange a date."

"Ok, that as well, but before we do I want some ideas. Who can I talk to for some background on Patrick Coltrane?"

"What about his parents?"

"You mean the adoptive ones? How's that conversation going to go? I think your son might be a murderer, I wonder if you could tell me about him?"

"I think you might have to be a little more subtle. What about pretending you were a school friend or something and you don't know where he lives now? Try getting them to reminisce."

"Ok, but if they've moved, how do I explain that I knew where they were but I didn't know where to find Patrick?"

"Why not start by finding out where they are? You might at least get to find out if there is a definite link to the victims. Now about that date. You could take me to the pictures tomorrow night. We can go and see 'Dorian Gray'."

"Wouldn't you prefer 'Cloudy with a chance of Meatballs'?"

"I'm guessing you're more used to going to films with your son. I was thinking of something a little more cultural."

"Ok. I'll do my best, but I might be going to Birmingham for the day. I'll let you know if I'll be back in time."

CHAPTER 19

Connor was surprised the telephone wasn't radiating its own little halo of heat.

The first call had been Fingers. "Yo, brov, I've managed to find some more stuff on Patrick Coltrane. Are you ready for this?"

Being given information by Fingers was always a game. "I'm ready." Connor had his pen poised above the telephone pad.

"He was a pupil in the school where Charles Gumby was head."

"Really?" Connor felt the smile spreading across his face.

"Would I lie to you, man? I got a phone number for Mr Daley's bird too."

"Widow, Fingers. Not 'bird'!"

"Sure thing."

Connor wrote the number on the pad. "One other thing, Fingers, could you try to find Patrick Coltrane's adoptive parents for me? This one may be a little harder."

"I'm on it."

As soon as he rang off from Fingers, Connor rang Alisha Daley he could feel his heart pounding as he made the call. Why should she talk to a complete stranger who said he was investigating her husband's death?

"I don't mean to intrude on your grief, I am sincerely

sorry about your husband. I'm a private investigator and I'm looking into some other deaths that appear to be linked to that of your husband. I was wondering if I might talk to you."

Alisha's voice caught as she tried to respond. Connor felt guilty contacting her so soon after her husband's death.

"I'll do anything if it will help find whoever did this. He was a good man. He was never in any kind of trouble. He just worked for the Lord. Why? Why him?"

Connor could hear the gulping sobs coming from the other end. He struggled to find the right words. "I'm sorry. If this is too difficult."

"No," she muttered through the sobs. "If I can help."

"I'll be in Birmingham tomorrow, could I see you then."

"I'm off work right now. I'll be around most of the day. What sort of time?"

Connor thought through what he wanted to fit into the day and remembering he'd promised to go to the pictures thought it had better be earlier rather than later. "I could be there about 11.00."

"I'll be here. Oh, do you need the address?"

"I have it already. You were in the phone book." Connor crossed his fingers and hoped that they were in the phone book and it had been that easy for Fingers to find them. Alisha didn't react so he breathed a sigh of relief.

He'd just put the phone down when Fingers rang back.

"Aren't you just the lucky one?"

"Why?"

"They're still at the same address. Still in King's Heath, same place that our Mr Coltrane grew up."

"That's brilliant. Now I can go for the line of having lost touch with him. It's amazing in this day and age to find people in the same place. Don't you just love the older generation?"

"I'm guessing you're not looking for an answer." Fingers gave him the details and hung up.

If he got to Birmingham early enough he could always have two shots at finding them at home, both before he saw Alisha Daley and afterwards if necessary.

Connor put aside all the notes from the case and dragged himself to his desk. He rummaged through the accumulating debris until he found the draft of an article he needed to finish for *The Press*. Tammy sat beside him. "Sorry old girl," he said, stroking her head. "I do have to get this finished."

Sensing it wasn't going to be an exciting afternoon, she trotted off to her bed and left him to it.

***

It was a cold start to the day when Connor got up to take Tammy out the following morning. "It won't always be like this, I promise." He looked at just how early it was on his watch and shivered. *All this to get a good walk in before their drive.* He scratched Tammy behind the ears and then threw the ball for her to chase after. He wished everything could be as simple as his relationship with his dog.

With all the long distances he was driving, he was beginning to wish he had a more economical vehicle, but the pick-up was useful on the odd occasions when he helped his dad or brother, not that that happened very often these days. His thoughts turned to seeing Maggie that evening and he smiled. *Perhaps it was time to think about moving in together. How would Mikey take that? He seemed to like having Maggie around, but that was based on one weekend. Maybe he should invite Maggie to join them for the coming weekend and stay over before asking her to move in.*

Once in the car, he listened to the CD player. He always thought it was an ideal time for some self-improvement and that he should be listening to something appropriate, but he thought about it when he was in the car and never when he was anywhere that he could do anything about it. He could just about have learnt a foreign language with the amount of time he'd spent in the car recently.

He decided to go round the M42 and then come back into Birmingham from the South, rather than going through the centre. It was always a close call as to which would be quicker. He made his way to Tenbury Drive and parked outside a generously sized semi-detached house. This was the childhood home of his supposed friend. He'd got about an hour before finding Alisha Daley, he just needed to act the part.

He could feel his hands damp and clammy as he rang the doorbell. He'd been rehearsing his story in his head as he'd driven that last few miles. He couldn't say he was a school friend as there was an obvious age difference. He could risk a guess that Patrick had gone to the youth club and that he'd known him from there, or he could try to say he'd lived nearby, but that risked a discussion of who his parents were.

He wondered whether the fact that there was no car on the drive was a bad sign. He rang again and stood back a little way from the front door to see if there was any movement behind the windows. He'd just about given up when an older lady with an apron over her navy elasticated trousers answered the door.

"I'm sorry have you been waiting long? I was hanging the washing out. I don't always hear the bell."

"No, it's fine. I don't know if you remember me. I was a friend of Patrick's from the youth club." He was thinking crossed fingers, even if he wasn't doing it. "I remembered he lived here and just thought I'd call to see if you could give me an address for him. You are his mum aren't you?"

A beaming smile spread across the woman's face. "Well this is a pleasant surprise. We don't often hear from any of Patrick's friends he didn't have that many. Do come in. I'll put the kettle on. Can I get you a cuppa?"

Connor smiled as much in relief as for the thought of a hot drink, although he was ready for that too. "That would be lovely. Yes please."

The rooms downstairs had been knocked into one and Connor was surprised how modern it seemed. He had expected a house that was at least to some extent out of date.

"This is very nice. I don't remember it being like this."

"No," she said. "Our eldest did it all for us while we went away on a cruise a couple of years ago."

Connor hadn't realised there were other children. That hadn't turned up on Fingers' information which surprised him. He felt at a loss not knowing the names of any other children and hoped he didn't get caught out.

Mrs Coltrane left the room and Connor found himself a seat on an easy chair. He was tempted to go and look at the bookcase at the other end of the room, but resisted.

When Mrs Coltrane returned she was carrying a plate of chocolate biscuits and two cups of coffee. For a moment Connor felt like a child again and as though he was visiting a friend's house and needed to be on his best behaviour. He wondered how he was going to ask any questions. He was hoping that Mrs Coltrane might be the talkative type.

"Does Patrick still live locally?" he asked.

"No, he's in Derby now. I think after all the trouble here, he was glad to move away. He said he wanted a new start."

"Oh, that's a shame. I could have called on him."

"I'm sure if you're ever in Derby he'd be pleased to see you. We don't see a great deal of him these days. I expect he's busy." She said it with a sadness that told Connor she didn't believe it herself."

He took a risk and asked, "I don't remember any trouble, what happened?"

Mrs Coltrane put her head on one side and looked at him as though she was sizing up whether he was being honest. "He was expelled from school part way through his O Levels. Not that he'd have passed them, I don't suppose. Then there was the incident at the youth club."

Having used the excuse of having known Patrick from the youth club, Connor stepped in so that he didn't blow his cover. "Oh yes, I remember that. That was a shame."

"Well I'm sure it wasn't Patrick's fault. He wouldn't hurt a fly. I'm sure he was provoked."

"What happened at school? We weren't in the same year and I didn't see him much once he'd left the youth club."

"It was always the same. Always getting into fights." She leaned forward conspiratorially. "It was his background you know. All very difficult. His behaviour was already formed when he came to us." She sounded as though she was trying to distance herself from the bad side of Patrick. "We did our best by him. Of course the church prayed for him a great deal. He never seemed to appreciate that."

Now that she had started talking about Patrick, Mrs Coltrane looked set to continue for some time. Connor stole a look at the clock on the old closed up chimney breast. He could stay another quarter of an hour, but then needed to be on his way.

"It's good to know he had a friend," Mrs Coltrane continued. "There were so many times he seemed to be too much of a loner. I always said to Bernard, that boy would be much better if he didn't spend all the time on his own. He never fitted in with our children. He always seemed so conscious of all the rejection he'd faced. He went about looking for it. Every new situation was a chance to be rebuffed. I suppose faced with that I'd go into my shell." She paused. "Deary me, just listen to me talking. I suppose I feel we failed him in a way. I don't get that many chances to talk about him these days." She looked up. The corners of her eyes looked damp. "I'd best be getting his address for you." She went over to the bookshelf and pulled out an address book. He could see her hand trembling. "It's hard to remember the addresses. He's moved about a bit. Here it is. This one's the latest." She scribbled it down onto a piece of paper. Connor accepted it smiling. Mrs Coltrane wasn't to know he already had the address.

"Do you know if he ever got round to finding his birth parents?"

Mrs Coltrane hesitated. "I tried talking to him about that. I said I thought it would be a good idea." She shook her head. "But he never seemed to think it would help. He was just scared there'd be more rejection waiting for him. Who knows, he may have been right. I never knew who they were. He'd been in care a long time before he came to us."

The more Connor talked to her, the more he couldn't see Patrick being one for premeditated crimes. He'd be much more a spur of the moment violence type than a man who would spend years brooding. He wondered whether to tell Mrs Coltrane the truth about what he was doing but decided against it.

"I'd better be going." He said standing up, clutching the piece of paper she'd given him. "I'll try to get over to Derby to see him."

Connor thought he'd managed to get away without even giving a name, when she said "I'll perhaps give him a ring later and tell him you called. I'm sure he'd be pleased. What name should I say?"

Connor found himself saying, "Steve Daniels." He had no idea what had come over him, but then he'd quite like to have seen Patrick's reaction to that one.

CHAPTER 20

As Connor walked away from the house he smiled at the thought of Patrick's reaction to Steve Daniels having called to see his parents. He wondered whether Fingers could stretch as far as a phone tap, but it was too late to get it set up in time. He wasn't sure whose phone he wanted to tap. At least if it were Patrick Coltrane's he'd capture calls both with his parents and Steve Daniels, although these days he was more likely to use a mobile than a land line, so perhaps he needed to tap both.

What was confusing Connor was the question, if Patrick Coltrane wasn't the murderer, who would want to frame him and threaten his half-brother? On top of that, what was going on for Steve to feel the need to hide his relationship with his brother?

Tammy was looking out of the window waiting for him to return to the car. She jumped down as soon as he opened the door and bounced round in a circle, then jumped back into the vehicle ready for them to move off.

"Have you looked at the map?" He asked her with a serious voice. "No, well not to worry. I'm sure the sat-nav will find it. He typed in the postcode and picked 'fastest route' from the options. It said he would be at the Daley's house by ten-fifty, which gave them ten minutes to find a patch of grass for Tammy to have a quick run round. "Come on then girl. What are you waiting for?" He drove off in search of a convenient park.

Alisha Daley lived the other side of the Alcester Road from Patrick's parents, in Melton Road. These were terraced houses with tiny gardens separating them from the pavement. Connor found a parking space about six houses away. He left the pickup's windows down hoping that Tammy would be a sufficient deterrent to burglars. Then he walked along to where Kenmore Daley had lived until the previous weekend.

He was struck by the overwhelming aura of sadness that surrounded Alisha Daley as she stood framed in the doorway of the house. She had been crying but looked demure and carefully groomed.

"Mrs Daley, I'm Connor Bancroft. I'm so very sorry about your husband."

She nodded and appeared to bite her lip, probably trying to keep the tears from flowing, Connor thought. She indicated that he should go straight down the hall to the kitchen, but still said nothing.

It was a small space with nowhere to sit down. At last she spoke. "I'll make a drink and we'll take it into the back. I can't face the front room yet. It was where it happened."

Connor thought how difficult it must be to live in a murder scene. "I suppose the police ..."

She nodded almost imperceptibly. "I've not been able to bring myself to clean in there yet. It ..." She didn't finish the sentence, but Connor could imagine how she must feel.

"I realise that this isn't a very good time for you and I know you will already have had the police to deal with, but my client has received a death threat on one of the devices that was left with your husband and it may be linked to your husband's murder."

As she nodded, Connor thought how beautiful she looked in her sadness. She must have been about 50, but her skin was flawless and she looked a lot younger.

"Were you about on Saturday when it happened?"

"No," her doleful brown eyes looked straight into his. "I'd taken our son to start university. He's never been away before. He came back of course."

"Did you see anyone hanging around outside when you went out?"

She looked to be thinking before she said, "The police asked me that. I've found it hard to think back. There might have been. I think there was a man leaning against the wall of the house along the road, but you don't notice." She was looking away into the distance as though searching to recreate the image of Saturday. "No, nothing's coming back." She hesitated, "you could ask Demaine or Jasmine, our children, although, I would rather they weren't involved if possible."

"I know this is difficult, but does the name Patrick Coltrane mean anything to you?" By now they had moved into the dining room, which was furnished with dark furniture that made the whole place feel very dreary. They sat in the dining chairs at the table.

Alisha Daley closed her eyes as she thought and her mouth puckered in concentration. "No, I don't think so. Where would Kenmore know him from?"

"Do you remember your husband ever talking about any trouble at the youth club? I think that Patrick may have hit him on one occasion." Connor looked across at the sideboard at the pictures of family outings. So many photos of smiling faces as the family unit went through every stage of life. They were clearly close and he wondered how Alisha would cope without Kenmore.

She smiled. "Yes, that was years ago. There was a boy who hit him. I don't know what his name was. It was before we got together, but I remember him talking about it. I'm afraid I can't tell you any more than that, although I could put you in touch with someone else that might be able to. The other youth club leader is still around, Ted Richardson. They've both been involved for years." She stopped. She was still talking as though Kenmore was around. "Had been involved. Oh I'm sorry." She broke down in tears and pulled a tissue from a new box.

Connor waited until she had composed herself again. "It would help if I could talk to him. It seems there is some sort of link between Coltrane and all the victims so far. If the other youth leader is around I could see him today." He wasn't sure what he was trying to prove. He already knew there was a link, but he didn't have anything that put Patrick Coltrane at any of the scenes. What would be useful was to test out his suspicion that Patrick was a spur of the moment type of person, a man who would react then and there and not wait for years before coming back.

Alisha went to get the phone leaving Connor to look around the room. Kenmore Daly looked to be a strongly built man and not one you'd get into an argument with. His attacker must have been known to him, otherwise there would at the very least have been signs of a struggle. Connor presumed that the attacker had found some way to sedate Mr Daly before administering the insulin.

When Alisha came back he asked, "Were there cups left out when you found your husband?"

"No there weren't, but I did think that the cups in the kitchen were in a different position. I didn't think much of it at the time as Kenmore might have moved them, but I can't see him putting them away as well as washing them up. He leaves them on the draining board. I managed to get hold of Ted Richardson on his mobile. He's shopping at the moment. He said he could come here if that's all right with you?"

"Thank you, yes, that would be great. Look, I know this is difficult, but would you mind if I take a look in the front room? You don't need to come if you don't want to. It's just that you said nothing had been moved and I'd like to see if there are any clues that jump out at me. I realise the police will have done all that, but there might be something."

She nodded, "I won't come. It's the next door along. Please close it when you've finished."

Connor went out into the hall and turned the door handle of the lounge. It was almost as though he was expecting someone or something to jump out at him.

The room was much lighter than the dining room. He noticed the fresh patterned wallpaper on a pale background. The three piece suite was of old-fashioned design, but in good condition. It was hard to tell its age. Everything looked to be in its rightful place with the exception of a magazine rack that had fallen onto its side next to one of the chairs. This Connor assumed was where Kenmore Daley had been sitting and perhaps there had been a limited struggle though nothing very significant.

Connor tried to work out what the order of events would have been. Mr Daley must have opened the door to his killer and then what? Did he come straight into the front room and sit down? Perhaps the murderer had been shown in here while Kenmore had gone to make some drinks. Connor wondered whether the other person had followed Kenmore to the kitchen in order to see what needed to be put away and where it went.

The lounge faced onto the road. It was possible that someone going past might have looked in and seen Kenmore Daley with the visitor. Connor wondered how much could be seen from the street and tried to work out which way the room faced so he could tell if there might have been sunlight streaming in or not. He didn't have time to call at all the surrounding houses and there was no knowing who might walk along that road. No one would use the road as a thoroughfare, on the way to the shops, as it ran parallel with the main road, but it was open at both ends and could have had passing traffic.

Connor started to look round the room in minute detail. There was a bookcase in one corner and a television in the other. Nothing looked to be out of place. From the fingerprint powder the police had already covered the room, but Connor suspected that it was unlikely that anything would yield fingerprints, except for those of the people who lived here. The only hope might have been the mugs, which the killer washed. He was just looking underneath the cushions when the doorbell rang and he jumped with a guilty start. Despite the fact that his search had been sanctioned by Alisha Daley, he still felt as though he were trespassing, snooping on other peoples' lives. If he was going to take on more work as a private eye he was going to have to get over those feelings.

He went back out into the hall to find Alisha Daley opening the door to Ted Richardson. Connor closed the lounge door and went back to the dining room to give them space to come through.

Ted Richardson looked like an aging rock star. He had long grey hair around the lower part of his head but was balding on top. His hair was tied back to keep it neat, but

Connor thought it would be neater still and more in keeping with his age, if he just had it cut. He wore a denim shirt and jeans and Connor wondered if he looked as bad as that in his. He'd ask Maggie later.

"I'm sorry to meet you under such circumstances," said Ted shaking Connor's hand. "If there is anything I can do to help, then I'm happy to."

"There was one thing in particular I wanted to ask you about, or rather one person. Do you remember a Patrick Coltrane from the youth club? I believe he might have been involved in an incident with Mr Daley many years ago."

Ted paused to think. "Sure I do. Wasn't he the one who hit Kenmore? He was an odd kid. The others didn't like him but he was a big kid so they left him alone. He always seemed very awkward."

Connor nodded. "That sounds like the same person. Do you remember what happened?"

"It's a long time ago and I don't think I was in the room at the time. Things kicked off and I think Kenmore had asked him to leave. After Patrick punched him we had to ask him to leave the youth club altogether. That was the last I saw of him. I may have seen him round the streets once in the while, but he never tried to come back."

"Did he ever talk about his past?"

"Not that I remember. He didn't talk about anything, not to me at least."

"Do you happen to know if he had trouble at school?"

Ted shook his head. "I'm guessing he did, from the way he behaved, but I can't be certain."

"I don't suppose you know of anyone who had a reason to kill Mr Daly do you?"

At that point Alisha Daly had to reach for the tissues

again. "I'm sorry. Do answer. I can't think, but that doesn't mean there wasn't anyone." She sniffed.

Ted Richardson pursed his lips. "No, he was a great bloke. Why would anyone want to kill him? He'd do anything for the kids. They loved him. He was one of life's greats."

"Thanks," said Connor not knowing where else he could take it. "I'll leave you my phone number, if you think of anything else, will you give me a call?" He took a card from his pocket and laid it on the table. It was the one with both his home and mobile numbers. There were very few people he gave those ones to. "I'll see myself out."

By the time Connor got out into the street he was glad to leave the oppression of the house behind. It was as though the secret it held was hanging as a heavy weight on its brickwork. Connor was convinced of one thing, he needed to find the courage to see Patrick Coltrane, but he couldn't think of a single reason why Patrick should talk to him.

CHAPTER 21

The metal bowl clanged to the floor as Connor dropped it in his haste to find Tammy's food. He'd still got to change and was due to meet Maggie in twenty minutes. He had no idea whether Maggie would have eaten, but there was no time for that right now.

The film wasn't the best production that Connor had seen and whilst Dorian Gray failed to age, his mind wandered back to the case. What were the chances of someone other than Patrick Coltrane replicating the links to all three victims and if it was him, should Connor perhaps warn Steve Daniels before Steve saw too much more of his brother? What he couldn't understand, apart from the styles of death not being in keeping with what seemed to be Patrick Coltrane's personality, was why Steve had lied about not knowing Patrick Coltrane when they were spending time together. He decided his next step was to visit Patrick in Derby before talking with Steve.

All that would have to wait until the following week. Apart from seeing Trevor Whitworth for lunch the following day, he had no choice but to finish the articles he'd been working on and ensure they were submitted by the deadline on Friday. Jayne had relented and Mikey would be with Connor for the whole weekend. He knew he could stretch his writing into Friday evening if he wanted to, but with Mikey there and the prospect of once again including Maggie in their plans, it wouldn't be a popular move.

As the credits of the film rolled, he wondered what Maggie was going to say if he admitted that he hadn't taken much notice of the second half. *The Picture of Dorian Gray* was a story he knew quite well, which would at least enable him to have a half decent conversation.

They were sitting in Chiquito's after the film waiting for their food to arrive when Connor said, "Would you like to join us this weekend?"

"Why?" said Maggie. "Are you having another day out?"

Connor shifted in his seat. He didn't find things like this easy. "Not exactly, although we'll probably go somewhere on Saturday. I meant would you like to stay with us for the whole weekend?"

Maggie put down her glass and stared at Connor. "You mean stay over with Mikey there?"

He smiled at her and nodded. "Yes, that's what I was asking."

"Wow. I mean, do you think he's ready for it? Do you think we're ready for it?"

"I think it's more of a big deal to us than it will be to Mikey. Kids take things in their stride. If you're ready."

Maggie picked up her drink and took a deep gulp. "I think I am. I'm terrified as well, but then I'm bound to be. I've got butterflies just thinking about it now. Will Jayne be all right about it?"

"It's none of her business. She's moved on, it's time I did."

"Then I'd love to. Shall I come straight from work?"

Connor felt relieved to have asked the question. He

was glad that Maggie seemed so positive. "I'm picking Mikey up at 19.00 so any time before or after that. Although I'm sure he'd love you to be there in time for a bedtime story.

***

Connor appreciated the lazy start to the day that he could have on Friday. He'd got three articles to finish off, but none of them demanded he was at his desk by 09.00. Still wrapped in his dressing gown, he sat down to his computer around 09.30. Tammy was happy to skip an early walk once in a while and he reasoned that he didn't afford himself this luxury very often. He sipped the strong black coffee in front of him and wondered what new information Trevor Whitworth might have for him at lunchtime.

He got stuck into the work and broke again in time for a shower and to drive into York. With Tammy having to sit in the car again he felt guilty about skipping her morning walk and promised to take her along the river as soon as he came back from seeing Trevor.

"Have you been waiting long?" He asked Trevor as he approached the bar.

"Long enough to make a well-earned start on my pint." Trevor laughed and raised his glass. "Cheers."

"Cheers. So what have you got for me?"

Trevor passed him an envelope. "I don't know what you'll make of it. There's an interview in there with the son of Charles Gumby. It sounds to me as though our guys are looking towards him as the murderer. At least of his father."

"Don't they think the murders are linked?"

Trevor shook his head. "They're looking at copy cats. No one can see a particular connection between them."

Connor looked up surprised. "But what about Patrick Coltrane? Did you tell them about him?"

Trevor looked down at his pint. "I've had a lot on. Give me some more details and I'll write them down this time." He searched his pockets for a pen and a scrap of paper.

"Well, the bloke I'm working for has a half-brother who lives in Derby. However, he grew up in Birmingham. He was expelled from Charles Gumby's school, thrown out of the youth club that Kenmore Daley ran and fired from the company that Paul Tranter managed."

Trevor let out a low whistle. "Have you got any actual evidence to link him?"

Connor shook his head. "I might try to talk to him next week but it's a bit awkward?"

Trevor tilted his head, showing interest.

"I had a bit of a run in with him myself when I went down to Derby. It turns out that he works for the Company that sold Steve Daniel's Lifetracer."

"You're having me on."

"It's still all circumstantial, but there are an awful lot of common denominators."

"I'd better tip my lot off and have them bring him in for questioning."

"That's fine by me. I'm not sure I fancy talking to him anyway. Although I'll give it a go."

"You're not such a bad risk with information after all. If this comes to anything, I might even go as far as buying you a drink." He raised his glass and clinked it against Connor's.

They spent a little bit of time catching up on general news and gossip before Connor excused himself and left Trevor to his second pint.

There was quite a breeze starting to get up as Connor walked Tammy. It was good to feel the wind on his face and Connor found himself looking forward to the weekend with Maggie and Mikey. He wondered what the weather forecast was for Saturday and whether they could enjoy another day outside. At least then Tammy was able to be part of the action. They headed for home so that he could finish his articles. He'd managed to complete and submit one piece but there were two that he still needed to do some research for, never mind complete. He just hoped the internet would have what he needed.

He was still deep in references when the doorbell rang and Maggie arrived.

"I hope you don't mind me coming round a bit earlier. I wanted to be here when Mikey arrived. I don't know why. It just seemed like a good idea."

"That's great." Connor's smile said it all. He was looking forward to a family weekend with the two most important people in his life. "Do you want to take your bag up to the bedroom? I'll just finish what I was doing and then I need to collect Mikey. Do you want to come or would you rather stay here?"

"I think I'd like to come if that's ok, although it will feel a little strange sitting outside Jayne's house." She hesitated. "You don't go in to the house do you?"

Connor put his hand on her shoulder for reassurance. "No you don't have to meet my ex-wife again into the bargain. The weekend's going to be quite enough. Are you sure you're up for it?"

"I think so. Ask me again on Sunday evening." She laughed and headed up the stairs.

Connor was following a link from Wikipedia on breathable liquids when she came back down. "I know this isn't great timing, but I've got to finish these two articles this evening. I've let everything slide a bit over the last few days with following up the Lifetracer. I need to get back on track. We can get a takeaway if that's ok with you and then I'll cook us all a nice meal tomorrow night to make up."

"You're a smooth talker, Connor Bancroft. What you're saying is that you are giving me and Mikey some time to get to know each other better."

"He's happy on the Playstation if you don't want to be too active."

"I can do Playstation. Has he got any good two player games?"

"I'll let him tell you that. Are you ready? He picked up his jacket, whistled Tammy and then headed out to the pick-up."

This week there was no delay in finding Mikey. He came running out to the vehicle to see Tammy, leaving his father to carry his little Power Ranger suitcase.

"Maggie!" He shouted in a gleeful voice. "Are you coming to stay for the weekend too?" He seemed unfazed by the prospect, as he climbed into the car and sat next to the dog. "Where can we go tomorrow?"

By now Connor was back in the driving seat. "From the weather forecast we need to be indoors."

"Can we go to see the trains?" Asked Mikey.

"What do you think of the Railway Museum?" Connor asked Maggie.

"It's ages since I've been." She smiled. "And it's free!"

"We went to see the Railway Children there in the summer." Mikey chipped in from the back. "It was good, with real trains. Can we go to see it again, Dad?"

"Yes, if it's on. The Theatre Royal has done it two years

running with the same cast. It's well worth seeing. Even I enjoyed it."

After they'd eaten their Chinese takeaway, Connor left Mikey to show Maggie the Playstation games and went to finish his articles.

He was still there when Mikey came and said "Night, Dad. Maggie says it's time I was in bed."

"Oh, Mikey, I'm sorry. I've nearly finished this. Shall I come up and read you a story?"

"It's ok, Maggie's going to read to me."

Maggie came up behind him in the corridor holding a book. "I'm quite enjoying it too," she said. "It makes me realise what I'm missing."

"I hope you're not going to get all broody on me!"

"Well I might." She laughed and ushered Mikey upstairs before Connor had time to reply.

Connor finished off in the study, smiling to himself and sent the two remaining articles. He then went upstairs to find how Maggie and Mikey were doing. He found Maggie curled up on the bed next to Mikey and snoring gently. As he went in Mikey opened his eyes.

"I think she fell asleep, Daddy. I didn't want to wake her."

Connor smiled at the role reversal and roused Maggie. Then he tucked Mikey in and kissed him before going back out of the room behind Maggie.

Saturday's weather was atrocious. Gale force winds were sweeping across the country and at intervals the rain was blustery in the extreme. All three of them agreed that it was a day for doing things inside and set off for the Railway Museum at Mikey's request.

Despite the fact that he had visited the museum many times, it never ceased to provide interest for several happy hours and the enthusiasm was infectious. Connor would have taken Mikey for a trip on the miniature railway outside, but today was a time to stick to the exhibits in the halls.

They'd finished looking at Mallard when Mikey said, "Can we go and see the model railway?"

"Ok, lead the way," said Connor.

By the end of the day Connor's legs were aching and Maggie looked quite ready to go home. Mikey was still full of energy although he fell asleep in the car on the way back to Haxby.

"I had a great time," said Maggie as they set off.

"I did too. Mikey seems to have taken to you being around and he didn't react at all when he came into bed this morning and found you there. Isn't it funny how much we worry about children's reactions and how often we are the ones who have a problem?"

CHAPTER 22

On Sunday morning Connor took Maggie breakfast in bed and Mikey helped him by carrying the box of cereal upstairs. It felt like being part of a proper family again and Connor smiled. It made him realise just how much he missed his old married life and the completeness of having his son with him all the time. He found Tammy curled up on the bed next to Maggie.

He had just put the tray down next to the bed when the phone rang. It was Trevor Whitworth.

"I'd got a bit of quiet before the day got going so I was doing some hunting around on HOLMES. You can tell someone at the Home Office has a sense of humour from the name. Anyway, rather than looking for the Lifetracer, I tried searching for murders that have occurred where Rohypnol has been present. These cases aren't that usual. Most of the murders we have are more violent in nature. The victim has to be overpowered or taken by surprise with a gun or a knife. The ones you've had are unusual in that there's no gore. All of them have involved the victim being drugged first."

"I'll be calling you Sherlock at this rate. Put me out of my misery. What have you found?"

"Well I've got another possible for you. This one was in March. A woman in Gloucester, name of Edith Monkton, she was 72 years old."

"I'll get on to it right away. Our Mr Coltrane started life in Gloucester. I wonder if he had any connection to Edith Monkton. I'm betting he did."

"I'm going to have to alert the forces working on these cases to what you've found. I can't leave you as the caped crusader doing our job."

"I know, but will you keep me informed?"

"Only if it works both ways."

"Deal."

Connor sat on the bed and looked at Maggie. He'd forgotten that Mikey was standing there.

"What is it, Daddy? Have we got some work to do?" Mikey looked solemn, but excited.

Connor gave Maggie an enquiring look, wondering whether she was up for turning their Sunday into part of the investigation. "Yes team, we've got a situation." He didn't want to say 'murder' in front of Mikey. Somehow it all seemed too frightening. He looked at Maggie. "I don't suppose you're up for a Sunday outing to The Press's offices are you? I wouldn't mind seeing if we could find any new background on this case."

"Oh that's it, bring me breakfast in bed to soften me up and then ask for the favour."

"I didn't know," pleaded Connor.

Maggie laughed. "I never was one to spend all day in bed."

"Can I come to the newspaper?" Asked Mikey, wide eyed at the prospect.

"As long as you're good," said Maggie. "We'll all go."

Tammy barked as though she understood the importance of the outing and didn't want to be left out.

Connor patted her and said, "You can come and wait in the car." Her tail wagged enthusiastically as he spoke to her.

At least today the sky was clear, even though it was still windy, although nothing like the previous day.

"You do promise you won't tell your mum about this don't you, Mikey? She doesn't like me involving you in what I'm working on."

"I promise," he said. "Can I tell her I went to the newspaper office with Maggie?"

Connor looked across at Maggie and smiled. "Yes you can tell her that."

Whilst Maggie tapped away at her keyboard calling up stories about the murder of Edith Monkton, Connor and Mikey looked at the photographs all around the walls of the office. They had been taken by the newspapers' photographers and depicted the many faces of life in York. There was a spectacular view of the Minster in the snow and others of places and people from all aspects of life. Connor was just passing a photograph of a formal dinner, when he stopped.

"Maggie!"

She got up from her desk and came across to him. "What is it?"

"This photograph, what do you see?"

"There are three couples posing for a picture at a charity gala. What's unusual about that?"

"That is," said Connor pointing at the middle couple. "I'll swear that's Harry Daniels, Steve Daniels' father."

"So, what's the problem?"

"If I'm right, that isn't Paula Daniels and if this date is anything to go by, it was taken before Steve's mother died."

"And you're thinking?"

"I don't know what I'm thinking, except that I want to

know some more. Is there any way of getting the names of the people in the picture?"

"It'll all be in the records. I'll be able to search and see what we've got on file. At this rate we're going to be here longer than I expected."

Mikey was starting to get bored and whilst a newspaper office is a fascinating place to a small boy he'd passed the stage of asking about everything and was now asking if he could have a McDonald's for lunch.

"I could stay and do this while you go for a Big Mac," said Maggie. "Or if you think you can wait for the other information, I could finish up on Edith Monkton and find a spare half an hour to do the rest tomorrow."

"Why don't you do that, if you don't mind? It seems a shame to leave you out of our weekend fun."

"I was hoping you'd say that. Give me five minutes and I'll be done. I'll put these documents in an envelope so you can read them when Mikey isn't around."

"Good move. Thank you."

***

It was the evening, after dropping Mikey back at Jayne's, before Connor first felt able to take the newspaper stories out from the envelope. He'd opened a bottle of Burgundy and was trying not to think about how quiet the house felt now he was back on his own.

He spread the stories out on the table. There was one from when the murder happened, one a couple of weeks later and an obituary. He started by reading the obituary.

Edith Monkton and her husband had fostered more than sixty children over a period of forty years. *What was the betting that one of them had been Patrick?* Connor turned to the story from the paper that outlined the murder. This time there was no mention of a Lifetracer. It didn't mean there hadn't been one, but in that detail, the case was different. Trevor had been right though, once again the murderer had used Rohypnol and once again there was no blood. This time the favoured method was asphyxiation. Connor wondered what the old woman had done to deserve that.

She had left two children of her own as well as the foster children, who had all long since grown up and set up their own lives. One of her children still lived in the Gloucester area, whilst the other had moved to Italy. Her husband had died three years earlier, so the daughter in Gloucester was the best bet to ask if the mother had kept a record of all the children that she had fostered over the years. It might of course be simpler just to ask Patrick Coltrane, although Connor preferred the idea of the police doing that.

Connor rang Fingers. "I need to find the details of another victim's daughter."

"Go ahead."

"The victim was Edith Monkton. She died in Gloucester in March of this year." He gave Fingers as much information as he had gleaned from the newspaper reports and hung up.

Connor sat sipping his wine with *Night at the Opera* playing in the background. He knew it was better listened to at high volume, but he needed to be able to think. What had he got? He seemed to have found four murders, all of which appeared to be linked to one man, presuming that the fostering link worked out. However, it still didn't feel right. Patrick Coltrane was not by all accounts a thinker, more a man of actions, although looks could be deceptive. If it wasn't Patrick, then why would someone be following the pattern of his life and killing people along the way and why would they now be threatening his half-brother?

He poured another glass of wine. Then there was the picture of Harry Daniels, presuming he was right identifying him in the picture. Who was the woman that he seemed particularly close to? If there was a dinner, wouldn't he have taken Paula with him?

He set to thinking about the week ahead. He would go down to Gloucester for a couple of days and come back via Derby. He was going to try talking to Mr Coltrane, even if it was in the hands of the police. Patrick might remember him from the other day, although it was possible that he'd paid more attention to the pick-up than to Connor himself. He decided to hire a car in order to be less conspicuous. He could always start with Derby so that he could set off the following morning, but that meant ringing Patrick Coltrane to make an arrangement now.

Connor took a deep breath. If Patrick was the murderer then he needed to meet him in a public place. It would be preferable to be in control of the location, but there was little chance of arranging that in advance of the meeting, unless he went back to the place he'd had lunch the other day, but he'd be better to find somewhere close to where Giftitatry was based. He wondered about ringing Cynthia from Higgins & Sons for a suggestion, but he didn't have her home number and there was a limit to how much he wanted to pay Fingers to find things for him. The one place he could think of was the Bull's Head from where Paul Tranter had been abducted on the night of his murder. It was as good a place as any and it would be interesting to see whether Patrick would react to the suggestion.

Connor got out the earlier notes from Fingers and rang

Patrick's number. He half expected him to be out, but then from what he gathered, Patrick didn't have much of a social life. He'd play it cool and see what Patrick said.

The phone rang several times before being answered and Connor was at the point of expecting to get an answer phone when a gruff voice said "Yes."

"Hello, is that Mr Patrick Coltrane?"

"Who else would it be?"

Connor crossed his fingers, "We haven't met. I'm Connor Bancroft. I've been employed by your half-brother to look into some problems he's having. I've spoken to the rest of the family and I wondered if I could perhaps buy you a pint tomorrow lunchtime in the Bull's Head off Waverley Road and see what your thoughts are?"

"What's it got to do with me?"

Connor hesitated. He didn't want to lose the opportunity. He opted for a downright lie. "It may have some bearing on the amount of money left to you by your mother when she died. There may be some more owing to you."

"What's that bitch got to do with anything? Hasn't she messed me up enough already?"

Connor raised an eyebrow. "Do you think we could meet tomorrow to talk about it? I'll be there about 13.00 if you'd like to join me."

There was a long pause. "Where did you say again?"

Well the pub didn't seem to be engrained on his mind, but maybe that didn't mean anything. Connor explained where the Bull's Head was and then hung up. "Ok Tammy, we'd better pack and book ourselves a Travel Lodge. We should have time to pick up a hire car in the morning and still make it to Derby in time."

CHAPTER 23

Edith Monkton started the day as she did every morning, by reading the day's bible passage and spending some time in prayer. The passage was Matthew 7 v. 1-2 *'Do not judge or you too will be judged. For in the same way as you judge others, you will be judged, and with the measure you use, it will be measured to you.'*

She smiled as she went about her morning chores thinking about how apt the passage was for many of the children she'd fostered over the years. They were society's waifs and strays, the unlovely and the unloved. She'd had the privilege of giving homes to so many of them and of showing them the love of Christ. And it was a privilege. She had received so much from the children. There had been difficult times and every so often there was a child who didn't settle, but for the most part, Edith and her husband, Eric, had provided a loving stable environment. Their own children were growing up by the time their parents had started fostering and had felt secure enough in their relationships with their parents not to be threatened by the care that had to go into each new arrival. Now, Edith's own children had left home, as had all the children she fostered and nothing brightened her day more than to meet up with one or other of those children and in many cases their own sons and daughters.

Today was a little different than normal. Edith was

expecting a visit from one of the children she fostered right at the start of her fostering time. She was struggling to remember much of the detail of his circumstances, but she could remember that Simon had stayed with her for about eighteen months before finding a permanent home for adoption. From what she could remember he was a happy child and when he had phoned her a couple of days earlier, she had been pleased to invite him over to see her.

Many of the children came to her with tales of mistreatment and woe, from the earliest part of their lives. Their behaviour was often wild to begin with and that was where not judging had come in. There wasn't a child out there that didn't need to be loved. She'd been good at that part. She had so much love to give that it seemed natural to her to extend it to all the children in her care.

She spent the morning tidying the house. She wanted everywhere to look its best for when Simon got there at 14.00. She had kept photos of all the children, entered in an album. She often looked through it and remembered their faces and thought about them in their lives now. She took the album down from the shelf and opened the pages at the beginning. There he was, Simon Edmonds. This would be the first time he'd ever come back to see her, after thirty-nine years. The more she thought about it the more excited she felt.

She turned the page of the album to look at the pictures of other children they had fostered around that time. Sometimes they had as many as four at one time. Her eyes fell on one on the right-hand page, Patrick Coltrane. A moment's sadness came over her as Edith remembered the very few children whose placements had not worked out. Patrick had been one of the few. He was a wild child when he came to her. If she'd only had him to deal with she might have had the chance of helping him to straighten out, but she had the others to think about. It was funny as she thought about it; Simon had been one of the ones she wanted to protect from Patrick's behaviour. If Patrick had stayed it would have been very difficult to have brought the order and stability that Simon needed. If she remembered, Simon had been abused and was having serious problems rebuilding his trust in adults.

Then there was Caroline. She looked at the smiling face of a little girl with pigtails. She and Simon had been inseparable for quite a while. She was a very quiet child and when Edith thought of the cruelty that Patrick had shown towards her, she shuddered. Yes, difficult as it was, she'd had no choice but to send him back. She wondered whether another family had been able to succeed where she had failed.

Edith made herself a cheese sandwich. She was in two minds whether to throw the end of the loaf away and start a fresh one. She decided that she'd wait and open the new one later. She was feeling excited as she watched the hands progressing round the clock. It would be good to see Simon and hear about how he was doing.

The bell rang almost on the stroke of 14.00. She went and opened the front door. He hadn't grown up as she had imagined. She'd thought he'd be stockier than this. He smiled and held out his hand.

"Remember me?"

"Of course I do," she said a little hesitantly. "Come through."

He followed her down the hall into the lounge.

"I suppose it's changed a little bit since you last saw it. I must have decorated at least?" She watched him looking around the room. She still felt there was something not quite right, but couldn't put her finger on it.

"This is new." Simon said, picking up an ornamental fishing well that was sitting on the sideboard.

Edith looked at him, "You probably wouldn't remember it. It used to be on the shelves in the hall. I was given it as a girl." There were a lot of things he didn't remember and it was a very long time ago. "Would you like to see your old room?"

"Perhaps we could have a cuppa first? I've had a long journey and I could murder a drink."

"Yes of course, tea or coffee?"

"I'll have tea please." Simon settled himself down on the settee while Edith went into the kitchen. If she didn't know it was Simon, she'd swear she had never seen him before. Perhaps it was age? Her memory wasn't what it used to be, although she'd always prided herself at being good with faces.

She brought the tea in and put it down on the small table in front of the settee.

"Do you have some sugar, please?" Simon asked.

"Oh yes, of course." She went back to fetch it from the kitchen. She didn't see what Simon was doing while she was gone and was none the wiser that he had slipped Rohypnol into her cup. She returned with the sugar and set it down on the tray. Simon was already holding his cup on his knee. He smiled at her.

"What made you get in touch after all these years?"

"I suppose I wanted to get some perspective on my past, put a few of the jigsaw pieces in place."

She was ready for the tea and drank it as soon as it was cool enough. She was starting to feel more comfortable around Simon and as he told her about his life more recently, she could almost picture the little boy who became the man.

They had been talking for about forty minutes when she remembered that she had been about to show him his old room.

"Do you want to go up on your own or would you like me to come?"

"I'd much rather you showed me. It's such a long time ago now. It doesn't feel as though this was ever my house."

She smiled. That wasn't an unusual feeling amongst those who came back. Sometimes they seemed to be looking to reclaim the missing years of their lives, particularly those who had had a more nomadic existence.

Edith led the way upstairs and to the bedroom at the back of the house. "You can't see the River Severn anymore, now they've built those new houses. I say new, but they've been up a good number of years." She was leaning across the bed and looking out of the window that was behind it as she spoke. Simon was behind her. She could hear his breathing.

She turned to look at him and found he had taken some gloves out of his pocket. He smiled at her and as she took her hand off the window sill, he took advantage of her not being balanced and pushed her down onto the single bed.

Edith's brain felt befuddled. She had no idea what was going on. She made to get up but he had his hands on her pressing her down. She was strong for her age and began to struggle but he hit her with the back of his fist across the temple and she fell back onto the bed. She felt drowsy, but knew that it wasn't the time to be sleeping. She needed to do something. She was starting to feel she was at risk and yet at the same time she felt incredibly relaxed. She just wanted to sleep. She closed her eyes and as she did she became aware of a pillow being brought down onto her face. She was fighting for breath, but fighting was too difficult. She needed to breathe, but the pillow was being forced down on top of her. Her final thought was that Simon had been a good child. He wouldn't have done this. Then all was darkness and there was no more thought.

CHAPTER 24

Connor collected the hire car as soon as the company opened and then went home to collect Tammy. He packed the car including everything for an overnight stay. *Dog bowl!* He rushed back inside with Tammy at his heels.

"Do you think we need some sort of weapon?" He looked down at Tammy wagging her tail. "Bread knife too obvious? Yes you're right, but we don't have many options." He hesitated fingering the handle but then closed the door and headed out. It was unlikely that Patrick Coltrane would be armed, but somehow he felt almost naked at the prospect of confronting him. One thing he was certain of was that he wouldn't be leaving his drink unattended for so much as a second. If he had any doubts, his drink would be left well and truly untouched.

As he drove into the car park of the Bull's Head, he got a sinking feeling. There were no other cars to be seen. It was just past twelve, but the place looked deserted. It might have been wiser to check on the internet for opening times before turning up, but he'd assumed that a pub in an industrial area would be open every day. He shut the car door and followed the path to the entrance.

'Closed for refurbishment. We will open under new management in two weeks' time.' He kicked the door making the metal hasp jangle. Two weeks was no use, he was meeting Patrick Coltrane now. He gave the door a second satisfying kick and made his way back to the car.

He'd still got an hour until he was due to meet Patrick, but he had no way to get in touch with him to agree a different venue. He decided to drive round to look for an alternative. The thought of meeting Patrick in a deserted area did not appeal. He wished he'd brought the bread knife. He drove around a few streets but found nothing suitable, so he headed back to the car park to wait.

Connor sat facing towards the car park entrance tapping his fingers on the steering wheel. Each time a car approached he took a deep breath and then let it out as each one drove straight past. It was 13.10 when a battered Vauxhall Golf turned into the car park and Connor recognised the bulky figure behind the wheel. His palms began to sweat and he could feel the hair on his neck standing on end.

"Lie down," he instructed Tammy out of the corner of his mouth. He didn't need her to be seen right now. He then got out of the car.

Connor dispensed with the formality of introductions. "It's closed for refurbishment. Do you know anywhere else nearby?"

Patrick looked him up and down with a quizzical expression on his face. For a moment Connor thought he'd been recognised, but he hoped that the cap and roll neck sweater would help to make him look different to the last time they met.

Patrick grunted. "There's a place round the corner. Get in I'll drive."

Connor felt cornered. His mouth went dry. "I could follow in my car. I need to get away afterwards."

"Whatever."

He relaxed a little. "I'm on my way." It sounded ridiculous as soon as he'd said it and he returned to the car, hoping that Tammy would not jump up in her excitement to have him back so soon.

Patrick pulled out of the car park with Connor behind. They drove to the end of the road and turned left. They passed some waste ground. *Please, God, no.* After several more corners and back in civilisation, Connor felt the tension drop back out of his tensed shoulders. They drew up in front of a pub that looked even more in need of refurbishment than the last one. Patrick parked first and lumbered over to where Connor was still parking. He saw Tammy as Connor opened the car.

"You're that bloke."

Connor wasn't sure whether to respond and confirm which bloke he was or whether to pretend he didn't know what Patrick was talking about. It was starting to look as though the cost of the hire car had been a waste, whilst the bread knife would have been a welcome presence. Patrick was starting to look annoyed. He was looking menacingly at Connor.

"At least let me buy you a drink and hear me out." Connor pleaded, hoping that Patrick wasn't about to get hold of him. He was standing facing Patrick with his arms spread in a disarming gesture, whilst biting the inside of his mouth.

"What's this really about?" Patrick took another step towards him. Connor was pressed up against the side of the car with nowhere to get away to.

"It's about your step-brother."

Patrick spat to the side, but said nothing.

Connor was thinking as fast as he could for what to say next. One false move on his part could be fatal. "He asked me to find you."

"That bastard knows where I am."

Connor thought the description was ironic, but chose not to point it out. "I just need to ask you a few questions. You may be able to help me."

"He told that copper didn't he?"

Connor didn't know whether to ask which copper or what he'd told him. What he did know was that he didn't want to be pressed up against the car by a potentially violent man. "Can we go inside and talk?"

"We can talk here," said Patrick.

"When did you last see your brother?"

"He said he'd got some more money for me. He came to see me last week."

"And did he have more money for you?"

"No, he just came to my house. He wanted to borrow money from me."

"What did the police want?"

"What's it to you?"

Connor thought that was a fair point. He had no idea how to proceed and wondered if Trevor Whitworth could access the police interview for him to save him the trouble. In the compromised position in which he found himself Connor didn't feel inclined to ask too many more questions. Then a thought struck him.

"Did you meet your mother before she died?"

Patrick deflated. He nodded but said nothing.

"What did your mother say to you?"

Patrick's head sank down and he backed away. "She said," his voice caught. "She said it was all her fault. That I was such a loser."

"Do you think you're a loser?"

"That's what Steve called me."

"What do you think?"

Patrick gave a deep shrug.

"Did you feel angry with your mother?" Connor was beginning to feel that he was getting into a flow and was off guard when a fist connected with his chin and sent him sprawling over the bonnet of the car. Tammy started barking angrily and before Connor could pull himself together Patrick had fled across the car park to his own vehicle and was heading away at speed. Connor felt dazed and wasn't sure whether his jaw was just bruised or broken. He pulled himself up and then leant against the side of the car again. He supposed he had been asking for something to happen with the sorts of questions he was asking, but what it did confirm to him was that something wasn't right with the idea of Patrick being the murderer. Yes he was a violent man, but he was an aggressive and impulsive man too, not someone who planned things and then executed them in a non-violent manner.

Connor sat in the car nursing his wound. He took a good look in the mirror and moved his jaw about. It was painful, but he didn't think he needed to find a hospital. He decided to go into the pub and wash his face to see how that made him feel. He'd also have a whisky. He thought he'd earned it and one shouldn't affect his drive to Gloucester. He still needed the number, for Edith Monkton's daughter, from Fingers, so perhaps he could give him a call too.

Using a carrier bag that he carried to clean up after Tammy, he made an ice pack with some ice from the bar and held it against his jaw. He kept it in position until the ice began to melt and drip out of the safety holes in the bag. Although it was very painful to move, he was convinced there was no break and proceeded to ring

Fingers.

"It's me, Connor," he said barely moving his jaw as he spoke.

"Who is this?"

"Connor! I got thumped in the jaw." He'd never been a very good ventriloquist and struggled to make any of his words clear.

"Sorry, mate. I don't know who you said it was."

Connor hung up and sent him a text message. It would be easier this way, but how was he going to ring Edith Monkton's daughter if he got the number? He would write her a letter explaining that he would like to talk to her and put it through her door that evening. He could then call round tomorrow, when he hoped his jaw would be a little better. His mobile rang, it was Fingers.

"You poor sod. Why didn't you say something? No, I'm joking. Grunt if you've got a pen and paper and I'll give you the details."

Connor grunted and then proceeded to write down what Fingers gave him.

"Thanks," he said at the end of the call.

"Pardon?"

"I said 'thanks'. Oh it doesn't matter." Connor hung up, Fingers would be able to guess what he meant.

He wanted to ring Maggie, but after the episode with Fingers he didn't think he'd got the energy to even try. He was sure she'd ring him later if she'd got something for him from that picture.

He went back to the car and set off. He was feeling hungry, but he had no inclination to try chewing anything. What he needed to find was somewhere selling Paracetamol. He decided to stop at the first service station he came to. Maybe they'd be serving some soup as well.

He arrived in Gloucester late afternoon and found the house of Joy Meredith with little difficulty. There were no cars on the driveway and he slipped the letter through the door without anyone seeing him. He breathed a sigh of relief. It was easier this way. He just hoped that she would be available the following day and that his jaw would be a little better.

He set off in search of the Travel Lodge and a good night's rest. Before he went looking for something liquid to eat, he sent a text to Maggie saying 'Am ok. Got hit in jaw. Hard to talk. Love Connor.'

His phone rang almost immediately.

"Connor, it's me, Maggie. What happened?"

Connor's jaw had stiffened up from earlier and he grunted out a few noises.

"Ok, if you can't talk, just listen. It's about that photo. The woman's name is Maureen Winter. She was a secretary at the place where Harry Daniels works. It's just that she's dead. She drowned in the River Ouse last year. I don't know if there were any suspicious circumstances, but I thought you'd want to know."

Connor grunted in what he hoped was an appreciative way.

"I'll see if I can find anything more and bring it over when you get back. You take care of yourself. Who hit you?"

Connor tried to say 'Patrick' but Maggie guessed.

"I suppose it was the half-brother. Be careful. Someone round here has got secrets worth preserving."

Connor was frustrated that he couldn't ring Trevor Whitworth and ask him to do some digging on the possible mistress. He tried to reassure himself that a day or two wouldn't make any difference. However, it might to Steve Daniels. The Lifetracer must now say twelve days.

CHAPTER 25

Connor looked in the mirror at his rainbow coloured jaw. He would have grinned at the excuse not to shave, but the pain was too much. He smiled and winced with pain. At least he could move it a little more freely than yesterday. "Good morning." He nodded. The words were almost coherent. He wondered whether he should phone Joy Meredith to arrange a time for their meeting, but he didn't want to face her saying no. He took Tammy for a walk along the road before breakfast. From the look she gave him, she was not enamoured with the tarmac pavement and car fumes.

"Sorry old girl. It won't always be like this." *But who was he kidding?* He had no idea how it was going to be.

He was on his way back when his mobile rang. The caller ID said Steve Daniels. It was his house phone.

"This thing is still ticking and I haven't heard from you."

"Good morning to you too. I'm working on it. I should have some news in the next day or two."

"You do that. I'll be expecting you."

Connor could almost hear the menacing curl of the lip in Steve's voice and wondered whether that was the effect of hearing from his half-brother

He let his mind wander to the other steps he needed to take when he got back to York. He was going to need to see Harry Daniels again, to ask about Maureen Winter, but he'd like to find some more background first. Maybe there was nothing in it, but apparent coincidences always sparked his interest.

It was 09.30 when he rang the bell of Joy Meredith's house. He hoped his appearance didn't make him look too suspicious. He almost smiled as he thought that if there were someone like that on his doorstep then he wouldn't open the door to them. He stopped himself just before he stretched the tautness of the damaged skin.

The door was opened by a gentleman, who from his proportions looked as though he enjoyed his food and had a smile as broad as his girth to go with it. Connor thought that all he needed was the white beard and the red suit to make the perfect Santa Claus.

"You must be Connor Bancroft, come through, come through. My wife's in the kitchen, round the corner to the left and through the end door."

Connor followed the direction and the smell of baking. The man who he assumed was Mr Meredith followed behind.

"Joy, darling," the man called ahead of him. "Our visitor's arrived."

"Oh you poor dear. Whatever happened to your chin?"

Connor resisted the joke that she should have seen the other bloke. He tried to grin. "I asked too many questions. It's good of you to see me," he held out his hand but took it away again as Joy Meredith held up two hands covered in dough.

"It's the W.I. this afternoon. I'm afraid I've got quite a lot of baking to do. Can we talk while I work? Gordon, dear, would you put the kettle on?"

Gordon went across the kitchen to the kettle.

"Do have a seat, Mr Bancroft," Joy indicated to the chairs near the table where she was working. He pulled a seat out and sat a little way away to avoid being in the firing line of the flour. "There will be fresh mince pies out of the oven in five minutes." She seemed as jolly as her husband. All of a sudden the jollity slid away and a much more serious voice said. "I believe you want to talk to me about my mother."

"Yes, please. As I explained in my letter, I'm investigating a number of murders that seem to be connected with that of your mother. I know the police are looking into it, but I wondered if there was anything you could tell me."

Joy nodded while kneading the dough. "It was a shock to all of us. She was such a good person. Oh dear, look at me." She wiped a stray tear away with the back of her hand. "We were very close. A day like today and she'd have been helping me with the baking."

"I'm sorry," Connor said. "This can't be easy."

"No," Joy sniffed. "I'll be all right, just give me a minute." She kneaded the dough with such ferocity that Connor was grateful she'd got that to take her feelings out on. "On the day she died, my Mother was meeting one of my foster brothers. At least that's what I thought. His name was Simon Edmonds, except when the police followed up with him, he was out of the country at the time and hadn't been in touch with my mother. I don't know who it was that went to see her, although it must have been someone who knew that she had fostered Simon."

"Do you remember back to the time when Simon was in your mother's care?"

"Not really. We had so many children come and go. I

remember the ones that stayed for quite a long time and even then, I can only place the time if I can link them to particular events."

"Did your mum keep a record of them?"

"She kept a photo album. I'm afraid the police have it at the moment. She wrote in there the years that the children came and went but not always the months, so it was still a bit vague. Simon was with us quite a long time so there were a fair number of other children around then."

"Does the name Patrick Coltrane mean anything to you?"

Joy shook her head. "I don't remember him. Was he one of the foster children?"

"I think so. If you don't mind me asking, can you tell me anything about how your mother died?"

Joy stared at him for a moment. "I can still see her body when I close my eyes. I had to do the identification. It was terrible. She looked so normal. I can't believe that a violent death can look so natural. The cause of death was confirmed through the bloodspots they found on my mother's lungs. Apparently that's common when someone has been . . ." Joy didn't finish the sentence. She brushed her hands on her apron and fled from the room, leaving a trail of flour as she went.

Connor felt awkward. "I'm sorry. I didn't mean to cause upset." He addressed his comments to Gordon Meredith who was still standing in the kitchen.

"I'll go after her. Excuse me." He left the room.

Connor wondered whether he should be taking the mince pies out of the oven as there was a smell of burning pastry starting to emanate from the cooker. He found some oven gloves on a hook to the side of the cooker and took them out placing them on a wire tray that he presumed had been put there for that purpose. Then he sat down and waited.

At least ten minutes passed before Joy Meredith returned, fully composed.

"Oh the pies, thank you."

"It was the least I could do. If you'd rather I went...?"

"No. It's difficult but I do need to talk about it and if talking to you can help to find the demon who did this..."

Connor wondered what else he could ask.

"I did see a car," Joy said. "I told the police. I don't know if it was relevant. The driver could have been going anywhere. It was parked on the road outside my Mother's house when Simon was supposed to be there." She looked at him guiltily for a moment. "I wasn't checking up on my mother, well not exactly. I drove by sometimes just to make sure everything was all right. It didn't do much good did it?"

"What was the car like that you saw?"

It was small. I'm sorry, I don't know what make it was. It was red though, I do remember that. I think it struck me as odd as it was parked outside my mother's house and there were spaces further along the road. I thought at the time that it must have been Simon's car."

"I don't suppose you saw the registration number did you?"

Joy shook her head. "I don't think it was that old, but I can't remember. I didn't want to linger outside in case Mum saw me and got cross." She smiled. "There were still times that she made me feel like a little girl who had been naughty. She never shouted. She just had this way of making you know when you'd displeased her."

"Was there anything left with your mother?"

"Such as?" Joy was frowning.

"A Lifetracer. It's a sort of electronic diary gadget. It's just that one was left at the scenes of the other murders and if your mother is linked, I thought it would be the same."

Joy shook her head. "No, there was nothing like that. Perhaps they aren't connected after all." She looked crestfallen, what little straw he was offering her being taken away again.

"There are a number of other similarities." He decided not to go into the details of the ways the killings had taken place for fear of upsetting her again. "If you think of anything else, will you give me a call?" Connor passed her a card with his numbers on.

"I will, but I don't think there was anything. I'm sorry."

The apology stung Connor. He felt as though he should be the one apologising that he hadn't got further with finding the killer. He needed a breakthrough, but it just wasn't happening. Everything was pointing to Patrick Coltrane, but he just didn't buy that.

As he left the house of Joy Meredith, he wondered about at least driving past the scene of the crime, but what was the point? There was nothing there he would see. There had been no point asking Joy to look round, the house would have been sold by now. He wondered how someone felt living where there had been a murder and thought of Alisha Daley, having to deal everyday with the knowledge that her husband had been murdered in the house the family were still living in. He shuddered.

Tammy barked with delight as she saw him approach the car. He let her out and walked her along the street before setting off. It was going to take him much of the rest of the day to drive back to York. It gave him some thinking time if nothing else.

He'd been driving for a couple of hours when Maggie rang.

"How are you today?"

"Sore and bruised, but I'll live. The worrying thing is that I feel I need to ask Patrick Coltrane another question."

"No!"

"I want to ask several. I want to know who knows enough detail of his former life to implicate him so effectively and I want to know whether he knows anyone with a motive to frame him."

"Can't you do all that by phone?"

"I could, but I don't know if he'd take my call."

"Why don't you ring him at work to see if you can get him to take the call there? He might be more off his guard."

"Yes, I'll do that."

He decided to wait for his next coffee stop, rather than trying to do it while he was driving. He stopped at Donnington services on the M1 near East Midlands Airport. He wasn't all that far from Derby, so he could always make a detour if it proved worthwhile. He rang through to Josh Thompson's secretary.

"Hi, it's Connor Bancroft here. I came in to see Mr Thompson last week to ask him about an investigation I'm undertaking in which one of your Lifetracers was found."

"Oh yes, I remember."

"That's great. The thing is, I'd like to speak to one of your employees if that would be ok. I've got a couple of questions for him."

"Which employee did you want to speak to?"

"Patrick Coltrane."

"I'm sorry, that could be difficult. Mr Coltrane hasn't arrived at work today. There's a rumour amongst the lads that he's done a runner, probably because he always seems a little bit shifty, but no one knows anything."

"Did he come back to work yesterday afternoon?"

"What do you mean 'come back'?"

"I met him at lunchtime. He nearly broke my jaw."

"Yes he did come back, but he seemed rattled. One of the lads said he thought he saw Mr Coltrane taking everything out of his locker at the end of the day. It looked like he wasn't planning on returning."

"Thanks. You've been a great help."

Connor sat back in his seat and looked at Tammy. "Now what do we do, girl? I don't think he's the guilty one, but he doesn't help himself does he? I wonder if he's still at the same home address."

Connor dug out the paperwork he'd got from Fingers to find the phone number. He had no idea what he was going to say if Patrick answered, but short of visiting the house, what else could he do. Then he made up his mind.

"Come on Tammy, we're going to Derby. He programmed the sat-nav and set off again.

CHAPTER 26

Connor rang the bell and then paced back and forth across the doorstep of Patrick's house. He waited for a couple of minutes. There was no reply. He rang again. This time he peered through the letter box to see if there were any signs of life. It was hard to tell from an empty hall. He could feel his pulse racing and looked over his shoulder to check no one was around.

He shouted through the letterbox. "Mr Coltrane. I know you're in there. I want to help you. I don't think you did it." He just hoped he was right and he wasn't trying to make his way into a murderer's house. There was still no reply. He had a sudden thought and looked around for the car that Patrick had been driving the day before, but there was no sign of that either. He could try breaking in, but what if Patrick caught him there?

He tried the gate across the passageway to the houses, but it was either bolted or blocked by something from the other side. He glanced around again and then went round to the back of the houses through an open passageway further along the road. He climbed over fences to get to the right one. It was broad daylight, someone was bound to see him. He hoped that the majority of people were still at work. He ran his finger round the back of his collar and swallowed hard. He reached the back of Patrick's house and made his way to the back door. He pulled his sleeve over his hand and tried the door. It was open.

He was breathing heavily as he entered the untidy kitchen. There were dirty pots filling the sink and the rubbish needed taking out. From the loaf of bread on the side, it looked as though someone was either at home or would return shortly. Connor had no idea what he was looking for, but he reasoned that he'd know it if he saw it. He went through to the front room, keeping clear of the window. It was as untidy as the kitchen but there was still no sign of life.

He tiptoed across the hallway and towards the stairs, trying to take in every detail as he went. As he climbed the stairs he was treading as lightly as possible, but the third stair creaked. He paused, hunched against the banister hoping he couldn't be seen from the turn in the top of the stairs if someone were to look round. There were no sounds of movement from upstairs so he carried on. The landing was dark, but he could still make out three doors, all of them closed. He started with the one nearest; the room at the back of the house. It was the bathroom. He was just pulling the door closed again when he heard a noise outside.

He paused, hardly daring to breath. Then he heard the sound of a wheelie bin being rolled out to the pavement and breathed a sigh of relief. He opened the door to the back bedroom and went inside. There were boxes piled in a haphazard pyramid in the centre of the room. He lifted the corner of the nearest one and found what he presumed were goods that had been stolen from the warehouse. There were at least two boxed Lifetracers included in the stash.

He was careful to hold everything through his sleeve. The last thing he wanted to do was leave a finger print.

He replaced the flap of the box and began to retreat towards the door. He was just stepping out onto the landing when he heard the slam of more than one car door. He froze, heart thumping in his chest.

Then the shout "Police, we've got the house surrounded. Come out with your hands up or we're coming in."

Was it too much to hope they were at the neighbouring property? Connor headed back into the bedroom and keeping to the wall as he went made his way towards the window. He looked at the small garden below. It was Patrick Coltrane's garden and it was swarming with police. He wondered if they were looking for Patrick or whether someone had called them to say there was an intruder. Either way it didn't look good for him right now.

He decided to give himself up. Waiting could make matters worse and he didn't fancy becoming a fugitive. Besides there was no way he could get out of the front of the house and he needed to rescue Tammy from the car. He headed back towards the stairway.

"I'm coming out. I'm unarmed." He shouted as he went.

He got as far as the front door and through the glass could see an officer on the doorstep. He tried opening the door, but he needed a key and a quick scan of the surrounding walls and table revealed nothing useful.

"I can't open it. I don't have the key. I'll come through the back door, it's open."

"Stand back." Shouted the officer outside and before Connor had time to say he knew the back door was unlocked, the door had been booted close to the lock and had swung open.

"Patrick Coltrane, you are under arrest on suspicion of

murdering Paul Tranter. You do not have to say anything but it may harm your defence if you do not mention when questioned something which you later rely on in court. Anything you do say may be taken down in writing and used in evidence."

It hadn't been a tip off from a neighbour. "I'm not Patrick Coltrane." Connor was almost laughing with relief that it wasn't him they were looking for. Then he realised that he was going to have some difficulty explaining what he was doing in Patrick's house and wondered if he should remain silent until he could get someone to sort this mess out. He was bundled into the back of a police car before he had any further chance to argue.

He had two concerns as they drove him to the police station. His first was how long it was going to take for him to explain his way out of this one and the second was that Tammy was sitting in a hire car near Patrick Coltrane's house. The windows were down, but she couldn't stay there for long.

When he arrived at the station, the real confusion began. The desk sergeant prepared to book him in. He listened to Connor explain he wasn't Patrick Coltrane. Then Connor produced his driving licence to prove it.

"Is there someone who can verify your ID?"

"Would an officer in the North Yorkshire constabulary be acceptable?"

"Yes, sir."

"Do you mind if I use the phone?"

Connor was given access to the phone and told he could make one call, other than to ring a solicitor. He was torn. He could do with ringing Trevor Whitworth, but he was also concerned about Tammy and wanted the reassurance that someone would be with her soon. He rang Maggie and crossed his fingers that she would answer.

"Maggie, it's me Connor. I've been arrested. Don't panic, it's all a misunderstanding, but I think it might take a while. I need you to do two things for me."

"Are you all right, Connor?"

"Yes I'm fine. Please, do you have a pen and paper?"

"Yes, go ahead."

"I need you to ring Trevor Whitworth and get him to talk to someone here in Derby to confirm my identity." He gave Maggie Trevor's number. "Then I need you to come down to Derby as soon as you can to rescue Tammy from the car." He gave Maggie the address of where Tammy was and a description of the car.

"Isn't there someone nearer who could get to Tammy?"

A sudden thought crossed his mind. "Yes, could you ring Bob Minton? If you explain what's happened he'll understand."

"Connor, be careful."

He hung up and was left to wait for Trevor Whitworth to ring the station. He was processed by the Custody Sergeant and then taken to a cell while he was waiting for his story to be confirmed. He spent his time trying to work out how to explain his presence inside Coltrane's house. He concluded that nothing short of the truth would explain it and set about deciding which precise version of the truth he was going to give and how exactly the truth should be worded. His mind wandered as he looked around the sparsely furnished cell. This was not somewhere he wanted to be held for very long.

He'd been waiting about half an hour when Detective Inspector Saunders unlocked the cell door.

"Well it looks like we might like to interview you in connection with all this anyway, Mr Bancroft."

"Do I need a lawyer?"

"You tell me. You've already used your phone call home. Are you now saying you want to call a lawyer?"

Connor wondered whether the hard man image was to compensate for arresting the wrong bloke or whether he was always like this. There wasn't much time for thought as the interview room was close to the custody suite and it wasn't long before he was being ushered through a door.

Detective Inspector Saunders put the tapes in the machine and signalled for the sergeant to join them.

"Interview with Mr Connor Bancroft on Tuesday 6th October 2009 at 15.51. Present are Detective Inspector Saunders and Detective Sergeant Rose. The interviewee did not ask for a lawyer to be present." He winked at Connor.

"Please can you explain what you were doing in the house of Patrick Coltrane earlier today?" The officer sat with his arms crossed, low down in the chair looking bored.

Connor spoke slowly, trying to give himself time to think about each word. "I was looking for Patrick Coltrane."

"Is that so? And why were you looking for Mr Coltrane?"

"I wanted to talk to him about the murders that he is being framed for." He said no more. DI Saunders raised an eyebrow and sat up a little straighter.

"And how do you come to have any knowledge of the crimes that Patrick Coltrane is alleged to have committed?"

"I've been working for his brother, well half-brother,

Steve Daniels."

Connor sensed that DI Saunders had started to drop the hard-man act and was now interested in what he was saying.

"Go on."

"I'm sure I'm not telling you anything you don't already know, but Patrick Coltrane was in some way connected to at least four people who have been murdered. He just doesn't fit the profile though. Have you met him?"

DI Saunders shook his head. Then he appeared to remember the tape. "No. And you're an expert in profiling are you?" There was a sneer in DI Saunders voice.

Connor paused thinking about how to handle his observations. "No. I'm no expert, but he's an aggressive man. He did this to me yesterday." Connor pointed to the bruising on his chin."

"Mr Bancroft is pointing to an area of pronounced bruising around his chin and jaw. And you went back for more!"

"I wanted to tell him I didn't think he'd done it. The style of the crimes isn't right. He's violent and although they're murders, they couldn't be less aggressive in the way they've been set up."

"Do you still think that when I tell you we found Rohypnol and a pair of gloves that we believe may have been used in at least one of the crimes in his house?"

Connor gasped. "I didn't know that."

"Unless you were planting those at the time we found you."

Connor sensed the mood changing and started to feel cornered. He wondered if he'd opened up too much. What had seemed a pleasant discussion felt quite a frightening situation to be in. "I was looking for evidence, not planting it." Perhaps he had been wrong to go ahead without the lawyer.

"We only have your word for that."

"You've had a call vouching for me haven't you? Isn't that enough?"

"Either that or a very clever cover. I could charge you for having broken into Patrick Coltrane's house. Hold you longer for questioning."

"I didn't break in. The door was open." Connor was tempted to point out that the forced entry had been by the police, but thought better of antagonising them.

There was a knock on the interview room door. A young constable poked his head round. "Can I have a word, sir?"

"Interview suspended at 16.09." DI Saunders got up and left the room, leaving Connor to wonder what would happen next. He smiled at DS Rose who didn't return the pleasantry, but looked away instead.

Ten minutes passed before DI Saunders returned and without a word of explanation said to DS Rose, "Take him back to one of our guest rooms. We may want to interview him again later."

Connor was led back down to the cells which he was pleased were fairly quiet, although he suspected they would become noisier as the evening came. It was odd, feeling that the tables had been turned. He knew going to see Patrick was a gamble, but after yesterday he thought he was more likely to be in physical danger confronting Patrick rather than in the cells. He was conscious that this was his own fault and yet if he went back in time he'd do the same again. Although with hindsight, he might have waited for the police visit to be out of the way before entering. Now he had to work out what he was going to do next. At least Maggie knew where he was and by now Bob would have rescued Tammy and be making a fuss of her.

If nothing else, he would be able to work this into an article for some magazine or other. He could call it 'my night in the cells', although he hoped it wouldn't come to a whole night. He was hoping the misunderstanding would be sorted out.

He'd been sitting there about three-quarters of an hour if his body clock was accurate, although it could have been almost any length of time for the lack of reference points. He heard some noises down the corridor and another prisoner being brought to the cells. He went to stand by the grill to see if they came past.

As soon as he saw who was on the other side he realised what had given rise to the interruption to his interview. It was Patrick Coltrane. Connor guessed they wouldn't be planning to put them in the same cell, but wondered if they might be near enough to communicate.

Once the cell door had been closed and Patrick was incarcerated Connor called out to him.

"They found you then?"

"Who wants to know?"

"It's the guy you punched yesterday, but before you start I think you're innocent and want to help you."

"What are you doing in here?"

This was awkward. Connor didn't want to get off on the wrong foot by mentioning his minor trespass.

"I was looking for you. They mistook me for you and brought me in."

"Why've they still got you then?"

"I told them I think you're innocent. I think they want

to know what I've got."

"How come you think I didn't do it?"

"It's just a hunch. I don't think the murders are your style. I think someone is framing you, but I don't know why someone would do that. Do you have any ideas?"

"Do you think I'd be here if I knew who it was?"

"Who knew the details of your life up to now?"

"Nobody. I don't talk about it to no one."

"Someone must know. Think about it. The only way the Police are going to believe you didn't do it is if there is someone else who might have done."

"They've got evidence." Patrick sounded very low.

"I'll do what I can but there isn't much I can do while I'm stuck in here. Is there anyone who would have it in for your family? I mean someone is threatening your brother too."

"He's not my brother."

"Ok, Steve Daniels. Someone is threatening Steve Daniels and now trying to fit you up for the crimes." Before Connor could say anymore an officer came to his cell and started to unlock the door.

"You're out of here."

"What, I'm free to go?"

"Sure are."

Connor was surprised but loathed to ask any questions of clarification. Instead he followed the officer out of the cell.

He called to Patrick. "I'll see what I can do for you. Have you got a lawyer?"

"I don't want no lawyer."

Before Connor had chance to reply the officer was ushering him along the corridor. Much as he needed transport back to where he'd left the car, Connor decided to get a cab and then thought of Bob Minton. If Bob had rescued Tammy for him, he was going to have to see him soon anyway, maybe he'd be willing to pick up Connor from the station. He rang Bob's number.

CHAPTER 27

"Yes of course we collected Tammy for you. She's here now, safe and sound. I can be there to pick you up in twenty minutes. Shall I bring Tammy with me or would you like to come back here to sort yourself out?"

"I'm really grateful, but I'll head straight back if you don't mind. I need to return the hire car."

"Not a problem to me. This is a fine dog you've got. We're on our way."

Connor went to find a coffee while he waited for Bob to arrive. His temporary incarceration had made quite an impression on him and however tired and grubby he was feeling, the air smelled sweet and he was glad to be outdoors. He got a takeaway coffee from a café and sat on a bench outside.

Twenty minutes later he found Bob and an excited Tammy waiting for him at the agreed meeting place.

"Good to see you again, although I must admit I wasn't expecting these circumstances." Bob waited for him to finish fussing over Tammy and fasten his seatbelt before setting off. "Where to?"

"Back to the car, please. How would you describe the size of the man who was talking to Paul Tranter at your retirement?"

"Average."

"He wasn't a big awkward man?"

Bob thought for a moment. "The hood was deceptive, but I wouldn't say he was particularly large."

Connor nodded. "We've all been going after the wrong man. At the moment the police have him under arrest, but I think the real question is why would someone try to frame him and then threaten his brother?" He fell into silence thinking and they soon arrived at the car. Connor looked at Patrick's house. It would take another ten minutes to finish looking round. He shook his head. He needed to get on the road home.

"Thanks, Bob. I owe you for this."

"Think nothing of it, just find out who killed Paul Tranter and you'll have given me all the repayment I need."

By the time Connor got home, he was worn out. Maggie met him at the house, but he had no sooner sat in a chair than he'd fallen asleep and was out of it for the day. He came to with Tammy pawing him on Wednesday morning. Maggie had gone without him knowing, but had wrapped a blanket round him and left an envelope and a note. He took Tammy out and sorted her breakfast before opening the envelope. Inside were copies of the picture of Harry Daniels with Maureen Winter, together with some news stories about the accidental death of Maureen Winter by drowning.

Connor stared at the paper. He would have liked to talk to Maureen Winter, but in the circumstances it looked as though he was going to have to track down Harry Daniels. He rang Maggie and left a message apologising for the previous evening and thanking her for the envelope.

He was contemplating what approach to take when his phone rang.

"It seems that everything has been resolved then."

"Pardon? Who is this?"

"Sorry, I thought you'd recognise the number. It's Steve Daniels. I hear that the case has been solved."

Connor was surprised that the news had filtered through. "Who told you?"

"I had a call from the police to say that Patrick Coltrane has been charged. Who would have thought it, my own brother? At least that's the end of my needing your services."

"Right." Connor was wrong-footed. If he didn't tell Steve that he thought Patrick was innocent then he'd have to go it alone with any further investigation and if he did tell him… Well he had no idea how Steve would react.

"I'll send your cheque to you. Where shall I send it to?"

"I'll collect it, if you don't mind." Connor was very careful not to give out his address. Although when he thought about it, he had no problem finding other people, so it was unlikely that anyone would have much difficulty finding him. "When will you be in?"

"I'll be around on Friday morning before 11.00."

When Connor hung up, he went to get a cup of coffee. So, the man he thought was innocent had been charged with murder and he was off the case. Without any money coming in for the investigation he couldn't afford to continue, but he couldn't leave an innocent man in prison, even if he had been punched in the face for his troubles. He sat and contemplated his next step. He wanted to talk to Harry Daniels but first he needed to find out a little more about Maureen Winter's death.

He rang the coroner's office to see if he could get a copy of the inquest report and although he could, it would take up to three weeks to obtain. He wondered whether the newspaper's court reporter would have sat in on the inquest and whether he could supply any of the details. He'd ring Maggie again later and see if she could find out. In the meantime, he was going in search of Harry Daniels.

Harry was a tax advisor with a small practice in York. Connor waited outside his office in the hope that he was the sort of man who liked to go out at lunchtime. He'd had a walk round and found a back entrance to the car park and a front entrance onto the street. He didn't think he'd manage to catch Harry if he went out by car, so he waited by the front entrance in the hope he'd come out on foot. He'd been waiting about half an hour and was starting to think his efforts were futile when Harry came out wearing a heavy overcoat and started walking towards the shopping centre.

Connor wanted it to look as much like him casually bumping into Harry as possible so he followed him through the crowds until Harry went into a sandwich shop. Connor decided to catch him on the doorstep as he came out. He had a few minutes to wait as the queue was served and then he saw Harry moving towards the door.

He walked towards him. "Mr Daniels isn't it?"

The man looked up frowning.

"I'm Connor Bancroft. I was doing some work for your son."

A look of recognition flooded Harry Daniels' face. "Oh yes." He looked as though he was about to move away.

"It's great news that they've caught the person behind the murders isn't it?"

Harry looked confused. "Er, yes."

Connor surmised that he had no idea that Patrick had been charged. "Can I buy you a drink to celebrate?"

Connor was relying on Harry being the lame character he appeared and not having the strength to say no. He wasn't disappointed and before Harry had chance to change his mind, Connor guided him into the nearby Harkers.

Connor bought the drinks and led Harry to a table away from the main bustle of the lunchtime traffic.

"Are you surprised to hear who's behind it all?"

Harry hung his head, "To be honest, I haven't heard." He looked up at Connor. "Who is it?"

"Patrick Coltrane, your wife's son."

Harry gasped. "Patrick was threatening Steve?"

"Well the Police think so. I'm off the case, but there are one or two loose ends I want to tie up."

"I never liked that son of a bitch." Harry's face grew red as he talked. "The way those boys took the money that should have been mine. I should have been able to retire by now. If they hadn't got their thieving hands on my money."

"Do you begrudge the money to your son?"

"Little squirt. Always a mummy's boy. Oh she loved him all right, but what about her husband? What did I count for?"

"There are some points you may be able to help me with."

"I'll help if I can."

"How long did you have a relationship with Maureen Winter?"

This time not only did Harry gasp, but the colour drained out of his face. "Who told you?"

Connor was in two minds whether to tell the truth. He didn't want Harry to brush the question aside, a photograph wasn't complete proof against the man. "I heard it on the grapevine."

"Some grapevine, I thought we'd kept that secret. It was a while ago. Can you blame me? There was no love for me at home."

"You mean it was whilst your wife was alive?"

Harry nodded.

"Is that why she committed suicide?"

"Who, Maureen?"

Connor was surprised by the response. "I thought Maureen's was an accident?"

"I should be going." Harry got up. "Goodbye, Mr Bancroft."

"No, wait. Are you telling me that Maureen Winter committed suicide?"

"It wasn't clear. It was put down as an accident to spare the family. Goodbye," and before Connor could say another word, Harry Daniels scurried from the room.

Was it possible that one man could be so unlucky as to have both his wife and mistress commit suicide? Connor wondered whether it was worth looking at the evidence from both of the inquests. Something didn't make sense.

If it wasn't Patrick behind the deaths was it possible that either of the suicides might shed some light on what was happening? Connor needed to find a quicker way of accessing the Coroner's records. Within three weeks, the Lifetracer would have reached zero and Steve's life could be over. There were two possibilities and Connor decided to try them both. He fetched his mobile out of his pocket and started to dial.

"Trevor, it's Connor."

"They let you out then."

"Yes, thanks for the phone call. It was all a case of mistaken identity, well that and the fact that I was in somebody else's house."

"I probably don't want to know. I hear they've arrested the bloke you mentioned."

"Yes, but if I'm not mistaken they've got the wrong man."

Connor could hear Trevor draw a breath in through his teeth. "And what makes you say that?"

"A number of things, not least of which is that he doesn't fit the description of the man that was seen leaving the pub with one of the victims."

"The victim didn't have to leave the pub with the same man that killed him."

"You mean there was more than one man?"

"Well that's a possibility, but it could have been a different man that picked the victim up later, or he could have left the pub with an acquaintance and met the killer later."

"I hear what you're saying, but I've got a hunch."

"And you want me to do some more digging. What is it this time?"

"I need the records from the inquests of two suicides. I want to see if there is anything suspicious about them."

"And who would the victims be?"

"Steve Daniel's mother and his father's mistress."

Trevor took a sharp intake of breath. "Sounds like the family are having a spell of bad luck."

"I think it may be more than that."

"Give me the details and I'll see what I can do."

Connor went through his information with Trevor and then hung up. One more call to make.

"Fingers, how's it going?"

"Not bad, my man. Not bad."

"Ok, so the things I've asked from you on this case so far have been relatively easy. This time I've got a real challenge for you."

"I like a challenge. What are you after?"

"I need the coroner's records from two inquests. Can you hack into their systems?"

"I might be able to come up with something, but you can't ask any questions about where it comes from and whether it's legal."

"I wouldn't dream of it. Go."

Connor smiled. He wondered who would win the race to the information, the almost legal route through Trevor or the suspect route through Fingers.

CHAPTER 28

It had been an almost balmy day, which was a pleasant change for that summer. Maureen was on holiday from work, a glorious week to do as she pleased. She'd tried to persuade Harry to take the week off with her, but he'd been worried that people would talk. What did she care about what people thought? She wanted them to find out, but even since his wife's death Harry still didn't seem to want people knowing about their relationship. He said it was because they worked together, but she suspected it was more than that. If he was so worried about it, why was he always so happy to meet her at lunchtime? Besides which, some of his family knew. She'd met his son, but that was because they bumped into him one day while they were out. She'd seen the son again the week before this one and he had recognised her and stopped to talk.

As she cleaned out some kitchen cupboards and potted some small herb plants to grow on the kitchen windowsill, she thought about all the good times they'd had over the last three years. She kneaded down the soil around the fragile stems. It could have been the tension she was easing out of Harry's shoulders. He had seemed very tense recently. He seemed worried that she might want them to move in together. In truth, she was happy with how things were. She still liked her own space and she'd lived alone so long now that she didn't fancy the idea of someone's dirty socks on the bedroom floor. She felt carefree and that made her feel young.

She finished cutting some dead heads off a beautiful orange rose bush and went inside to get cleaned up ready for her date. For Maureen there was a thrill in the clandestine nature of their affair. It had been more accentuated when Harry's wife, Paula, had been alive, but she'd committed suicide earlier in the year and with her passing, so did a little of the danger of their meetings. She often wondered whether Paula had found out about them before she died. Women knew these things. It was years ago now, but she'd known when her own husband was having an affair. Having an affair herself didn't put right the past, but she felt it evened things up a little.

Meeting Harry still made her feel like a teenager. She looked in the mirror drawing a careful line with the eyeliner, smiling at the care she was taking. It wasn't as though they were going anywhere special, just to the Castle Museum and for a bit of lunch. There wasn't time for anything more. Harry could stretch his lunchtime to an hour and a half, but never any further.

Maureen looked at herself in the hall mirror. *You'll do girl.* She picked up her car keys and went outside. Her little white Peugeot wasn't new, but it got her around as well as any car. She'd become quite attached to it over the years. She'd take it as far as the Park 'n Ride and then catch the bus into the centre.

Harry looked distracted when he met her outside the museum.

"Have you been waiting long?" She wanted to kiss him, but knew that had to be reserved for their rare moments of privacy.

"About five minutes, shall we go in?"

They would start with the cafeteria and then look round the exhibits with any remaining time. As they got their food, Harry picked up a sandwich, while Maureen went for a salad. She couldn't help but notice that Harry seemed to be fidgeting, which wasn't like him.

"Is something wrong?"

"Let's find a table. Then we can talk."

She thought it sounded ominous, but had known him long enough not to probe. She said no more until after he had paid for their lunches.

"Maureen," he said as they sat down, a tone of seriousness in his voice that she didn't like. "I think we should stop seeing each other."

She hadn't seen that coming. "Why? Now there isn't Paula to worry about there's no problem?"

He was fiddling with the corner of his sandwich. "It's not that. I just think that Paula's death has thrown me off track and I need a bit of time to myself."

"But you didn't love her. You always said that you were planning to divorce her. We had plans."

"Her dying was different. I suppose I feel guilty."

"Well it's a bit bloody late for that. We've been seeing each other for over three years. All that time, I thought you loved me, but all you wanted was a bit of excitement on the side. I suppose now there's nothing to hide from, it doesn't seem so exciting." Maureen could feel the tears welling up, but didn't want to show them in front of him. She didn't want his pity. If he didn't love her, she didn't want anything from him. She got up, then hesitated a moment looking at her cup of tea. She picked it up and threw it at him before rushing for the door. See how he explained that one at work this afternoon.

"Maureen," he called after her, but she didn't turn

225

round. She kept hurrying out and into the fresh air. She felt numb, empty. She'd thought it was a matter of time until they'd be together permanently. She wanted the world to know. She was looking forward to telling everyone and now, thank God that none of her friends knew. At least she wasn't going to have the ignominy of having to explain to people that he'd dumped her.

She made her way back to the bus stop. What she needed was a good brisk walk for the afternoon. That would blow away a few cobwebs. She'd go home and change and then go and walk down by the river. She loved walking along by the water. It always gave her some perspective and she could use some of that right now.

As she pulled up outside her house, she was unaware of the red car parked on the opposite side of the road with the driver sat in his seat watching her. She went straight into the house to get changed without bothering to get anything for lunch. She wasn't hungry. She felt as though she would never be hungry again.

It was half an hour later when she drove away, with the red car following her. She was oblivious to it, lost in her own world of memories and grief. She headed for Beninbrough she wanted to pick up the footpath near the hall and walk towards York for a while. It was quiet except for the odd dog walker and they were few and far between at this time of day.

At least with the dry weather she wouldn't need her walking boots. She kept them in the back of the car for occasions such as these, but found the training shoes she'd put on more comfortable. It was still a sunny day and the warmth coming down onto her face was welcome. She walked away from the hall, looking for a nice spot to sit and watch the river go by. She wanted some shade to sit in and maybe a stick or two to throw into the river and watch floating away, the way her dreams were doing right now.

Harry hadn't been the greatest of catches, but she'd loved him and enjoyed his company. She could imagine growing old with him and since Paula had been off the scene, she'd thought of little else than when the time was right, they'd be together, not hidden from the world.

Maureen had walked about a mile and a half when she came to a deserted spot and sat down. The sun was glinting on the water and the scene was peaceful and restorative. She closed her eyes and leant back against a tree. This was the life. She'd be fine on her own. She'd managed before Harry came along, she could manage again. She didn't hear the footsteps approaching and was unaware she had company until the man spoke.

"Hello, Maureen."

She jumped and opened her eyes. "What are you doing here? Aren't you supposed to be working?"

The man didn't answer, but took out a flask. "Tea? You look like you could do with one."

"How did you know I was here?"

"I didn't I just happened to be visiting Beningbrough Hall and came for a walk. Everyone needs some time out now and again."

She took the tea he offered and sipped it.

"You look sad. Do you want to talk?"

"Probably not to you." She took another swig of the tea, which she needed. "I used to come here as a girl. My mother hated it, because I couldn't swim and she always thought something bad would happen to me. I used to tell her, I'm not stupid." She could feel herself becoming much more relaxed. Perhaps this was what she needed, but what an amazing coincidence. She hadn't told anyone she was coming here. She continued to sip the tea, surprised that he hadn't poured one for himself.

"Shall we walk for a while?" He stood up and brushed some grass off his trousers.

Maureen got to her feet unsteadily. She hadn't felt like this earlier. She wondered whether it was delayed shock, but the strange thing was she didn't seem to mind anymore. In fact she was quite happy and her day seemed to be progressing nicely. She started to walk along the path and put her arm through the one her companion offered to steady her. They hadn't gone far when Maureen stumbled and had to sit down.

"I don't feel quite myself. Can we just stop here for a moment? Perhaps I should have eaten something."

Within a couple of minutes of sitting down, she was completely out of things and somewhere between sleep and coma.

The man who was with her looked around and confirmed that they were out of line of sight from any of the properties that littered the countryside. He pulled on his gloves, then filled Maureen's pockets with as many of the belongings from her bag as he could manage and then put the bag round her neck for extra weight. He thought about filling the bag with stones, but the more this was seen as an accident the better, although it might be seen as suicide, which would give a sort of symmetry to the situation. Then lifting Maureen's sleeping form he carried her to the water's edge and threw her in.

Whilst the weather was bright that day, there had been an awful lot of rain over the previous few days and the river was fast flowing. Maureen floated out to the middle of the river not stirring. He stood and watched as she started to bob beneath the surface and then came up gasping. She had come to and was feebly calling for help, but other than him there was no one around. He watched her flounder and then dip back below the surface. After a few minutes she didn't surface and he wondered whether she had floated out of sight or become entangled in some rubbish under the surface.

His work here was done. He packed up the flask and without a second glance walked back towards the parked cars. No one had seen him arrive and no one saw him leave. Maureen's abandoned car would be found at some point later and her body would float to where it would be seen. By that time, all evidence that she had had company would be long gone. The man smiled. This was almost too easy. He could get to enjoy killing.

CHAPTER 29

Connor was barely through the door before he reached for the phone to ring Mikey.

"Hey there little chap, how's it going?"

"Fine. Where are you Dad?"

"I'm at home, why?"

"You just sound different."

"Oh I got hit in the jaw by a nasty man, but I'm ok now." He skipped the 'and I got arrested' bit, thinking what Jayne's reaction to it would be. "What do you want to do this weekend? I'd wondered about going to the horse racing."

"Oh, yes, Dad. Can we?"

"I would think so. Oh, and I've already asked Maggie and she's coming too."

"YES!"

Connor was delighted by the enthusiasm in his son's voice. It was great to have found a wonderful girlfriend that his son seemed to think the world of. "I'd better talk to your mum, sort it out with her."

"Ok." Mikey passed the phone to his mother saying, "Dad got hit," as he did so.

A frosty voice came on the line. "What's been happening? Mikey said you've been hit."

"It was nothing. Just a little misunderstanding."

"I'm warning you, Connor, I don't want my son

around things like that."

"He's my son too and don't you think I care about what happens around him? I'm not too keen on getting hit myself."

"Hmmm."

"I'll pick him up as usual."

"Just make sure you keep your work away from him. Otherwise…" She left the sentence hanging, but Connor knew what she meant.

He washed and changed and rang Maggie to see if he could go over. This time he remembered to pack Tammy's breakfast and they set off.

It had been a long day, but despite his tiredness, Connor wanted to talk through where he'd got to and read the articles about Maureen Winter's death for himself.

"If you're off the case, does it matter?" Maggie asked as she rubbed his shoulders, her slender fingers smoothing out the knots in the muscles.

"The way I see it, the man who employed me to find his potential killer is still at risk. I'm almost certain that despite his arrest, Patrick Coltrane is the wrong man. What would you do?"

"I guess for professional pride as much as anything, I would carry on."

"Precisely."

"And where do you think the death of Maureen Winter fits in?"

"I don't know if it does, but I can't help thinking someone is targeting the whole family. What if Paula Daniels didn't commit suicide? We've got her death and the death of Maureen Winter who just happens to be Harry Daniels' mistress. We've got the threatening of

Steve Daniels and the framing of Patrick Coltrane. Who is connected to all of them?"

"Well there's the father."

"Yes, and there's the sister and brother-in-law. I don't think these crimes have been committed by a woman, unless she's a very strong woman and Claire Suffolk didn't strike me as that. Of course she could be working in partnership with someone, but two people are twice as likely to be seen as one and so far there only seems to be suggestions of a man meeting some of the victims."

"But it could be the brother-in-law."

"There seemed to be enough resentment. I might try asking whether the family knew about their father's mistress when I see Steve on Friday."

"And in the meantime?"

"It depends whether Trevor or Fingers come up with anything for me. If not, it's back to the day job for a while. I've got to do something to pay the bills."

"I'm glad you're safe," said Maggie running her fingers down his bare arm. "There are days when I wish you'd stick to the writing."

"There are days I wish I did too," he said smiling. "Yesterday wasn't one of my better moves. He leant in to kiss her and pulled back sharply. "I guess getting hit in the jaw wasn't one of my best days either!"

It was later when they were lying in bed that Connor couldn't stop thinking. "Are you awake?"

"Well if I wasn't, I am now!"

"Can you see a motive for either Harry Daniels or David Suffolk?"

"This is going to take a while, isn't it?" said Maggie rolling over and turning on the bedside light. She sat up, plumped the pillows and put them behind her back.

Connor rested his weight on his elbow. "Can't you think in the dark?"

"Yes, but when I'm tired I can also fall asleep and I'm guessing you're not looking for snoring as a response."

Connor smiled, reached up and very gently, without putting any pressure on his mouth, kissed her. "Has anyone told you recently that you're wonderful?"

"No and I wouldn't believe them if they did! Hmmm . . . Harry Daniels. You said he didn't inherit all the money?"

"No, some went to Steve Daniels and some to Patrick Coltrane."

"He might be trying to get money through Steve dying."

"Presuming that he stands to inherit. But that wouldn't explain trying to set up Patrick Coltrane."

"He might resent that Patrick Coltrane even existed."

"I suppose so. What about David Suffolk?"

"Possibly the same reasons, but then I don't suppose he stands to inherit if anything happens to Steve and why should he resent Patrick Coltrane?"

"Money again. Paula Daniels left money to Patrick Coltrane but didn't leave any to Claire Suffolk."

"Maybe. What about the murder of the mistress?"

"Maybe it wasn't murder. Maybe it was just an unfortunate coincidence."

"You don't believe in coincidences. Remember?" Maggie started to run her fingers across his chest.

"Are you trying to put me off?"

"Well it would be good if you'd stop thinking about the case for five minutes. Besides I need some sleep."

Connor entwined his limbs around her naked body and started kissing her. With his left arm he reached across and turned out the light.

"Doesn't that hurt your face?"

"I'm willing to be a martyr," said Connor circling her belly button with kisses.

Maggie giggled and moved back down the bed.

***

On Thursday Connor set about selecting which markets he would write some articles for. He needed income and until this case was sorted, he didn't want to take on any of the other investigations he'd been approached for, besides divorces were going to seem somewhat tame after this. It was pleasantly strange to be working at a desk for the day, with Tammy curled up by his feet.

"No long journeys today, Tammy." He reassured his long-suffering dog as she nuzzled up to him. It felt like a lifetime since he'd started working on Steve's case. In reality it had been a couple of weeks. He'd done more travelling in that time than he was used to.

When the phone rang, it was a welcome break from the computer screen.

Connor looked at the display before answering. "Hey Trevor, what have you got?" Connor had been expecting it to be Fingers that came up with something first.

"I don't know if it's any good to you, but I've got copies of the original notes of the police investigation into Maureen Winter's death. I've got nothing from the Coroner yet."

"Anything you've got may help. Where shall I see you?"

"I'll drop them off with you later. I'm coming out that way. There was one other thing. I thought you'd like to know that Patrick Coltrane has not been granted bail. He's being charged with four counts of murder and they're holding him pending trial."

"Well that will at least keep him away from Steve Daniels, but I still don't think it's him."

Long after hanging up from Trevor, Connor continued to ponder how he might prove Patrick Coltrane's innocence. Why was he doing it? The man had thumped him for heaven's sake, but pride was a strange thing. He'd set out to discover who was behind the Lifetracers and payment or no payment he was going to succeed. He pictured Mikey and grinned as he thought of the same level of determination that the little boy showed. It was always great to see your better qualities reflected in the next generation. Of course the times he was tenacious to the point of stupidity were an altogether different matter.

With that thought in mind, he dug out the mobile phone number for David Suffolk and began to dial. He was preparing himself to leave a message when David answered the phone sounding less abrupt than he had when they met. For a moment Connor felt optimistic.

"David, it's Connor Bancroft. We met with regards to the investigation I'm undertaking for your brother-in-law."

There was silence at the other end of the line. Connor hesitated, uncertain whether to push on with the questions or arrange to meet him. His decision was made for him when a measured voice came back on the line.

"I'm listening."

Connor took a deep breath. "Have you ever met Patrick Coltrane, your wife's half-brother?"

"Oh yes. I met him. We all did. Paula thought it would be 'nice' if we could all be a family."

"And what did you think?"

"I think she was nuts. None of us wanted anything to

do with him and from his reaction I'd say the feeling was mutual."

"Have you seen him since then?"

David hesitated. "No. Look, Mr Bancroft, I've not got much time…"

"Just one more question then, if I may?" Connor ploughed on before David had chance to say no. He wondered from the good mood whether David's luck with the cards had changed, but he was reluctant to ask in case it broke the spell. "Did you know that Harry Daniels was having an affair at the time that Paula died?"

"Yes."

Connor waited for David to say something more, but instead there was a heavy silence that eventually he had no choice but to fill. "Did you ever meet Maureen Winter?"

"Who?"

"The woman the affair was with."

"No. I'm sorry that is all the time I have. Thank you for calling." And David ended the call.

Connor was left feeling as though he'd been conducting some survey rather than a possible murder enquiry. He scratched his head and went to make some notes on the computer.

It was late afternoon when he heard the door knocker.

He looked through the spy hole before answering. "Trevor, come in."

"I can't stop, we're on our way to a crime scene."

"What, out my way?"

"It happens. Just because someone lives in the country doesn't make them a saint." Trevor handed him an envelope. "I had a quick look. I don't know if it will be any use to you. Let me know what you think. We found nothing to indicate it wasn't suicide or an accident."

Connor took the papers back to his desk and spread them out. There were a few sheets covering things such as the initial report on attending the scene, a handful of interviews with people who had been in the area, though none of them close to where the incident happened and an initial assessment of the state the body was found in. Connor turned to the last one first.

To all appearances, Maureen Winter had been dressed for an afternoon summer walk. There was little of any significance at all. The water was deep and at the time it was quite fast flowing. She was carrying a shoulder bag that had been found with the body. The contents of her pockets were also listed. Connor read the report through twice. Something was wrong but he couldn't put his finger on it.

In her pockets, Maureen Winter was carrying her purse, a diary, a make-up compact and a large bunch of keys. There was nothing abnormal about any of them. Then he had a thought. He reached for the phone and rang Maggie.

"If you were going for a walk would you put your diary in your pocket?"

"Not usually, why?"

"What about your make-up?"

"Well I wouldn't, but you might if you were particularly vain. It would depend on whether you were carrying a bag."

"And if you were?"

"You'd put everything in the bag, so that they didn't pull your pockets out of shape."

"Thank you. So if Maureen Winter was carrying a bag, but had loaded most of the things into her pockets, it would be a bit odd?"

"Yes, I'd say so. Is that what she did?"

"If you buy that she had an accident or killed herself, then yes. But if you start to wonder if someone murdered her, then it might make more sense to weigh her down."

"You're sure you're not just trying to turn it into a murder when it wasn't?"

"I don't know. I suppose that's possible, but something doesn't seem right. Oh I forgot to say, Mikey wants to know if you can stay again this weekend?"

"Just Mikey? Or does his dad want to know too?"

"Ok, I admit it. I'd love to have you around, if you've got nothing else planned."

"If I had, it would be worth cancelling for such an irresistible invitation. I'll see you tomorrow."

Connor went back to puzzling over Maureen Winter's death. Would you fill your pockets with everyday things in order to commit suicide? He supposed it was possible if it was a spur of the moment decision, rather than something she planned for. It was always hard to put yourself in the desperate mindset of someone about to end their life, but if you'd planned to do it, even if you planned to drown yourself, then you might take other precautions than to fill your pockets with a diary.

Connor was left with two options. Either Maureen Winter committed suicide as a spur of the moment act, or this was another murder. He began wondering about what might lead a person to kill themselves without any planning for it. The most obvious thing was that she had received bad news. It was possible she had been reflecting on her life and concluded it was hopeless, but somehow the circumstances didn't make sense. If she'd received bad news then either she had met another person, in which case why weren't they on hand to save her, or she had received a mobile phone call.

Connor rang Fingers. "I know I've already got you working on one thing, but can you get me a mobile phone record too, please? I want to know of any calls that Maureen Winter made or received on her mobile phone on the afternoon that she died." He gave Fingers the times and the phone number, which had appeared in the police record. "When do you think you'll have it all by?"

"I'll ring you back in half an hour with the phone record. The Coroner's papers are going to take a while longer. In fact you might be almost as quick to go through the official channels for those."

Connor was frustrated. He wanted to know anything there was on Maureen Winter's state of mind at the time of the accident. There must have been something to make Harry Daniels refer to it as suicide rather than an accident. He just had to hope that Trevor would be able to come up with some more detail.

Fingers rang back in less than twenty minutes. "There were no calls after first thing that morning. There was one to a mobile that belongs to Harry Daniels at 9.30, but nothing either outgoing or incoming after that."

"Thanks, Fingers. Are you sure you can't get those Coroner's records?"

"I'm relying on someone who works in that department and they're on holiday for a few days. I'll give them another call and see if they could call into the office. Are you willing to pay a premium?"

"Sure am. Just get them for me, please."

CHAPTER 30

Connor loved Fridays. It was the day he could look forward to seeing Mikey and the expectation of it gave him renewed vigour every week. Of course, he was glad it was almost the weekend, but his primary concern was 19.00 hrs and collecting someone who was to Connor the single most important person in the world. There was a lot to get through before that could happen. For a start he wanted to make some notes of the thoughts he'd had last night as he was trying to get to sleep.

If Maureen Winter had been murdered then her killer must have known where she would be, even if that meant he'd followed her. Unlike the other victims, she had got there by her own transport. What he presumed she did have in common with the others, was knowing her attacker as there had been no records of a struggle in the police notes.

Connor thought he might take Tammy for a walk by the scene of the incident, if it stayed fine. More than anything he wanted to get a sense of the place. But first, he'd got a meeting with Steve Daniels to think about.

As he got ready, he realised that he needed to get his hair cut at some point and added that to the list for the day. He also thought his jeans were getting a little on the tight-side and presuming they hadn't shrunk after all this time, he wondered whether more exercise might not be a bad idea. There wasn't time for that today as well, walking Tammy was as much as he could manage.

Connor arrived at Steve Daniels' house and wasn't surprised to find Steve ready and waiting for him. Once again he was shown into the lounge and took a seat. The Lifetracer was still in full view, now saying '8 days to death'. It gave Connor a jolt to see it in single digits.

"I would have thought you'd have got rid of that now that Patrick has been arrested." Connor said as Steve sat down, watching Steve's reaction.

Steve didn't rise to the comment. "I've got your cheque," he said coming straight to the point. "I don't want you sniffing round anymore. I think your job is done."

"Even if I think you might still be in danger?"

"How can I be? It's over now."

Connor could hear the rattle of washing up in the kitchen and wondered if it was Betty or Emma, at this time of day he presumed it was the housekeeper. If she was there, this was perhaps not the best time to be asking Steve questions, but it was the only chance he had.

"What do you know about Maureen Winter?"

Steve shot him a look which said 'don't go there' but answered with "I don't know a Maureen Winter."

Connor wondered how far to push it. "He was your father's girlfriend."

"This is nothing to do with my father. I don't want you pestering him."

"Not even if it will protect you?"

"As you said, they've arrested Patrick. Your work is done. Goodbye." Steve stood up.

"Did Maureen Winter commit suicide, the same as your mother?"

241

Steve's eyes bored into Connor like two gimlets. "You leave my mother out of this. She was a good woman, not like that tart."

"So you did know Maureen Winter?"

"Get out of my house. Our business is done."

Connor decided that being punched once in the week was enough for him and he got up to leave. As he got to the door Steve had already opened it.

Connor said "Is that why your mum killed herself? Was it because of your dad?" He could see Steve's nostrils flaring and almost expected him to breathe fire.

"Just get out." Steve's voice was trembling but determined and Connor decided not to push his luck any further.

When he got back to the pickup he sat in the driver's seat and took a few deep breaths. He'd touched a nerve, but it could have been for a number of reasons. He relaxed and put his hand on Tammy's head. "What do you think, girl?"

As always Tammy replied with a wag of the tail.

Once he felt calm again, Connor set off in search of a barber.

He was on his way home when the phone rang. It was Fingers.

"I've got it."

For a moment Connor wasn't sure what he was talking about, but then remembered. "You beauty. I presume you mean the Coroner's report?"

"I do and as soon as I can scan it, it will be on its way to your email. Along with my bill. I was going to make you wait for the report until you'd paid, but I thought that might be seen as cruel."

"I get the hint. I'll send the money over immediately."

"You understand I've got to pay my sources."

"If they've come up with the goods, who am I to complain?"

"Ok, Tammy, we forget the haircut." From then on the traffic seemed heavier and Connor felt frustrated wanting to get to his email. He even wondered about stopping off to download it, but there was little to gain. He'd be home soon enough. He stopped to fill up with fuel and bought Maggie some flowers from the petrol station. It felt good to be this close to each other. He never wanted it to end.

Once they were back in the house, Connor opened the back door for Tammy to go out and turned on his computer. As the mail downloaded he held his breath. It wasn't that this death was key to the whole thing. It was just that it was local and it felt more tangible. For all he knew if there were a crime involved, it could be separate from all of the others, but right now it felt crucial.

He started to scan the report for anything that would tell him Maureen's state of mind at the time she died. Had she received bad news? Was she ill? He hadn't gone far before he reached the interview with Harry Daniels. Connor was almost surprised to see him there, if their relationship hadn't been common knowledge. He read it through twice. Harry Daniels had ended their relationship on the lunchtime of the day that Maureen Winter had taken her life. No wonder he thought it was suicide. As he went through the evidence, Connor was surprised that there was no comment made about the odd contents of her pockets. He felt sure it was relevant and if it was he felt confident it indicated some sort of foul play rather than suicide or an accident. He needed to see Harry Daniels again and wondered what sort of reaction he might get. It was still possible that Harry was behind her death, which might explain why he was so prepared to promote the idea of suicide

There was little time left to arrange something for the same day, but Connor thought if he rang now, he might be able to meet Harry Daniels on Monday. Connor found the number and dialled.

"Mr Daniels, sorry to bother you, it's Connor Bancroft here. You said you'd help if you could. I've been reading the Coroner's report on Maureen Winter's death and I do have one or two questions, if you'd be prepared to discuss it?" Connor held his breath as he waited for a reply.

"I don't know that there's anything I can add."

"Would you mind meeting me to talk about it?"

Harry hesitated before answering. "I don't suppose it would hurt. How about lunchtime Monday, same place?"

"That's fine. I'll be there."

After he'd hung up, Connor looked at the clock. It was 4.30pm. He could think of nothing else of pressing importance and decided that the weekend would start here. He went in search of a bottle of wine. One glass before picking up Mikey would be fine.

It was another good weekend for the three of them. Mikey was comfortable with having Maggie around and they had a great time. After the excitement of the horse racing they had a quiet Sunday watching movies and playing together. By the evening it was as though they'd been together for ever and taking Mikey home was the last thing Connor wanted to do.

"Shall I stay here for when you get back?" Maggie asked.

Connor was grateful that she realised how hard he found it. "Yes please. It's always worse to come back to an empty house, without the sound of children's laughter."

When he did return, Maggie had sorted out some pizzas from the freezer and they were almost cooked.

"Did I tell you that I have to go away on a course this week?"

"No." Connor felt alarmed at the thought of not having her around. "What all week?"

"No just Thursday, Friday."

"Where is it?"

"Just outside Leicester, a hotel near the motorway. I promise I'll call you."

"I should think so." He said, kissing her on the nose. He poured two glasses of wine from the open bottle.

Once they were sitting down, Connor said, "Maggie."

"Oh dear, this sounds serious. What have I done?"

"It's not that you've done anything exactly. I was just wondering whether you'd like us to move in together?" He'd been careful not to say 'move in with me' as he didn't want her to think he was assuming that they would live at his place. He would rather it were that way, but he didn't want her to feel pressured.

"Wow. I wasn't expecting that. Things have certainly been good recently and I do get on well with Mikey, but do you think it's a bit soon?"

"A bit soon for what? I know you make me happy and Mikey is obviously ok with it. Will you at least think about it?"

"Yes, I'll do that. I think I want to say yes, but give me some time to think it through." She relaxed with a broad grin on her face that was enough for Connor to be going on with. I'll give you my answer next weekend."

"That sounds like a deal." He tucked into his pizza and was quiet for a while.

"I do love you, you know. I just need to think about

things before I make decisions."

Connor looked up. "That's ok, it's just that for me, for the first time in years I feel complete. A family again. The three of us. I wish I didn't have to take him back."

Maggie rested her hand on top of his on the table. "I know. It's tough, anyone can see that. Have you thought of fighting for custody?"

Connor wiped the corner of his eye. "I'm too frightened to do that. What if the decision went against me and Jayne refused to let me see him at all?"

"Yes, I can see that. The system's not fair. Maybe one day."

"Maybe."

They sat in silence for a while, Maggie was watching him and Connor's thoughts had drifted back to the case. "Can I run an idea past you?"

"Are we still on living together or have you moved on?"

"Sorry, I was just thinking about Steve Daniels. Someone has threatened to kill him and at the moment we don't know who it is. The police think it's Patrick Coltrane."

"But you don't."

Connor smiled. "No, it could be Harry Daniels, but I can't get all the cards to stack up on that one either, or it could be some unknown person."

"That you're no nearer to finding."

"But what if we set a trap?"

"What sort of a trap?"

"Well we know that Steve has been threatened with death in another six days."

"Six! I hadn't realised it was so soon."

"Hmmm. What if we sit tight until 'Death Day' and

then watch what happens?" Connor was drawing a little mousetrap on a scrap of paper by his side.

"Because we might miss the key moment and your client might end up dead."

"Ok, so there's a risk, but technically I'm off the case. There's no more risk than if I walk away altogether?"

Maggie fidgeted with a pizza crust that she'd left on her plate. "Do you think it's ethical?"

"Probably not, but then neither is obtaining inside information or hacking someone's mobile phone bill."

"Would you tell Steve?"

"I don't know. What do you think?" Connor had progressed to drawing a little hangman on the paper next to the trap.

"Well if Steve knew he'd have his wits about him, but if he didn't the killer is less likely to get wind of the plan."

"I think ethically, we'd have to tell him."

"Oh so you've gone ethical!" Maggie was smiling. "It might work. If Steve is willing to do it. Do you think the killer has been watching him?"

"For all I know, he could be watching me." Connor shivered and got up to close the curtains.

"Now there's a thought I didn't need when I'm about to go home on my own to an empty flat."

"Sorry. You can stay here if you like."

"Thanks, but you've given me a lot to think about. I need to do it in my own space if I'm to give you an answer. I'll go now before I lose the courage altogether. Will you be all right on your own?"

Connor smiled. He liked it when she started to look after him. "I'll be fine. I'll phone you tomorrow after I've seen Harry Daniels."

CHAPTER 31

Connor scratched his head. *What was he going to say to Harry Daniels? He wanted to know what he and Maureen Winter had argued about and whether Harry thought it might have left her suicidal, but could he start there? Of course if Harry had killed her he was bound to say she was suicidal to cover for his actions.*

It was quieter in the centre of York than it had been when he saw Harry the previous week. He arrived at Harkers early and found a table where he could see the bar. Harry Daniels scurried in shortly after 13.00 and acknowledged Connor as he went to the bar. Once he'd bought a drink he took it over to the table.

"Have you been here long?"

"No, just a few minutes. Thank you for seeing me again." Connor had a good look at Harry. *Was it possible that this ineffectual man could be a killer?* He looked at Harry's hands. They were small, with stubby fingers. The deaths had all been non-violent. *But then, you never knew what another man was capable of.*

"I wanted to ask you a few questions about Maureen Winter's accident, if I may?"

"I'm sorry yes. I could have told you more the other day. It was all a bit of a shock. Fire away."

"The Coroner's report said that you had argued with Ms Winter before the accident happened. Can you tell me

248

what that was about?"

Harry looked down at his hands and fiddled with a beer mat. "It wasn't so much an argument. I told her I didn't want to see her anymore."

"Oh, I see." There were a number of new questions that came to Connor's mind. He didn't know in which order to ask them. "Why was that?"

"It was just one of those things. The relationship had run its course. I didn't know what I saw in her."

"And how did Ms Winter take it?"

"Well she wasn't happy. She hadn't seen it coming. I think she had in mind that we could move it up a gear since Paula wasn't on the scene anymore. I think that was what perhaps drove me the other way. I didn't see it going anywhere else."

Connor had a panicky feeling wondering whether that was how Maggie might react to his proposal. For a moment he found it hard to concentrate. "Did anyone know about your relationship?"

"Well of course there were some. It's never possible to keep something like that to yourself, however hard you try, particularly when you both work in the same office."

"What about outside of work? Did any of your family and friends know?"

Harry hesitated a little too long. "I don't know. Maybe. Well to be honest, yes. We bumped into Steve one time when we were out. I don't know about the others."

"Did your wife know?"

"I don't think so, but then they say they always do, so I can't be certain." Harry was looking uncomfortable.

"What do you think happened to Maureen Winter? Do you think she was capable of killing herself?"

"I don't know. I've had it on my conscience ever since.

Is it my fault that she killed herself? Or was it just a dreadful accident? She couldn't swim you know. The river can be very dangerous when there's a lot of water in it. I'm sorry. I think I'd like to leave it there, if you don't mind."

Connor had saved the most difficult question and for a moment saw the opportunity to ask it slipping away. He grabbed the chance before Harry could leave. "Do you think there is any possibility that Maureen Winter may have been murdered?"

Harry had been in the process of getting up when Connor asked the question. He fell back into his seat. "What did you say?"

"Could Maureen Winter have been murdered?"

"My God, I thought that's what you said. Why? Who in God's name would want to kill Maureen, other than herself? The Coroner didn't say anything like that, did he?" The colour had ebbed away from Harry's face and his hand was shaking. "Do you know something?"

"No, Mr Daniels. It was just a question. I have to look at all the possibilities."

"But I thought you were off the case. Surely, you don't have to look at anything?"

"I'm still investigating. I don't believe that Patrick Coltrane is guilty. I'm trying to find who the real killer is before they carry out their threat on Steve."

Harry snorted. "That mother's boy will be all right. He always is. Little runt always lands on his feet. I need to go." Unsteadily Harry got to his feet and made his way out of the bar. Connor stayed where he was and finished his drink.

As he watched the lunchtime traffic milling around him, he wondered what Harry Daniels was capable of.

Could he kill? It was after all Harry who was promoting the idea that Maureen Winter may have committed suicide. Connor thought that if Harry were the killer, he would have left the verdict to look like an accident, rather than bring that into doubt? Connor supposed that at the point he was interviewed by the Coroner the verdict wasn't apparent and it could have gone in any direction.

Harry was a man with a grudge against both Steve Daniels and Patrick Coltrane, but was that enough? He tried to think through the case to pick out what definite information he had. Then he remembered the car, it had been a small red one. He needed to find out what Harry drove. There were two approaches he could take. He could find out the old-fashioned way by watching Harry Daniels and seeing what he came out of the car park in, or he could get in touch with Fingers. Fingers was the obvious option, but with no more money coming in from the case he needed to keep his costs down. Connor decided to kill the afternoon in the Art Gallery and then wait outside the garage of Harry's work to see what he drove. As long as he wasn't seen, there wouldn't be a problem.

There was one small flaw in Connor's plan that he thought of as he was walking round the painting exhibitions. He didn't know what time Harry Daniels finished work. It was easy to assume it would be 17.00 or 17.30, but for all he knew they might have some sort of flexitime in the office. At least it would still be light so that he could see the car colour.

Connor took up his position by 16.30. The road at the back of the car park was closed at one end so it was reasonable to assume that the car would have to leave in the other direction. There was nowhere by the car park that was concealed. Connor scouted around for the nearest shelter that still afforded a view. He found a position by some bins. It wasn't the sweetest smelling hiding place and he did feel very self-conscious that he would be asked to move on because he appeared to be loitering, but he thought that if a man couldn't loiter around garbage, where could he loiter? Connor smiled to himself, glad he wasn't due to meet anyone that evening. He would at least have chance to shower and change before he encountered another human being and Tammy was never as fussy. She was more likely to have a good sniff and work out where he'd been.

Connor was bored standing in the shadows of the oversized wheelie bins. There was little to watch while he waited and very few cars were coming to and fro. There had been a brief flurry of traffic around the time he arrived and another around 17.00 but other than that there was little going on. He waited until 18.15 and then decided to go back to have a poke around in the car park to see if Harry was working late.

The car park was little more than a parking area behind the building, big enough to hold around a dozen cars. It dawned on Connor that there wouldn't be enough space for all the employees to park there and it was possible that Harry was amongst those who parked off site. He might even use the bus to get to work, a possibility that hadn't previously occurred to Connor. There was one car left in the parking. It was a large Mercedes and Connor couldn't imagine that it belonged to Harry. There was nothing else for it but to call Fingers.

As he made his way back across the city to his own car he dialled Fingers' number and left a message. Then he went back to Tammy, who hadn't seen him since after lunch when he'd walked her before going to the Art Gallery. While he was fussing her, Fingers rang back.

"You've never found it already?"

"No, I need some more detail. If it was as easy as that, I could never justify my fees."

Connor told him what he could, but Fingers would have to find the home address details of Harry Daniels, before he could trace the car.

"How long do you think it will be?"

"About half an hour."

"Fine, I'll be waiting."

Connor then set off back to Haxby and wondered what Maggie was doing and whether he should call or give her some space to think. He decided to wait until she called him and picked up a takeaway for one, on his way home.

He was tucking into a spring roll when Fingers called.

"There are two cars registered at that address, one in the name of Harry Daniels, a blue Volvo and the other in the name of Paula Daniels, a green Renault Scenic."

"Odd that it's still in Paula Daniels name, given she's dead."

"Not strictly legal I wouldn't have thought. Are either of them the one you're after?"

"Not unless they're able to don a disguise. The Volvo would be too big, but the Scenic might be described as small, by some people anyway. I wonder if there is any way someone could mistake the colour."

"If they were colour blind."

"Don't you think they might have said something if they were?"

"Probably. I'd best get on. Good luck, mate. I'll add it to the bill."

"You do that and don't be in too much of a hurry to

send it, will you?"

Connor wondered if the cars ruled Harry out, then thought if he'd got one that was still registered to Paula he might have any number of others still in the wrong names and even with the wrong addresses. It was easy not to get round to sending the paperwork off when you bought a second hand car and all it took was assuring the naïve seller that you would send off their part as well and no one was any the wiser, unless you picked up a speeding or parking fine.

There were another five days until the Lifetracer reached Death Day. Connor wondered what he needed to do to prepare for it. It would be a weekend, so there was Mikey to consider. Jayne would never forgive him if he took Mikey with him to stalk a killer. He wondered if he ought to trail Steve Daniels in advance to get used to his movements. *People tended to have a regular time slot for their driving lessons.* Following him was going to be difficult and as to setting him up as bait, that was going to be very difficult to achieve. In the interest of safety, he ought to tell Steve what he was planning. It wasn't the same as if the target was going to be in one location and the killer had to come to him. The killer could strike at any time and in any place during that day. He might tamper with the car or gun him down while he was out. Tampering with the car wasn't a guaranteed method and from that point of view was unlikely. Connor was going to find trailing Steve at close quarters impossible if he was out and about on driving lessons. Either way other people could be in danger, but that wasn't the killer's style.

Connor had a sleepless night. By morning he was ready to sleep for the rest of the day, but had at least concluded that his conscience wouldn't let him go ahead with the plan without Steve knowing. If something went wrong and Steve hadn't known, then Connor was still going to have to live with himself, a prospect that he didn't find attractive.

He got up to let Tammy out then got back into bed and snuggled under the duvet. Tammy was content to curl up at his feet. He dozed off and didn't wake again until lunchtime, by which time he felt refreshed, but concluded that it would be too late to start trailing Steve. Instead he settled down in front of the computer to catch up on some writing.

He was absorbed in an article he was writing for a family history magazine on professions from the past when his phone rang and made him jump.

"Hello, Connor Bancroft," he said once he'd scrambled to get it out of his pocket and answer the call.

"I've told you that I don't want you on the case anymore. Stay away from my father."

Connor couldn't help thinking that given the apparent animosity between the two, news travelled fast. He took a deep breath and tried to put the feeling of intimidation aside. "I've been meaning to ring you."

"Oh?" Steve Daniels sounded thrown by the response.

"Yes, I want to talk to you about Saturday, the day that the timer reaches zero."

"What about it?" Steve sounded as though he had recovered his composure and was trying to sound tough.

"I think we can use it to catch the murderer."

"But he's already under arrest." Steve faltered again.

"Do you know at what time of day it flips over to the next day? When did it go down to four from the five days it would have shown yesterday?"

"About 19.30 last night."

"I don't know if our killer is being as accurate as that, but I want to set up a trap to try to catch him. It could be dangerous though."

"I'm warning you. Leave this case alone or you'll regret it."

"Don't you want the killer caught?"

"He already has been. Now I want you to leave it in the hands of the police. If you don't . . ." Steve didn't finish the sentence, but from the menacing tone, Connor was left in little doubt as to the meaning.

CHAPTER 32

Mikey was panting as he shot behind a gatepost to hide from Luke. School had finished and he was playing tag with some of his friends. He never went very far from the house, but this time when they were running around they had gone a little way before he realised. His mum knew roughly where he was and as long as he went home before it got dark, she'd be happy.

He liked the rough and tumble of street play. Sometimes they kicked a football around and he was never happier than when he'd rolled on the grass and got grass stains all over his trousers. He stayed behind the gate until Luke ran past and then came out again. He was sidling along the street waiting for his friends to run back in his direction. Then he would start running again to get away. It was a good opportunity to catch his breath. He was just looking around to make sure the others weren't coming back his way, when a car pulled up beside him.

"Hey, Mikey, how you doing?"

Mikey stared at the man. "Mummy told me never to talk to strangers." He made to walk off, but the man called after him.

"I'm not a stranger. I'm a friend of your Dad's. Listen, I know you like playing with Tammy and that your Dad lives in Haxby. I know loads about you. Anyway, your Dad sent me to pick you up. He's taking you out as a surprise. I'm not to tell you where you're going, that bit's the surprise. In any case, your mum told me where I'd find you. She knows you're coming with me. It's fine."

Mikey was hesitant. He wished that the others hadn't run off down the road even if it would have meant they'd have tagged him again. The man seemed to know a lot about them and if his dad had sent him then he must be ok. Mikey opened the back door to the car.

"You haven't got a kid's seat."

"Oh, don't worry. We're not going far. I'm sure the police won't stop us on this little journey."

Mikey climbed in and fastened his seatbelt.

"Ready?"

He nodded so that the man saw him in the rear view mirror and they set off.

"Your car is very small. Not like Daddy's."

The driver laughed. "It's not everyone that can afford to drive a pick up."

Mikey felt himself relaxing. The man seemed to know a lot about his dad.

"Where are we going?" Mikey could recognise that they were off the roads of the estate and he'd got a vague idea that this road did go towards his dad's house.

"It wouldn't be a surprise if I told you. Why don't you have a little sleep and then we'll be there before you know it."

Mikey didn't want a sleep. He wanted to know how soon he would see his dad and Tammy. As the car drove past Tesco's Mikey started to realise that this wasn't the right direction for his dad's house and they must be going somewhere different. He wondered for a moment if they were going to McDonald's but they drove past that turning and carried on.

"I want a drink."

The man continued to sound gentle and patient with him. "You can have a drink when we get there. We'll be a little while yet. Why don't you go to sleep?"

Mikey was no longer feeling relaxed. Something didn't seem right.

"I want my mummy."

"Well Mummy isn't here." A note of menace had crept into the voice.

Mikey began to cry. "Then I want Daddy."

It was beginning to get dark and being so low down in the seat Mikey couldn't see very much around him.

It isn't easy when you're eight to think what you ought to do, but instinct was telling him that this man wasn't what he said he was and that Mikey needed to get away from him. He knew his address and he knew to ask to see a policeman if he was lost. The only thought he had was getting out of the car the next time it stopped and running away from this man.

It wasn't long before they stopped at a roundabout. They were in a whole queue of cars, although Mikey couldn't see what was ahead. He took a deep breath and tried the door handle. Nothing happened the child lock was on. He wondered about the other door, but Mummy always told him not to get out on the side of the traffic. What else could he do?

The man turned round to him. "You're not going anywhere. You are staying right there and coming with me." The smile was gone now. The man wasn't even pretending to be nice.

"You're not a friend of my daddy's are you?"

"Oh I am, in a way."

"Mummy doesn't know where I am does she?"

"Ah, now you've got me there. I might not actually have told your mummy, but maybe we can ring her later."

Mikey began to cry silent tears. He felt very tired and desperately frightened. He wanted Daddy to be there to wrap his arms around him and make him feel safe. Instead he looked out at the falling rain and the headlights flashing by in a rhythmic pattern and little by little he was overcome by sleep.

***

Jayne Bancroft was getting tea ready for her and Mikey. He was always hungry when he'd been out playing. There were days when he had two lots of food, one before he went out and another when he came back. She was cooking macaroni cheese with bacon, one of his favourite dishes.

She looked outside at the gathering gloom and wondered why he hadn't come in yet. It was too early to be worried. Very often the games they played got out of hand and it was almost dark by the time he came in with rosy cheeks and stained clothing, a picture of happiness.

She put the macaroni cheese into the oven to keep warm and went to look out of the front window. There was no sign of him running down the road. Jayne felt her first pang of concern. There would be some satisfactory explanation, there always was. Maybe they'd gone round to Luke's house or Jamie's.

She went to the telephone list in the hall and dialled Luke's number.

"Oh hello, it's Jayne Bancroft here. I just wondered if Mikey had come home with Luke?"

"No, I'm sorry. Let me just call Luke and see if he knows where Mikey went."

Jayne could feel her heart pounding as she waited for

Luke's mum to come back to her.

"No, I'm sorry. Luke says Mikey just went off when they were playing. They didn't see him go."

"Thanks." Jayne hung up, her hand starting to tremble. She dialled Jamie's house and the whole conversation was played out again. The difference was that Jamie's dad shouted at the top of his voice to summon Jamie to him rather than put the receiver down and go in search of his son.

Jayne made herself take a few deep breaths. What if Mikey was hurt? What if he'd got stuck somewhere and couldn't get out? They were always hiding in places they shouldn't be. Her mind was racing. She couldn't decide whether to get the torch and go looking for him on foot or to take the car. She needed some help. Loathed as she was to admit it, right now she needed Connor's help. She could call her own boyfriend but he wasn't close to Mikey and he'd tell her not to fuss. No, right now she needed Connor. She dialled his mobile.

***

Connor was out walking Tammy down by the river when his mobile rang. He'd had a quiet couple of days developing some ideas for a few articles. He'd also started to go through the requests for his more routine services that had come in while he was working on Steve Daniels' case. That was one thing with infidelity, it was never likely to dry up as a source of work.

He fumbled in the pocket of his coat to find his phone and was surprised to see that it was Jayne's number calling him. His first thought was that it was going to be Mikey at the end of the phone.

"Connor," Jayne said sounding out of breath. "Thank goodness you're there."

"Why what's happened?" He was imagining that some disaster had befallen his precious child. "Jayne, tell me what's happened."

"I don't know. Mikey hasn't come home for his tea."

Connor felt himself breathe again. "He's probably lost track of time and he's playing at a friend's house."

"Don't you think I've thought of that?" Jayne snapped at him.

"Ok, I'm sorry. I just know what I was like as a boy. Why don't you start from the beginning and tell me what has happened so far."

As Jayne ran through the events of the afternoon, Connor started walking with Tammy towards home.

"And you're quite sure that neither Luke nor Jamie know where he is?"

"Yes. Will you come and help me look for him?"

"Of course I will. I'm already on my way. Tammy and I need to get home to get the car keys and we'll be there. Jayne, just stay calm. We're going to find him. Have you called the police?"

"I thought we ought to search the neighbouring streets first."

"Good plan. We'll do that and if we don't find him we'll call the police."

***

Jayne drove round some of the roads while Connor set out on foot with Tammy. Connor had never trained Tammy to be a scenting dog, but he knew that if Mikey was within a reasonable distance, Tammy would find him. They walked up and down all the streets around Jayne's house, passing Luke and Jamie's houses on the way. They'd been out for about forty-five minutes when Jayne pulled up in the car beside them.

"Any luck?"

Connor shook his head, "Nothing. What about you?"

"Oh Connor we've got to find him."

"I think it's time to call the police. I'll just walk this last bit and then meet you back at the house. If you call them when you get in, I'll be there as soon as I can."

As he walked, Connor took out his mobile phone. He just wanted to hear Maggie's voice. He looked at his watch. She'd be driving down to Leicester to her course by now, but at least he could hear her answerphone voice. He was right. It went straight to message service.

He could feel the tears of panic welling up in his eyes as he left a message. "Maggie it's me. Mikey's gone missing. Call me when you can. And Maggie, I love you." He pocketed the phone and walked briskly back to Jayne's house with Tammy trotting along beside him. He wiped the corners of his eyes on his shirt cuff as he went.

By the time Connor got back to Jayne's house she had called the police and was waiting for them to arrive. She looked haggard as she opened the door to him.

"They aren't here yet. What else can we do?"

Connor spoke quietly. "I don't know. Can you think of anywhere he might have gone? Is there any other friend he might be seeing or any places that he likes to play that we haven't thought of?"

Jayne shook her head. She was clutching a screwed up tissue and little by little pulling pieces off it as she twisted it in her hands.

"Connor, this can't be happening. Our little Mikey."

"I know. I keep thinking that I'm going to turn round and his happy little face is going to be right there looking back at me."

"Have you told Maggie?"

"I've left her a message. Have you told, I'm sorry, I don't even know his name?"

"Iain." She shook her head. "He doesn't take much notice of Mikey."

Connor felt a quiet satisfaction that Iain wasn't trying to replace him in Mikey's life, but said "I'd have thought he'd have been here for you though."

The doorbell rang and Jayne jumped. Connor put his hand on her arm. "It's going to be ok." He was as much trying to reassure himself as he was her.

She pulled away and went to open the front door. There were two police officers, a man who introduced himself as DS Wainwright and a lady, DS Jameson, who explained that she was family liaison and would stay with Jayne whilst they waited for Mikey to show up. Jayne showed them through to the lounge and Connor followed with Tammy still trotting at his heel.

DS Wainwright took out his notepad and began to ask the questions.

"What's your son's name?"

"Michael Bancroft, everyone calls him Mikey. He's eight year's old."

"When did you last see him?"

Jayne paused looking as though she was thinking. "He went out straight after school. It would have been about 16.00."

"What was he wearing?"

"Dark jeans and a blue striped sweatshirt. It was sort of thick light blue and dark blue stripes."

"Was he upset in any way when he went off?"

"No," Jayne snapped the answer. "Sorry, no. We hadn't had any arguments or anything." She gave a quick look across to Connor. "Nothing except the usual request to go to his dad's."

"Would he know the way to his dad's house from here?"

"I don't know. Maybe."

"Have you looked there?"

Connor felt stupid for not thinking of that. "I'll go and do that now shall I?"

"That would be helpful, Mr Bancroft."

"I'll let myself out."

Connor got up to go as DS Wainwright asked Jayne "Has he ever done anything like this before?"

"No never…" Connor didn't hear any more as he'd closed the door behind him.

CHAPTER 33

Connor drove slowly along the roads, scouring the pavements as best he could in the darkness. *Wouldn't Mikey have rung him if he was going to do something like this*? Connor supposed Mikey might have been concerned that he would say 'no', as well as his mother having done so.

As he drove round the short stretch of ring road to get to the turning for Haxby he thought that they should ring the hospitals. *What if Mikey had been injured and taken to hospital and was too ill to give them his name? What if he couldn't remember his name?* Connor was living all the nightmare scenarios of what could befall his child.

It was less than four miles from Jayne's house to his. Even an eight year old could walk that in under two hours, if he'd had enough reason to. By now he would have arrived and had time to realise Connor wasn't home. *But he had been home. He was there until Jayne called him and if Mikey had gone straight there without getting lost, he'd have arrived before Connor went out, but of course, he was out walking Tammy then.* He decided to walk the route to Jayne's on the way back so that he could have a better look round, but first he'd ring Jayne and tell her he'd found nothing.

Jayne sounded breathless as she answered the phone. Connor almost felt guilty to be the caller and have no good news for her.

"He's not here. Have you thought about ringing the hospitals?"

"The police have already been in touch with them. Nothing."

"I'm going to walk the route on the way back. Call me on my mobile if there's any news. Giving time to look around, it'll take me about an hour and a half. I've got a decent torch and Tammy will have a good sniff. I'll see you later."

It was already around 20.00 when Connor set off. He was glad that Tammy rarely got tired. She had certainly had her walks for the day. He walked, shining the torch into hedgerows and driveways as he went. He wondered whether he was looking on the right side of the road and wished he'd got someone with him who could do the other side.

Progress was slow, but steady and easier for the stretches that had street lamps. When he came to a length of road without any lighting he wondered how Mikey would have coped if he had tried walking it. He'd have been frightened in the dark and alone, but he was a very determined little boy.

By the time he reached the ring road, traffic was still heavy and he kept on the grass verges as he walked. The going was rough and slow, but there was no alternative. He wished he'd brought an extra jacket to wrap round Mikey if he found him. By now, the boy must be freezing.

It wasn't long before he was back in the built up area of Rawcliffe and going over the same roads that he had searched earlier. He was clinging to the desperate hope that he'd missed something. It was 21.40 when he arrived back at Jayne's road and as he did so his mobile rang. Connor's hands were shaking as he tried to extract the phone from his pocket. In his haste to answer it the phone dropped to the ground, but continued to ring. He grabbed it up off the pavement.

"Hello."

"Connor, it's me Maggie. What's happening?"

He was delighted to hear from Maggie, but still gutted that the call wasn't news about Mikey. "Oh Maggie, he's gone missing."

"He's not turned up yet?"

"No. No sign at all."

"I'm coming back. You need me there."

"No, Maggie. There's nothing you can do that we aren't already doing. I appreciate the support, but you can still give me that by phone, even staying there. You've been looking forward to this course, please stay."

"How am I going to concentrate? Oh Connor, please say he's going to be all right."

"I hope so Maggie. I hope so. I couldn't bear it if anything happened to him. He means so much to me."

"I know, Connor. He's a very special little boy. I've grown really fond of him too. What are you going to do now?"

"I'm just arriving back at Jayne's. I guess I'll stay here for a while, although I feel I'd be better doing something."

"Ring me in an hour."

Connor hung up and wished more than anything that he hadn't told Maggie to stay in Leicester. He needed her more than ever at the moment. He'd give anything to be in her arms. He rang the bell of Jayne's house.

It was DS Jameson, the family liaison officer who opened the door to him. She nodded him through to the lounge.

"What have we got so far?" Connor asked, looking

from DS Jameson to Jayne and back again.

"Nothing, so far," was the police officer's reply.

"What else can we do?"

"I'm afraid there's not a lot. We need to give it a little longer before we take it up to the next level?"

"And what will that mean?"

"House to house enquiries, a wider search team."

"I don't just want to sit here not doing anything."

"Most parents feel like that in situations such as these. Most of the time the child comes home of their own accord and it is just a matter of waiting."

Connor got up and paced the room. "I don't think I can just sit here. Even if all I can do is walk back to my house on the other side of the road to the one I covered coming this way. I've got to do something." He looked at Jayne, who nodded to him. "I'll drive back over here as soon as I get home."

"Would you like a cup of tea before you go? There's a pot made." DS Jameson got up and made to go towards the kitchen.

"That's very kind of you, thank you. A quick cup would go down well. Although if truth be known I'd rather be drinking whisky and that isn't like me." He laughed a hollow laugh.

Connor went to the bathroom while DS Jameson made him a cup of tea. When he returned, he drank it in one gulp and then headed back out into the night, leaving Tammy with Jayne.

As he walked along the side of the road, Connor thought he could remember almost exactly the places that he'd crossed the road. As he retraced his steps he worried that his memory might be playing tricks on him and that he might be missing critical stretches of pathway. He retraced his steps for fifty yards and then re-crossed the road. He began to feel hopelessness creeping over him. He had to carry on. His Mikey might need him. He couldn't stop.

Connor paused and took a few deep breaths of the cold night air. He shivered. The thought that Mikey was somewhere out there, lost in the night, was unbearable. He felt conspicuous shouting Mikey's name into the darkness, but he wanted his son to know he was there. His precious, precious son.

He'd got back as far as the bypass when his mobile rang.

"Connor, it's me Maggie. Is there any news?"

He felt himself exhale the deep breath of anticipation that he had drawn in. "No, no news. I'm still looking."

"I'm coming back."

"No!" Then more quietly he said. "Stay there, I will let you know if there's anything you can do. At the moment, I'm as much trying to keep myself occupied as anything." They said good night and Connor carried on. He'd gone about twenty paces when his phone rang again. This time he presumed it was Maggie ringing back with something she had forgotten to say.

"Hello again," Connor said in an almost cheerful voice.

The caller's opening words stopped him dead in his tracks. "I've got your son." The words were said in a flat tone.

"Where, who, what? Can I speak to him? He is all right isn't he?" Then the light began to dawn on Connor. This was no hero ringing him to say he'd found Mikey and was returning him safely. It was that one word 'got', not found but got. Connor felt his whole body drain of warmth.

"Who are you?"

"The police are not to be involved. I'll ring you in an hour with my demands." Then the man rang off.

Connor hadn't recognised the voice. It was as though the man was talking through a handkerchief, muffled, but with the gruffness still coming through. He was sure it was a man, but even there he couldn't be certain. Connor sank down onto the wet grass. He had no idea what he should do next. The police were already involved. He should tell them about the call. He had an hour to wait before the next call. He needed to use that time effectively. The first thing he needed to do was get home and collect the pickup. Wherever Mikey was, Connor had to get to him. He had to save his son.

Connor dialled Maggie's number.

"Maggie, he's been kidnapped." His voice was urgent. "What am I going to do?"

"Connor, calm down. Take a few deep breaths and then tell me what's happened."

Connor paused for a moment, gathering his thoughts. "I had a phone call, just before I rang you. It sounded like a man's voice. I think he was trying to disguise it. I didn't recognise the voice. He said he'd got Mikey. He didn't say much more, just that I wasn't to go to the police and he'd ring again with his demands in an hour."

"Connor, why do you think they rang you and not Jayne?"

Connor stopped walking. He hadn't even begun to analyse the information he did have available. "I suppose somehow this is about me rather than Jayne."

"Do you think it's to do with one of your stories?"

"I'm only working on the murders at the moment and I've even been asked to stop investigating those."

"But you haven't have you?"

"No. What are you driving at?"

"What if you were getting too close? What if this were some kind of warning?"

"But I haven't got anywhere. I'm just sure it wasn't Patrick Coltrane. Beyond that it could be just about anyone."

"Is anyone on your list of suspects?"

"Honestly? Apart from Harry Daniels and David Suffolk there's no one. I'm still back at base."

"All you can do is wait to see what they say. Ring me as soon as you hear. Are you going to tell Jayne?"

Connor was quiet, thinking. If he told Jayne it would just give her ammunition to stop him seeing Mikey, but if he didn't tell her she would find out at some point. "I guess I have to tell her. But what if she tells the police?"

"Maybe you should tell them anyway."

"What and risk my son being his next murder victim. Are you crazy?"

"I'm sorry. I was just saying. Ring me when you hear some more. You'd be best to keep the line clear. And Connor, I love you."

The circumstances were dreadful, but his heart missed a beat hearing those words. It was just what he needed right now, that and a hug.

He walked more rapidly. He felt as though he had a purpose. He had to find out where Mikey was being held, then as soon as he knew he would set off in search. When he got back to the pickup, he put his phone on charge from the cigarette lighter and started the engine. He might as well go straight back to Jayne's house, there was no more searching he could do at the moment and yet driving round was calming and at least he was doing something.

Connor wove his way through the dark, deserted streets. He went north then west and then soon turned back south. He was weaving his way to nowhere. Jayne should at least know that he'd heard something. He turned his Sat-nav on and was surprised to find he was now fifteen miles from Jayne's house. She'd be wondering where he was. He started to follow the directions given by the electronic voice and very soon recognised where he was again.

He had been trying to rehearse what he could say to Jayne when he got there, but nothing sounded quite right. In the end he decided to stick with the truth and even that depended on whether the police officer was still present. If she was then Connor would maintain a façade of ignorance and wait to see what happened when his phone rang again. It was now a quarter of an hour before midnight and many of the houses were cloaked in darkness, yet at Jayne's house it looked as though every light in the place was on. It was as though by illuminating everywhere they could see beyond the evil that had taken Mikey.

Connor rang the bell. Tammy started to bark from inside the house. As soon as DS Jameson opened the door Tammy threw herself at Connor. After having a big cuddle with his dog, he made his way through to the lounge then saw DS Wainwright standing by the settee.

"Any news?" As he asked the question he realised how ridiculous it was. He was the one with news, not the policewoman and yet he was hesitating to say anything. What if his phone rang whilst he was in the house? How was he going to explain that one? He looked at Jayne's anxious face and decided to tell her the truth. He reasoned that the police must be experienced in situations in which they are asked not to intervene.

He looked from one of them to the other and said, "Sit down. I need to tell you about the phone call I received."

CHAPTER 34

"Connor, what have you done? You've put our son in danger because of your lousy work." Jayne's fists were balled as she yelled. The admission of the phone call had opened the floodgate to let her tension out.

"I know, Jayne, but at least at the moment we know he's all right." Connor knew how feeble the words sounded as soon as he'd said them.

"All right! All right! You call being kidnapped by a murderer all right. You're not fit to be a father."

Her words stung and right at that moment Connor didn't feel fit to be a father. Neither one of them noticed that DS Wainwright was on the phone, until he hung up and spoke to them.

"Your mobile is being monitored. If they call again we'll know where they're calling from."

"But he said no police. You can't go rushing in."

"Mr Bancroft, please don't worry. We aren't about to put your son's life at risk. Please trust us."

He didn't like to say that bearing in mind their decision to arrest Patrick Coltrane while the real killer was free to kidnap his son, there was no possibility of him trusting them. Instead he nodded and paced the floor as he waited. He couldn't sit still or even stand in one place. He needed to be doing something. Jayne had disappeared upstairs to lie down for a while, unable to cope with his constant action.

It was almost 01.00 when his phone rang. As he answered it, DS Wainwright slipped out to talk to his colleagues without his voice being heard by the caller. Connor stood by the doorway, his phone pressed hard against his ear. He was determined to identify the voice this time. He was breathing heavily as he answered.

"Hello."

"There's no point trying to come after me. You'll never find me or your precious son." There was a hollow laugh. "I can hide very well when I want to. I want you to drop the Lifetracer case. I want all your notes to be put in an envelope and sent to the following address." He read out a Post Office Box number in Cardiff. Connor wondered if Cardiff was a clue. "Once I receive them I will give you further instructions."

"But that could take days. What about Mikey? How do I know you are holding Mikey and that you will keep him safe? Can I talk to him? At least let me give him some reassurance."

"Each day at 10.00 I will send you a photo of your son. If I find that you have continued to work on the case I will send you photographs of parts of your son." A cruel laugh followed and then the phone was disconnected.

Connor turned to find Jayne standing just behind him on the stairs.

"You're right. I'm worthless. This is because of my work. How could I let Mikey become involved?"

Jayne gave him a cold stare. "What did they say?"

He was about to update her when DS Wainwright came back in.

"We've traced the call."

They both turned their attention to the police officer.

"It was coming from an office in the centre of York. We've got officers on the way to the scene now."

"Can I come?" Connor wanted to be close to the action. "I can't do anything about sending my notes to him until the morning."

DS Jameson looked uncertain, whilst DS Wainwright shook his head.

"It can't do any more harm than your people being there. He's told me not to get the police involved."

"I think you should stay here, Mr Bancroft. We'll be in touch as soon as we know something."

"I've been following this murder case. I might be able to help. I might know something."

Jayne spoke for the first time. "Don't you think your work has caused enough problems? Perhaps it's time you left it to the professionals." She almost spat the last word at him.

"Ok, but shout at me later. At the moment I just want to get our son back." And with that Connor walked out of the house calling Tammy to follow him into the pick-up. He planned to follow DS Wainwright to wherever he was heading. York wasn't a large city centre. It shouldn't be too difficult to keep up.

DS Wainwright scowled at him as he went out to his car. He turned and came over to his window. "Look if you must do this, at least keep a safe distance away. We don't want two of you at risk."

"Where are we heading?"

"I'm not sure. I need to ring in again while we're on the way."

Connor started the engine. "I'm right behind you."

DS Wainwright went back to his car and moved off. Connor followed a reasonable distance behind him. At first they could have been heading for anywhere. Then as they wound their way into the city centre, Connor realised that this was the route he'd taken to Harry Daniels' office. He began to get a sinking feeling. He wanted to tell DS Wainwright what his suspicions were, but he had no way of getting in touch with him. The closer they drove, the more certain he became, until they pulled up just outside a cordon that surrounded that block of offices.

Connor left the pick-up badly parked at the side of the road and ran across to where DS Wainwright had parked.

"I thought I told you to stay at a safe distance away."

"Yes, I know. But I've got some information that might help. I know who works here. It's Harry Daniels. He's the father of the man who received the death threat. He's one of my suspects."

"Ok, I'll inform the officer in charge. Now please go back to your vehicle and stay there."

Connor moved away his shoulders down. His eyes were fixed on a line of officers at the front of the proceedings. That was where he wanted to be. He wanted to know what was going on.

He walked up and down outside. He couldn't just sit in the pick-up. The building was in darkness. It seemed an odd place to hold a boy hostage. What would happen in the morning when the office workers arrived? They would be discovered. It didn't stack up. He hoped the same thoughts had occurred to the police officers. He was convinced that this was a wild goose chase. So if they weren't here, where could they be?

It was the middle of the night but Connor knew that Fingers kept strange hours. He dialled the number but it went straight to answer-phone.

"Fingers, it's me Connor. I need the address of Harry

Daniels. It's urgent. I think he's holding my son."

He rang off and went back to pacing. They had been there about half an hour when DS Wainwright came over to him.

"There's a phone in there that has been set to divert calls out of the building to your mobile. There's no one around. It means that our kidnapper can call a telephone line here and it goes through to you. What we traced was the leg of the call from here."

"Well there's a surprise. Now let me guess, the desk belongs to Mr Harry Daniels?"

"We don't know yet. We're waiting for the personnel manager to arrive and confirm that to us."

Connor was frustrated that he didn't know Harry Daniels address. He wanted to be the one to find his son. He was also worried that the police presence might lead Harry to take Mikey's life as well. He didn't want to wait around and follow the police so he got into the pickup and drove in the direction of Steve Daniels' house. Steve could tell him where his father lived.

The house was in darkness when he arrived. He imagined that Steve would be asleep and wondered if he would be better ringing. He stood on the doorstep and took out his mobile phone. He got the engaged tone, but there was no other sound. Someone must be inside, on the phone. He tried Steve's mobile but went straight to the answer service. There was no movement or the suggestion that someone was stirring, maybe the phone was off the hook, but that would be an odd coincidence and he didn't believe in those. He rang the bell as well, but there was still no response. He shrugged. He was in no hurry to be caught breaking and entering again. He wondered if Steve was staying at his girlfriend's house. He'd got her number somewhere. He scrolled through the contacts in his phone until he found the right one.

"Come on, come on, come on." He stepped from leg to leg with impatience as he waited for someone to answer. Eventually there was a sleepy voice at the other end.

"Emma, it's Connor Bancroft. I'm sorry to wake you in the middle of the night. The man who has been threatening Steve Daniels is holding my son and I have to find him."

"What!" She sounded more awake. "But how can I help?"

"I need to know where Harry Daniels lives. I thought Steve might be with you as he's not at home."

"No, he's not here. I haven't seen him for a while. Why Harry?"

"I don't know," he hesitated, "but it looks as though he may be caught up in it all somehow." He was reluctant to suggest that Harry might be the killer, but it was beginning to look that way.

"I've been to Harry's house. I don't know the address and I'm not sure I'd find it again, but it was over somewhere near Fulford. You know, as you go out of York to the south. I'm sorry I can't be any more help. I hope you find him. I didn't want my daughter caught up in things. That was why I stopped seeing so much of Steve. If anything happened to her . . ." Her voice trailed off.

"I know how you feel, except its happening to my son. I'd better go." Connor rang off. He could feel the tears welling in the corners of his eyes. He just wanted to sit down and cry. He wanted Maggie to be there to put her arms round him. He pulled himself together. He couldn't give up. He'd got to find Mikey.

Connor got back into the pick up and started driving south towards Fulford. He had no idea where to look, but he just needed to be there. As he drove a police car with its lights flashing overtook him. It was a slim chance that they were heading to the same place, but Connor decided to follow them. He knew there had been a good turnout at the offices in the centre of York and they'd have to go this way to get to Fulford. It was a calculated gamble.

His mobile phone rang as he was driving. It was Fingers.

"Sorry I didn't hear you, man. I was busy on the computer. You know what it is with these games. You get engrossed."

"Fingers, I need Harry Daniels address. You must have it with the phone records."

"Sure have. Have you got a pen?"

"Fingers, I'm driving a car. Sure I've got a pen and it won't be at all dangerous to use it. Why don't you tell me what it is and then send me a text so that I've got it in case I forget."

"Good plan." He read out the address in Grants Avenue, Fulford and wished Connor luck in the search.

Connor put the address into the sat-nav and stopped worrying about keeping up with the police car. He was five minutes away. He wondered whether anyone was keeping Jayne informed of what was happening, but assumed that DS Jameson was still with her. Not that there was much to tell her.

By the time he turned into Grants Avenue, there were already blue flashing lights marking out the position of Harry Daniels' house. Connor brought the pick-up to a stop at the side of the road and climbed out. He looked at the officers for any sign of DS Wainwright, but she was nowhere to be seen. He could do nothing but wait outside the immediate circle of activity.

As he stood there, two officers escorted Harry Daniels' to a police car and Connor could stand the tension no longer. He rushed to the nearest officer.

"Have they found my son? Is Mikey here?"

"I'm sorry sir, I don't know. I'll talk to the officer in charge and see what I can find out. Please wait here."

Connor didn't want to wait. He wanted to rush into the house looking for Mikey. He wanted to sweep Mikey up in his arms and tell him everything was going to be ok. He never wanted to let him out of his sight again. He started walking in circles. His nervous energy channelled into going nowhere. It felt like about half an hour before anyone came back to him, but it was probably little over ten minutes. It was the young officer he had spoken to before. He was shaking his head.

"I'm sorry there's no sign that he was being held here."

"But what did Harry Daniels say?"

"I don't know, sir. They've taken him to the Station where he'll be interviewed."

Connor's shoulders sagged. He could think of nowhere else to search, other than perhaps David Suffolk's house. He couldn't imagine Mikey being held there though, not in the middle of David's own family. If David were involved, Connor suspected that Mikey was being held in another location, somewhere he would never find his son.

CHAPTER 35

Connor toyed with his phone, wondering whether Trevor Whitworth would forgive him for ringing in the middle of the night. For something as extreme as this surely any friend would. It was even possible that Trevor was already awake and involved in the case.

He dialled his friend's number and got the answer phone.

"Trevor it's Connor. I don't know if you know, but Mikey has been kidnapped. Some of your guys are working on it now and I wondered if you knew anything? Call me if you can."

Connor stared into space feeling sick. This is what it meant to love someone. To have his life so tied up in Mikey's that he wanted to feel every heartache instead of his son. He wanted to take all the pain, while Mikey sailed through life in nothing but happiness. This was what it meant to be powerless. He put an arm around Tammy's neck, grateful for the warmth of her body. Right now he'd give anything to have Mikey home safe with him. He was driving on autopilot and was jolted back to the present by the phone ringing.

"I'm sorry. I should have called you earlier. I've been working on Mikey's case. We've got nothing so far." Trevor sounded as though he was having difficulty admitting this to his friend.

"What about Harry Daniels?"

"Nothing."

"But his phone was diverted to mine."

"He says it wasn't him. He doesn't divert his phone so he wouldn't have known. I asked when he last remembered getting a call on it and all that he could offer was that Friday had seemed a bit quiet but he couldn't remember if the phone rang at all."

"Well that was the first call I got on it. I didn't receive any of Harry's calls on Friday. Won't the company's phone records show anything?"

"We've asked for them, but it needs someone to go in and run the right reports for us. We've had difficulty getting the right person in the middle of the night. They're thought to be staying at a girlfriend's house or something. We'll be on it first thing in the morning. Until then, there's very little we can do. You'd be best to go home and get some sleep."

"Sleep!" Connor laughed an empty laugh. "How can I sleep when my boy is in danger?"

"I'm sorry. Just try to get some rest. It could be a long day tomorrow. We're going to need to wait until the kidnapper calls you again and try to trace the first leg of the call. We're doing our best, Connor."

"I know." Connor said before hanging up. "I know."

He continued to drive towards Jayne's house. It wasn't Jayne he wanted to see it was Maggie, but he felt he ought to tell Jayne what was happening.

When he arrived, the lights were out and he wondered if Jayne were sleeping. He didn't know whether to ring the bell or phone her instead. She saved him the dilemma by opening the door. She was dressed in a dressing gown and looked gaunt. Her hair was scraped back off her face into a band, leaving her sallow skin more evident. Connor felt a stab of guilt that this was what he had done to her. She had been right to leave him. How could he expect Maggie to live with him when this was the impact he had on those around him?

"I was sitting watching out of the window. I don't know what I expected to see. Do you want to come in?"

Connor didn't want to go in, but it seemed inappropriate to talk on the doorstep. He hung his head as he started to talk to her.

"I'm sorry. This is all my fault. You were right. I have put our son's life in danger."

He saw a flash of anger spark in Jayne. "We'll talk about that when this is all over. For now I just want him back safely. What have you found out?"

He felt like a scalded child, pulled into line by an impatient teacher. "Not much. The path of the phone call was a misleading clue. It doesn't seem to be anything to do with the man whose phone was used. Although, the case I'm working on does appear to lead back to him. Perhaps that's all been set up to mislead me too. There's nothing much more I can do until morning when he makes contact again. I'm going home to get some 'rest'."

"Right." She said no more than that one word.

Connor would have been happier if she'd shouted at him, even hit him. In his own mind there was no escaping the intense feeling of guilt. He'd let his son down and he'd let Jayne down and he wasn't sure he could live with himself for it.

***

It was shortly after 07.00 the following morning. Connor was dozing in a chair in his lounge with Tammy stretched out in her basket near his feet. He had been dreaming of happy times. The day on the North York Moors Railway had rolled into swimming and walking with Tammy. It was the dream of the perfect day. He had been clutching his mobile phone in his hands when he'd gone to sleep and it had slipped down the side of the chair. The sound of it ringing was muffled by the cushion. It took Connor a moment to wake and realise where it was. He fumbled to get to it before it stopped ringing, but was too late.

He looked for the missed calls and found that Maggie's had been the last number. He rang her straight back.

"I thought I'd call before I went down to breakfast. Is there any news?"

Connor told her about the night before and the false hopes that had led to Harry Daniels. "I've just got to wait until they ring again and see where it takes us."

"Will you ring me when you hear?"

"Won't you be in your conference?" Connor felt self-conscious that their call may be being listened to and shied away from the more intimate comments he might have made. Yet now, more than ever he wanted Maggie to know how much she meant to him.

"Yes, but I'll set the phone to vibrate. I'll pick your message up as soon as I can."

When she'd gone, Connor went up to the bathroom to have a wash. He looked dishevelled and unshaven. He splashed water onto his face to wake himself up, but shaving could wait until later. He decided that walking Tammy would do both of them good.

Connor hated waiting. Once he was back from the walk he was like a caged animal. Then he remembered that he had to put his notes together and send them to a PO Box. He started to go through the things on his desk, taking copies of the vital documents before putting them in an envelope. He wondered what good was served by handing them over. The killer must know he had a lot of material on the computer and would take copies of the documents that weren't there. He wondered whether it was just a gesture or whether it served any useful purpose. Perhaps the killer saw this as his glory moment, the point when the eyes of the world would be on him and he could go out in style. If that was the case, it seemed to Connor that Mikey was unlikely to go free. He couldn't think that way. He focussed back on the task in hand, then walked down the road to the Post Office. When the killer rang him again, he would feel better if he could say he'd met the demands.

He wondered if he ought to go to Jayne's house to receive the call from the killer, but little would be gained by that. The police could monitor the call wherever he was and he would speak to them straight afterwards. He couldn't face her overwhelming disappointment in him.

His phone rang on the dot of 10.00.

"Have you sent them?"

"Yes. What about my son?"

"I will send you a picture in five minutes and every day until I receive your parcel." He rang off. Connor wondered if that had been long enough to trace the call.

His phone rang immediately. It was Trevor Whitworth.

"We've got a position on the call. I've got men on the way there now."

"Do you have an address?"

"Connor, I don't think you should go."

"Trevor, just tell me."

When Trevor read out the address, Connor laughed.

"He's got us on another wild goose chase. That's Steve Daniels' house. There was no one there when I called last night. When I rang I got the engaged tone. I was ringing myself."

"He may not have been answering the door. It doesn't mean he wasn't there. We'll soon find out. When that picture comes in, will you forward it to my phone?"

"No problem. Good luck."

Connor was in two minds whether to head for Steve Daniels' address, but he was convinced it would just be another call forwarding set up on the phone. This guy was clever, too clever to make a basic mistake. He thought of the Lifetracer sitting in Steve's lounge, which must now say two days to go. However much danger Steve Daniels might be in, his only focus now was Mikey. Steve would have to fend for himself.

The picture arrived shortly afterwards. Connor was impatient for it to download to his phone. As he opened it, he had tears in his eyes at the sight of Mikey gagged and tied to a chair. How could someone do that to an eight year old? He forwarded the picture to Trevor Whitworth and then started to enlarge it to look for clues to the location.

As he zoomed in, Connor recognised the setting. He'd been there recently. The killer couldn't have known he would recognise it. There in front of him on the screen was the pile of boxes in Patrick Coltrane's spare room. For a moment Connor was torn wondering whether he should tell Trevor Whitworth what he knew. Then he made a decision. This was personal. The killer hadn't wanted the police involved and they wouldn't be. It would be the two of them. He wasn't going to put Mikey's life in more danger than it was already in. Whilst Trevor Whitworth investigated the house on the outskirts of York, Connor would drive to Derby to confront the killer.

Taking Tammy could be difficult so he bundled her into the car and sped off to Jayne's house. He had no idea what he was going to say to Jayne. It was too late to play the hero and he didn't want her telling the police.

"There's somewhere I want to check." He said as Jayne opened the door. His voice was urgent and uninviting of questions. "Can Tammy stay here?"

Jayne's mouth opened as though to ask him something, but she nodded and he dashed back to the pick-up.

As he drove, he rang Maggie and got her message service. He left a message, hoping she would have chance to call him back. If the traffic was ok, he should get to Derby around lunchtime. The nervous tension made him feel alert despite the lack of sleep.

It was around 11.00 when Maggie rang back.

"You've found him?"

"I wouldn't go quite that far but I know where he is."

"Where?"

"At Patrick Coltrane's house in Derby. You remember I went in? Well I recognised it from the picture."

"What's the address?"

He gave it to her and then stopped himself. "Why? What are you planning to do?"

"I'm nearer to Derby. I can get there faster. I want to save Mikey as much as you do."

Connor doubted that anyone could want to save him as much as he did but he appreciated the sentiment. "But you can't go. It's not safe."

"Try stopping me. I'll see you there. I'll ring you when I'm in the area." He realised that if the police were monitoring his phone, they would now be aware of both the location and the plan.

Connor shook his head in disbelief. What was Maggie thinking of? She couldn't just go into Patrick Coltrane's house and yet that was what he was planning to do. He sped up, trying to get there before her, but the faster he tried to drive, the more frustrated he became until he reached an interminable length of road works with average speed cameras littered along the way. The traffic all around him had slowed and he had no choice, but to join them. He would happily have risked losing his licence for speeding but there was just no way through the lines of cars.

He watched the clock moving round and wondered how Maggie was getting on. He shouldn't have agreed to Maggie doing something so dangerous, but he wasn't thinking straight. All that mattered was getting to Mikey. Deep down Connor was glad that someone might get to Mikey sooner than he would, but it shouldn't have been Maggie. He should have told the police, this was stupid. He wondered whether Trevor Whitworth was aware of the elaborate hoax that had been set for him with the phone call yet.

The roadworks ran on for miles and Connor felt hemmed in and desperate to put his foot down as soon as the speed limit sign changed. It would take him about another three quarters of an hour from where he was. Then Maggie rang.

"Connor, I'm here. How did you get in?"

"I went round the back of the house. You might be best to climb over the fences. There'd be less risk of being seen."

"How many?"

"I think it was five. Check how many houses down it is at the front and then count how many fences there are." He could feel that he was holding his breath, anxious for Maggie to make progress but at the same time regretting that she was putting herself in danger and wishing he was the one who had arrived first.

"I'm going to have to close the phone. I can't talk and climb fences. I'll ring you as soon as I can."

"Maggie, I love you."

CHAPTER 36

Maggie put her mobile phone in her pocket; it was already turned to silent. It hadn't been the right time to tell Connor that she would like to move in with him. There'd be time for that later, once Mikey was safe, but even before this crisis she had known that was what she wanted. She knew when Connor asked her, but she didn't want to rush into anything. She had loved her weekends with Connor and Mikey as a real family and although she hadn't known him long, Mikey had already become special to her too. It wasn't just for Connor that she wanted to rescue the little boy it was a deep rooted protective instinct that she'd never experienced before. *Please God let Mikey be safe.*

She looked at what lay ahead of her. From the holes through which she could see daylight, some of the fences looked more stable than others. She smiled as she remembered a course she'd been on that set a series of outdoor challenges. 'Team building' was what they called it. Well this time there was no team and the task she had to complete at the end mattered more than any made up goal. This was real. This was life or death. Failing or bottling out were not options here. It wasn't something she would laugh about with her colleagues in the pub later. She breathed deeply to calm herself and mentally prepare for what lay ahead.

She was glad that she was wearing jeans rather than a suit. The front door of Patrick Coltrane's house had been easy to find. It was still boarded from where the police had kicked it open to get to Connor. Maggie decided that her best means of access had to be around the back. There were passageways between each house, but by approaching Coltrane's place directly, she was more likely to be seen than by crossing some of the gardens. She started at the end of the row, finding dustbins, garden chairs and anything solid to climb on to scale the fences. There was a risk of being seen, but she stayed as far away from the windows of the houses as she could get. She could feel the adrenalin coursing through her body making her more alert than she could ever remember being. She could hear the quietest of sounds and smell the grass and flowers of the gardens.

As the splinters from the fencing got caught in the palms of her hands, Maggie wondered whether a direct approach might have been worth the risk.

Eventually she reached Patrick Coltrane's house. There was no sign of movement and she stayed pressed in beside the fence, behind a bush, as she surveyed the scene. She could almost hear her heartbeat. Connor had told her that the picture of Mikey was taken in the back bedroom. She looked up at the window for signs of movement but saw nothing. It was possible that the killer was in a different room from Mikey, or that he had taken Mikey there for the photograph.

Until now, Maggie had formed no real plan of action. She was relying on the elements of surprise and stealth. She had no weapon, but then doubted that she would be prepared to use it if she had. She decided that at the very least it would be sensible to have something she could use to stun the man holding Mikey. She looked around the end of the garden for a suitable object and saw a broken wooden chair lying on a pile of earth. One leg of the chair was missing. If she could find it, that would be ideal. It would be light enough to carry and easily concealable.

Maggie kicked at the dirt but found nothing. She left her hiding place long enough to collect the chair and began to work one of the other legs loose. They were badly glued into position and it took very little force to remove another leg from its socket. Maggie discarded the rest of the chair and tucked the leg into the back of her jeans, below her jumper. She tried not to think about the mud and dirt that encased the leg. Having it in her waistband made moving awkward but at least she had the comfort of having some sort of weapon with her. Although from the quality of the chair she couldn't help but think it would fracture if put to any real use.

The back door was on the other side of the garden, but there were few shrubs on that side that she could use for cover. Her heart was pounding so hard that her whole body seemed to move with every beat. Her hands were trembling. *So this was what it meant to feel the fear, but do it anyway.* She couldn't remember ever being as frightened as this. She concentrated on the thought of Mikey. If she was frightened, how must he be feeling? She'd do anything to set him free.

Maggie began to creep along the fence, one shrub at a time. The fence looked rotten in places and she could see through to the neighbouring property. There were lace curtains at all the windows and she watched for any sign of movement, but saw none. The angle of vision from the house was leaving her position more exposed. She needed to break cover. Fortunately, there were no windows on the back end of what she presumed was the kitchen.

Maggie looked at the path she was planning to take. The ground looked even; there was nothing to trip on. She had left her shoes in the car, knowing that this wasn't the time for heels. The ground felt cold and damp under her feet, but it was no use being soft about things. She took a deep breath and ran to the cover of the wall behind the kitchen. From that position there was no immediate possibility of being seen so she paused and regained her composure before readying herself for the next step.

She would have to pass the kitchen window to get to the back door. She would also be in view of both the dining room and bedroom windows as she crossed. She needed to get inside quickly and hoped that no one was in the kitchen. It dawned on her that the back door might be locked, in which case she had no idea what to do next.

As she peered round the corner she could see that the door was slightly ajar, so being locked wasn't going to be a problem. Maggie steadied her breathing and made a dash for the kitchen, stopping only when she was safely inside. As far as she was aware she'd made no noise. She listened, but could hear nothing. She ran through the layout of the house in her mind. There appeared to be a room at the end of the kitchen on the ground floor, but without windows she presumed it was a toilet or maybe a pantry. She would need to pass both the dining room and lounge doors on the way to the staircase and then the door she wanted was the one facing her at the top of the stairs.

Maggie took in her surroundings. There was a milk carton left out on the draining board. She noted that it was long life milk and wondered if the kidnapper was expecting to be there for some time. There was also a newspaper, but it was out of date and could have been there for some length of time. The cupboards were grubby white laminate and looked as though they had seen better days, whilst the lino had ragged edges and cuts in several places. She remembered that Connor had talked about the rubbish that was piled up outside and realised someone had taken the trouble to do a clearing up exercise on the house before using it. Time and effort had gone into the location, but it gave her no clue as to who was behind the murders and the kidnapping.

Maggie was calm now. She was ready for the next step. She looked at her watch. It was 12.15. She wanted to ring Connor to find out how far away he was, but she couldn't take the risk. As quietly as she could do it, Maggie turned the door handle to the kitchen door and opened it just far enough to give her a view of the hall. She was holding her breath as she did so and let it out when she saw there was nobody there. The doors to the dining room and lounge were slightly ajar. They were open too little to detect any movements inside. She listened, but heard nothing. Maggie took the chair leg from the back of her trousers and tested her grip on it. She wanted to be prepared.

She began to inch her way along the hall, listening intently as she went. There were no sounds coming from anywhere. Maggie could have believed that she was the only person in the house. She was focusing on the upstairs of the house, looking up the stairway hoping that Mikey was safe at the top. She had passed the dining room and was half way across the lounge door. She was almost at the bottom of the stairway.

Suddenly, an arm came up tight around her neck. Her assailant must have come out of the dining room. He had been watching her after all. He was stronger than Maggie. As his left arm tightened around her throat, in one sweeping movement his right hand swung round and stabbed her. She was too slow to move the chair leg. In her mind she knew she should have swung it over her shoulder as fast as she could, but it was too late for that now. She could feel her grip on the leg weakening. Then he stabbed again. Maggie felt as though the delayed, searing pain was in some way disconnected from her body. She clasped her chest feeling the thick warm blood flowing from the wounds. She knew she needed to stop the bleeding. But the breath was being crushed out of her. Then as suddenly as the stabbing started, it stopped. Her assailant thudded to the floor behind her, hitting the hall table as he went down.

Maggie flopped forwards onto the floor, choking for breath from where her throat had been constricted by his arm. She was fading fast. She tried to put her hand to her pocket, feeling for her mobile phone. With one hand pressed to her wounded chest, she used the other one to feel for the number nine on the phone key pad. She pressed it three times and tried to move her finger to find the send button. She was starting to feel confused and struggling to breathe. She brought the phone round towards her face and tried to concentrate. It was no use, Maggie slipped into the relief of unconsciousness.

***

Connor was becoming less and less calm as the traffic on the outskirts of Derby slowed his progress. He'd last heard from Maggie sometime before 12.00. He was so close. He almost hoped that she hadn't entered the property yet, but the thought that someone was on the way to rescue Mikey was reassuring. It was now 12.30 and he was nearing Reeves Road. He saw Maggie's car and parked behind it. He didn't want to waste the time it

297

would take to climb over fences. If Maggie was already inside then he could at least act as a diversion to get attention away from her. He walked along the road and tried the gate, which opened easily. He looked over his shoulder as he went through the passage between the houses.

All was quiet as Connor entered the kitchen. He could see no clue that Maggie was already there, but he had to assume that she was, otherwise she would have called.

As he opened the hall door Connor could see a man lying prostrate in the hall. His head was bleeding. Connor rushed towards him and was stunned to see it was Steve Daniels. Connor wondered what he was doing there and why he had been attacked. Then his eye caught sight of another body, doubled over on the floor a pool of red darkening the beige hall carpet. Connor gasped. It was Maggie. He rushed over to her and lifted her head. It was then he realised the extent of the bleeding and reached her wrist to find a pulse. Her arm was warm to the touch but there was no sign of a heartbeat.

Steve Daniels was starting to stir, but assuming that he too had been attacked by the killer, Connor paid no attention. His concern was his beloved Maggie. This was his fault. It was because of him that she was there. He reached her neck to find a pulse there and again found nothing. He grabbed his mobile and dialled 999.

As he did so, Steve Daniels got to his knees and was starting to get up. He was wielding a large letter opener in his right hand and had a leering smile on his face.

He began to speak but his words were slurred. "Not ssso fast." He was clambering to his feet.

Almost too late Connor realised what he was seeing in front of him.

"You!" he was incredulous. "You killed Maggie."

Steve smiled a gruesome smile. "Who else did you think it was? I thought you'd worked it out. I thought that's why you were going to set me up in two days' time, on the day the Lifetracer reached zero. I had to stop your little game somehow."

"My little game! You bastard. How could you?" He lunged toward Steve. "Where's my son? Where's Mikey?"

CHAPTER 37

"You don't think I'd give him up quite that easily do you?" Steve was now steady on his feet and was holding the letter opener in front of him.

"Where is my son?" Connor was now surveying the situation as best he could. There was little he could do for Maggie who still lay slumped by his feet. He just had to hope that the emergency call centre had heard enough of their conversation to trace his location and get help to them. In the meantime he needed to disarm Steve Daniels. At least if he could keep him talking it might buy enough time for help to arrive. He wanted to know what had happened between Steve and Maggie. Had Maggie hit Steve?

"What's this all about, Steve? Why did you do it?"

"Hasn't the great detective even worked that out? I chose you because I thought you wouldn't be able to work the case out and it looks as though I was right."

Connor could feel hurt pride mixing with the anger. He hadn't known it was Steve, but he didn't think he was that bad a private eye. He liked to think he would have worked it out.

"Why don't you tell me?"

"Why do you think my mother committed suicide? We were close, very close and they took her from me, my father with his fancy woman and my so called brother."

Steve snarled the words. "He came to see my mother. Oh yes. Patrick Coltrane found my mother and came and told her what a failure his life had been. At every step of the way he'd been rejected and it all started with my mother. At least that's what he said. He convinced her of it too. She'd just found out about my father and that woman and Patrick Coltrane made her feel a failure. She wasn't. She was a wonderful woman. But she couldn't take it anymore. She couldn't face a world where everything around her was failing. And my love wasn't good enough for her then. Oh no. I told her she'd still got me, but that wasn't enough."

Connor was frantically thinking how he could get away from Steve to find Mikey. He needed some sort of weapon.

"But the car? Your car has writing all over it."

Steve laughed. "Don't you know you can buy removable magnetic strips? I don't have to drive round as a driving instructor all the time."

It was then that the chair leg caught Connor's eye. It was partly hidden by Maggie's body.

"So you did this?" Connor knelt down to where Maggie was lying, putting his hand on her hair.

"Yes I did that. And all the others," said Steve taking a step forwards. "I did all of them and without you, the police will put it all down to Patrick Coltrane."

Connor's mind was racing. How did Steve think the police would explain this lot with Patrick Coltrane in prison? Quite apart from that, Steve's prints must be on the letter opener and all over the house. Connor moved his right hand down, feeling for the end of the chair leg while trying to keep Steve talking. His stomach lurched as he felt the congealing wetness of Maggie's blood.

"What happened between you and Maggie? Did she hit you?"

"Poor sweet Maggie. She rather got in the way. It's a silly little thing. I've always fainted at the sight of blood. Didn't you wonder why none of the other murders involved those lovely people bleeding? It was all rather unfortunate. I fainted when I saw that bitch's blood and must have hit my head on the corner of the table on the way down." Steve patted his head where it was bleeding. He looked at his hand covered in damp red blood and began to reel again. He tried to steady himself, but in the split second where he faltered, Connor pulled the chair leg from under Maggie's body and brought it crashing down across Steve's shoulder, sending him cart wheeling to the floor. The letter opener spun away from his hand and Connor rushed over bringing his foot down over the blade before Steve could take hold of it again. He didn't want to touch the opener and risk replacing Steve's prints with his own. Connor was loathed to hit Steve over the head with the chair leg but could think of no other solution. He needed to disable him altogether.

Steve was starting to recover. Connor was left with no option. He brought the chair leg down squarely across Steve's skull making a terrifying cracking sound. Steve slumped to the floor and lay motionless. Not daring to consider whether he was dead or unconscious, Connor started looking around for something to tie his hands and feet. In the end he removed his shirt and tore it down the middle. It didn't tear easily and Connor was losing precious seconds. He had to go and hunt for Mikey but it was imperative that Steve couldn't come after them. The ties were crude but would have to do. Connor didn't fancy their chances of holding for any length of time. He hoped he would have time to find Mikey and then find something better with which to tie Steve.

Connor ran upstairs. "Mikey!" He shouted for all he was worth. "Everything's going to be all right. I'm here now." Then Connor thought of Maggie's body lying at the foot of the stairs, his Maggie. Everything was far from all right. It was never going to be the same again. He opened the back bedroom door. The boxes were still piled much as they had been the last time that Connor was here, but there was no sign of Mikey. Connor went round the back of the boxes towards the window. He pushed a couple of the lighter boxes aside, their contents tumbling out, but Mikey was not in there.

Connor clambered over the wreckage of the room towards the door. Once out on the landing he tried the handle of the front bedroom. The door was locked.

"Mikey, stand away from the door."

He lifted his foot and brought it crashing down into the centre of the door, only to recoil in agony. The door was made of some reinforced material. He wasn't going to be able to kick it open.

"Mikey!" Connor put his ear to the door listening for any sign of movement but heard nothing. "Mikey, it's me, Dad. If you can hear me, just hang in there little fella. I'm going to find the key."

Connor limped downstairs to where Steve still lay unconscious on the hall floor. He began to search through Steve's pockets for the key. After pulling out a wallet and car keys he found a separate key ring with a set of house keys on them. He ran back upstairs and began trying them in the lock. It was the third one that fitted the lock.

Connor's hands were shaking as he undid the door and opened it to reveal Mikey gagged and bound to a chair. There were tears running down his cheeks and he looked imploringly at Connor.

Connor threw his arms around his son. "Everything's going to be fine." He untied the gag, his fingers fumbling on the knots.

As soon as the gag was out of his mouth, Mikey wailed "Daddy!"

Connor could feel the tears in his eyes as he set about undoing the rope that held Mikey's hands and feet. If he was quick, he could use the same rope to retie up Steve. As soon as Mikey was free, Connor wrapped the child in his arms and held him close, rocking him for comfort.

"It's ok Mikey, you're safe now." As he did so, he heard the sound of shouting from outside and the front door being kicked in once again.

Connor thought of the scene downstairs and didn't want Mikey to have to see Maggie's body. "You wait here. You'll be safe now. I need to talk to the officers."

"Daddy!" Wailed Mikey. "Don't leave me." He reached out to hold on to his father.

"Mikey," said Connor. "I have to tell the police officers what's happened." He hugged his son. "Be my brave little soldier just a little while longer." As Connor let go of him, Mikey began to howl, sending a chill through Connor. *How could he put his son through so much trauma?* He didn't want armed police coming into the room and confronting Mikey. On top of everything else he had been through, that would be too much.

It was as he walked to the top of the stairs with his hands raised that it began to occur to Connor that he looked suspicious being the one adult conscious in the house.

Once again he was escorted into the back of the police

car. "Please let me see my son before we go? Let me explain what's happening."

"One of our officers will take care of him. You need to answer some questions before you do anything else."

As they bundled him into the car, he saw the red Nissan Micra parked nearby and realised if you looked carefully you could see the cleaner paintwork where the signs had been removed. How could he be so stupid not to have noticed before? Calling him in to investigate the death threat had all been an elaborate hoax to set up Patrick Coltrane.

This time when Connor arrived at the station there was no Maggie to call to sort everything out for him and he had to hope that his one call to DI Whitworth would be answered.

"Trevor, I need your help." He explained as best he could the detail of what had happened and then hoped that other calls could take place to straighten things out. His most desperate thought was of Mikey, terrified in the bedroom of Patrick Coltrane's house, left in the company of the police. Then there were the things that Trevor couldn't sort out. His own dear Maggie. He felt a tightening in his chest and wanted to find a corner to curl up and grieve for the woman he loved. How could he have let this happen? He should never have let her go to Mikey. He should have been the one lying dead, not Maggie, but it was too late for thoughts like that. For the time being he needed to focus on Mikey.

***

It was Friday morning. Connor had been released late the previous evening, while Steve Daniels had been charged with six counts of murder including that of Maggie Fisher. Connor had identified Maggie's body and felt sick seeing her lying in the clinical surroundings of the mortuary. He still had no idea how he was going to tell Mikey what had happened and that Maggie wouldn't be joining them for any more days out. The police had contacted Jayne to collect Mikey the previous afternoon having ensured that Mikey didn't see Maggie's body on his way out. Connor felt numb. All of this was his fault. He shouldn't have got either Mikey or Maggie involved. If only . . . but it was too late for if only.

Connor's first task was to go to Jayne's to collect Tammy. His one consolation was that his beloved dog hadn't been involved too. At least she would have been company and comfort to Mikey.

When Jayne opened the door Tammy pushed past her legs and gave Connor an enthusiastic welcome. It was in stark contrast to the look on Jayne's face.

"How's Mikey?"

"Not doing too badly all things considered," said Jayne, narrowing the opening of the door as she spoke.

"Can I see him?"

She shook her head. "He doesn't want to see you right now."

"He doesn't want to or you won't let him?"

"Does it matter which?"

Connor could feel himself becoming angry. "Yes, it matters quite a lot." *Had Jayne no compassion for the loss he'd already suffered? Didn't she understand his desperate need to see his son?*

"The result's the same. You aren't going to see him."

"Don't you think I've suffered enough, what with Maggie being dead as well?"

There was a flicker of softness across Jayne's face, replaced by a look of steely determination. "I didn't know.

I'm sorry, but it doesn't change anything. You aren't seeing him. You put our son in danger and for that I cannot forgive you."

Connor nodded. "I'll ring him. I presume that will be all right? In the meantime perhaps you could give him a message from me. Please tell him I called and that I love him." Then with Tammy at his heels, Connor walked back along the path to the waiting pick up. As he turned to the house, he saw Mikey with a tear stained face reaching out his palm against the bedroom window. Connor stood there reaching out to his precious son, tears pouring down his cheeks. "Tammy, we're going to fight for custody. I might be a lousy detective but I'm a good father and Mikey belongs with us. This is just the beginning."

ABOUT THE AUTHOR

Rosemary J. Kind turned to writing after a 20 year business career, although she has written as a hobby for many years. Initially she focussed on non-fiction. Her main passion, however, is fiction. She also writes her dog's daily diary as an internet blog www.alfiedog.me.uk. She has won a number of prizes and short listings for her poetry and short stories. Her main hobby is developing the Entlebucher Mountain Dog breed within the UK. She has published 6 books including both fiction and non-fiction.

She is managing director and editor at Alfie Dog Fiction, which she set up in 2011.

Other books by Rosemary J. Kind

Poems for Life
Alfie's Diary
Alfie's Woods
Lovers Take up Less Space
The Appearance of Truth

Alfie Dog Fiction

Taking your imagination for a walk

For hundreds of short stories, collections
and novels visit our website at
www.alfiedog.com

Join us on Facebook
http://www.facebook.com/AlfieDogLimited

Printed in Great Britain
by Amazon